FOR HOSTILITIES ONLY

FOR HOSTILITIES ONLY

Eric Grimshaw

The Book Guild Ltd.
Sussex, England

The Book Guild Ltd.
25 High Street,
Lewes, Sussex.

First published 1990
© Eric Grimshaw 1990
Set in Baskerville
Typesetting by Key Origination,
Eastbourne, Sussex.
Printed in Great Britain by
Antony Rowe Ltd.,
Chippenham, Wiltshire.

British Library Cataloguing in Publication Data
Grimshaw, Eric
    For hostilities only.
    I. Title
823'.914 [F]

ISBN 0 86332 495 9

To my wife Vicky
for her help and encouragement

1

Able Seaman Ted Grainger had already decided, after seeing the length of the bus queues, that Shanks's pony was the only way he was going to get back to barracks that night.

It was a late evening in March 1941. Business had been brisk in the cinemas and pubs of Plymouth and their customers, who were now emerging into the blacked-out streets, were pleasantly surprised to see a clear night after the heavy rain which had driven them indoors. Queues for the last buses had begun to form in the town centre. Outside some of the numerous pubs which lined both sides of Union Street, people were laughing and talking, apparently reluctant to accept that the evening's entertainment had ended.

As he walked past the late-night revellers, it seemed to him that there was an atmosphere of forced joviality amongst them. It reminded him of mourners at a funeral trying to console themselves afterwards with whisky, ham sandwiches and the philosophy that life must go on. Perhaps the improvement in the weather had inspired a feeling of optimism that the night was still young and there to be enjoyed. Grainger smiled to himself, maybe they thought the war would soon be over with that bloody man Hitler calling off a war he didn't have a price of winning. The RAF had given that fat bastard Goering something to think about. Since the Battle of Britain the word was that Germany would not last more than six months. Well, six months was about up and, who knows, the real celebrations could be starting any time.

Stop kidding yourself, Grainger, he chided, with Europe under Nazi control and the Luftwaffe parked on French airfields, this could be the lull before the storm.

He looked up into the blackness of the night, and wondered if the weather had kept the Luftwaffe grounded. News film of the

London inferno was still vivid in his mind. He approached the front entrance of a sleazy-looking amusement arcade aptly known as the Snake Pit. An elderly woman was clinging to the arm of a sailor who looked young enough to be her grandson.

'Never mind going back to barracks with that bloody lot,' she was saying as she glared at the other three sailors. 'Come with me, dearie, I've got a comfortable bed and I'll give you a good time. You'll forget all about that rotten lot.'

'She's right there, Brum,' shouted one of his mates. 'You'll be too occupied with a dose of clap to think about us!'

A stream of abuse from the prostitute was drowned in the roar of laughter which followed and Grainger smiled to himself as he walked past the group. But the laughter and his amusement were short-lived.

Suddenly, the darkness disappeared in the blinding glare of magnesium flares floating slowly downward from the night sky. The curiosity and bewilderment of the spectators quickly turned to panic as the menacing drone of aircraft engines filled the air, closely followed by the belated wailing of air raid sirens. Searchlight beams lanced across the sky then flames from the first fall of incendiaries writhed and licked inside surrounding buildings, outlining targets for the shrieking high explosive bombs to destroy.

People were running blindly in all directions seeking to escape the fires which threatened to engulf them, only to find exploding gas pipes and shattered water mains blocking their way. The narrow streets became death traps. People were being blown to pieces by the exploding bombs, but they were luckier than others who suffered prolonged agony under the huge slabs of masonry which had crashed down on them from collapsing buildings. Showers of debris and sparks spewed through shattered windows and roofs on to the carnage below. Shrieks of the dying and injured rose with blood-curdling intensity above a background of roaring flames, the bell-clanging of fire engines and ambulances and the dull explosions of bombs blending with the sharper crack of ack-ack guns. A blood-red glow reflected in the clouds completed this scenario from hell. The Luftwaffe circled overhead as their bomber crews waited impatiently to start a return run over the fiercely-burning target area.

'Red sky at night, sailor's delight, my bloody arse!' muttered Grainger as he ran blindly for his life. The furnace behind him was searing his skin. His eyes narrowed to slits against the intense heat and thick smoke choked his lungs. The will to survive fought against the paralysing fear which gripped his stomach and forced him to keep on running. He came to a side street leading away from the main road and decided to risk using it as a possible escape route. The noise behind him began to fade as he ran down the street, and with a sense of relief he slowed down to a walk.

What the hell was that? He paused and peered into the dark shadows surrounding the buildings ahead, trying to identify the rustling noise which had attracted his attention. There was nothing to be seen, even with the illumination from the fires still raging at the end of the street.

'Move, man, move!' he shouted, willing himself to start running again but then looking upwards he saw something more terrifying than the furnace behind him. Suspended by its parachute harness from the roof of a tall building was a huge black canister.

'Christ, it's a mine!' he shrieked to the empty street, then stood transfixed wondering which way to run. He cursed himself for having run into the side street. The choice now was cremation if he turned back or being blown to pieces if he went forward. Then he heard voices and the sound of running feet behind him. He recognised the voices of the four sailors who had been talking to the prostitute outside the Snake Pit. Another glance upwards confirmed his worst fears. The parachute harness which appeared to be tangled round a chimney stack was slipping. He shouted to the sailors as they approached – 'Land mine in front!' He pointed to the mine which was now slithering slowly down, scraping the side of the building as it fell.

The leader of the group stared at the descending mine as he continued to run. 'Come on, Jack, run for it – it's your only chance!' he shouted as he and his mates ran past.

Grainger was of the same opinion and prepared to sprint after them, but the descent of the mine was quickening as its weight pulled the harness from the chimney stack. Suddenly, the harness came free and the mine plummetted downwards. There was a hissing sound like that of a lighted firework fuse and Grainger instinctively flung himself on the pavement and rolled quickly into the gutter. As he pressed hard against the high kerb the mine exploded and he glimpsed a blinding white ball of light centred with varying shades of violet-coloured rings expanding towards its circumference. A blast of air followed with hurricane force and the excruciating pain in his ears made him cover them with his hands as showers of rubble and dust blew over him. Successive blasts which threatened to burst his head open abruptly died away. He struggled to his feet and saw that the tall building on which the mine had been entangled was crumbling in a mass of flame and debris.

A voice groaned in agony. Grainger peered in the direction of the sound and in the glare of the flames saw the crumpled shape of a sailor amongst the broken cobble-stones and bricks. He staggered towards him, intending to help him to his feet, but drew back in horror when he saw the man's terrible injuries. His tunic and jersey had been torn from the upper body revealing deep wounds in his chest and neck. The man's eyes in a blackened face were open and fixed on Grainger with a look of incomprehension and shock.

'Hang on, mate, I'll get help!'

Grainger was about to rush away when he saw the man's lips moving. He bent down to catch the words '. . . had it . . . others . . . fucking thing to happen . . .' There was a deep sigh of breath being expelled for the last time. His head fell backwards but the sightless eyes remained open, staring upwards.

Grainger clambered over the piles of rubble hoping to find the other three – but there was nothing – no movement – no bodies. They'd be under this bloody lot – still alive as far as he knew, but he couldn't reach them – not with his bare hands. The heaps of rubble seemed to be spinning round and he slithered on his backside. God!, he felt so bloody helpless. He shook his head, trying to throw off the dizziness and attempted to get on his feet. His legs gave way and he went down again. What a bloody mess! He should be trying to get some help, not sitting on his arse like this. He tried to struggle to his feet. 'You been injured, lad?' Grainger turned in the direction of the voice and saw the smoke-grimed face of an air raid warden staring down at him.

'I'm okay. There's four besides me. One's dead back there. The other three could still be alive – farther up.' he pointed vaguely in front of him.

'Reckon they've bought it, lad, and so will you if you don't get moving.'

'Bollocks!', shouted Grainger. 'They could be up there – still alive – we've got to find out!'

'Easy lad, they're up there alright. I've seen 'em. Mates of yours, were they?'

'Never seen them before tonight. They ran past me before that bloody thing dropped off the building.'

'Think yourself lucky you didn't keep up with them – it's a miracle you're in one piece as it is. Reckon it must have been one of Gerry's secret weapons – one of them bloody land mines.'

Grainger looked at his torn uniform covered with dirt from the rubble he'd been lying in. God knows where his cap was – lucky his head hadn't gone with it, he thought.

'Here, did you say were?'

"What you on about, lad?'

'Those three up there — you asked if they *were* mates of mine. Are they dead? I can't see anything up there.'

'Not much left to see — just enough to account for three bodies. Yes — they're dead alright.'

Grainger felt sick. He wiped what he thought was sweat from the back of his neck and was vaguely surprised to see that his hand was covered with blood. The sirens began to sound the all clear. Behind them the fires were beginning to die down.

'You alright, Jack?'

Grainger nodded, then turned his head and vomited. The warden's arm supported his shoulder.

'Hang on, lad, there's a first-aid post nearby. At least there was a few minutes ago. Come on, they'll have you cleaned up in no time.'

'You haven't seen my cap?' asked Grainger still in a daze. 'I'll be in the bloody rattle without it.'

The warden looked round at the shambles which had been a street then turned to Grainger with a wry smile.

'Don't worry, Jack, I don't suppose those lads back there would have minded the rattle — given the choice, that is.'

2

The Plymouth train was already late as it waited in the station at Newton Abbot. Carriage doors had been slammed some time ago behind the last passengers on board.

Grainger looked impatiently through the window and watched the guard passing the time of day with an ancient-looking porter. From the occasional glances they kept giving towards one of the entrances he assumed that the reason for the delay would appear there at any moment. Like all railway stations throughout the country, name signs had been removed — presumably to confuse the enemy if they invaded. It seemed to Grainger that the absence of the signs was causing passengers more confusion than ever it would the Germans who would probably have updated Baedeker guides of the British Isles to help them. Several weeks had passed since his narrow escape from death in the Plymouth air raid. The cuts and bruises were healed but he had experienced continuous pain in both ears and had difficulty in hearing. It was thought at first that his eardrums may have been perforated by the blast, but further examinations revealed no permanent damage. To his great relief, the pain eventually receded and he regained his hearing.

What the bloody hell was holding this train up? Those two out there seemed to think they had all day to waffle. Don't they know there's a bloody war on?

Grainger moved impatiently in his seat. He was in no hurry to arrive in Plymouth but he needed to stretch his legs after nine hours of travelling in an overcrowded and stuffy compartment. A squeal of brakes announced the arrival of a post office van alongside the platform and the elderly porter ambled across to help transfer parcels to the guard's van. Grainger breathed a sigh of relief as a whistle sounded and the train suddenly jerked forward in response to the guard's green flag.

The other passengers in the compartment were servicemen with the notable exception of a girl sitting near the open doorway leading to a crowded corridor. Her white raincoat, tightly belted at the waist, emphasised the curves of a trim figure. Dark brown hair of medium length, parted at the side, provided a perfect setting for her attractive face. She reminded Grainger of a girl he had met on a previous leave. He would have been alright there, he reflected, if it hadn't been for his stupid shyness. Never mind, better luck next time — if there was a next time. He'd been lucky to escape in one piece from the air raid. Who knows what would happen next? He shrugged his shoulders into a more comfortable position. Didn't pay to think too much about it. What was it father used to trot out? 'Worry not over the future, the present is all thou hast. The future will soon be present and the present will soon be past.'

Grainger glanced across at the girl. A sailor in the corridor seemed to be making the most of the present as he chatted to the girl.

Joe Myers, facing Grainger in the opposite seat, leaned forward.

'Bit of alright, eh?'

Grainger smiled as the girl turned and looked across at him. She half-smiled back before the sailor diverted her attention.

'Competition a bit fierce,' smiled Joe, then he assumed a thoughtful expression as he looked out of the window.

Leading Seaman Myers was twenty-three years old, a navy regular signed up for twelve years with seven to complete. He was a stocky, dark-haired man with a decisive manner and an air of competence. He looked spruce in naval uniform resplendent with gold badges. Grainger was the younger by only two years but there was a maturity about Joe's manner and a hardness in his eyes which made him look much older. They had met on the train, both returning to Plymouth. Grainger from sick leave — Myers from seven days' draft leave.

Myers frowned as he recalled his visit to the Drafting Office in barracks a week ago. The chief petty officer, an old retired sea-dog brought back to a desk job for the duration, informed him that he had been drafted to HMS *Velperton*.

The chief had grinned maliciously as he said. 'You're lucky, lad, you've got seven days' leave before you join her.'

Sadistic old bastard, thought Joe, if that old Yank managed to move again under her own steam she'd be sure to spring her plates on the way out of harbour.

HMS *Velperton* was one of fifty last-war American destroyers loaned to Britain in exchange for a lease on British naval and air bases in the West Indies and Newfoundland. Like her sister ships she had been laid up for many years unmodernised, equipped with obsolete weapons, and with more than her fair share of mechanical defects. Joe had seen her a few times in the dockyard where she'd become part of the fixtures and fittings for the last three months. The boilers needed sorting out but there was no doubt she'd be brought into service as soon as possible on the convoy routes. The heavy losses in destroyers suffered in Norway and at Dunkirk made *Velperton's* return to sea a matter of great urgency.

Grainger hadn't much to say for himself but he didn't seem a bad sort of bloke, mused Joe, even if he is 'hostilities only'. Joe, in common with the other navy regulars regarded the 'hostilities only' recruits as bungling amateurs when it came to working aboard ship, but they would learn with experience — those who lived long enough. Grainger had already gained some of that experience. His last ship, a Hunt class destroyer, had been on east coast convoy work not far from waters which held nightmare memories for Joe.

In June 1940 Joe's ship had been sunk by German gunfire in the withdrawal from Narvik. He was one of the few survivors who were rescued from the sea before their blood froze to ice. Joe did not talk about the experience. Insufficient time had elapsed since he had seen the bodies of dead shipmates flopping amid the wreckage of the ship in the cruel Arctic Sea. It would be a long time before he could talk dispassionately about it. He had recognised the drawn look on Grainger's face and although nothing had been said, he understood and did not ask questions. Shore based, Joe had escaped the holocaust of the blitz, having been assigned to a defence station several miles from Plymouth. All good things come to an end, he reflected ruefully, as he thought about the *Velperton*.

As the train approached North Road station, the girl rose to her feet. Willing hands assisted her to lift a small suitcase from the luggage rack. She smiled her thanks and disappeared from view as she made her way down the crowded corridor to the platform followed by a chorus of wolf whistles.

14

'Pity about that,' grinned Joe as the girl disappeared from sight.

'The story of my life,' replied Grainger with a laugh.

3

'Christ, what a mess!' exclaimed Joe Myers as he walked with Grainger through the ruined streets of Devonport towards the barracks.

Buildings had been split from top to bottom, leaving gigantic heaps of rubble. Off the main road leading to the dockyard there were great gaps where houses and shops had disappeared and those that were left had been badly damaged by blast. Aggie Weston's, the sailors' club and rest centre, was razed to the ground and all that remained were heaps of smoking rubble. The front of the pub opposite the barracks had been blown out leaving the bar, bottles, glasses and the mirror behind the bar intact. A chalked notice on a board propped against a pile of bricks promised *business as usual.* The atmosphere everywhere was filled with the stench of burnt-out fires and desolation.

The high-gated arches and grey stone buildings of HMS *Drake* looked like a prison to the two men as they approached the main entrance. From the main road there was no sign of damage to the barracks from the recent bombing.

'Home sweet bloody home,' muttered Myers as he and Grainger walked through the single gate into the office adjoining the guardroom. The Master-at-Arms, Chief Petty Officer Barson, fifteen years in the navy with three red stripes on his sleeve to show for it, leaned over his desk and glared at them.

'*Velperton* draft, chief,' explained Joe Myers handing over his leave warrant.

'And you, lad?' asked Barson looking impatiently at Grainger.

'Sick leave,' said Grainger producing the required authority.

'Sick leave, eh?' scoffed Barson, 'Not swinging the bleeding lead by any chance? If you were, you chose a bloody good time to scarper from this place.'

Grainger's face went white with anger and he looked as if he was about to give a scathing reply but Joe's hand on his arm had a restraining effect and he said nothing.

Barson had noticed Grainger's reaction and his mouth twisted in a contemptuous smile. 'Going to have a go, lad, were you?...Why not?...Speak up, it's a free country, so they say...That's what we're fighting for, ain't it?' He paused then grinned. "At least some of us are, eh, lad?'

This time Grainger kept his temper under control and did not react. Barson stared at him for a few seconds.

'No answer was the stern reply, eh? Right, we can get down to business then.'

He turned and while he checked the leave authorisations against a thick file, the sound of the guard's measured footsteps could be heard outside. Suddenly a loud voice shouted a sharp command and the footsteps stopped abruptly with the thud of stamping boots and the sound of a hand smacking hard on a rifle butt. Grainger glanced through the window and saw the sentry presenting arms, acknowledged by a salute from a tall gunnery school lieutenant who was striding through the gate.

Barson looked up from the file. 'Right, Leading Seaman Myers, you're to report to the drafting office and Able Seaman Grainger you're in Exmouth block for the time being. Report to petty officer in charge. On your way then.' He handed them their leave cards, then called out as they were about to leave the office. 'Keep away from Boscawen block.'

'What's wrong with Boscawen block, chief?' asked Joe.

'You might well ask, Myers,' replied Barson. 'While you two were enjoying yourselves last week Gerry paid us another flying visit as you probably noticed on your way in. Plymouth, Devonport and the dockyard – usual routine.'

'Has *Velperton* been hit, chief?' asked Myers.

'No, most of the damage is in the South Yard area – bloody near flattened it by all accounts. But *Velperton's* alright, as far as I know.'

'Pity,' muttered Myers. 'Where does Boscawen block come in then, chief?'

'I'm coming to that, if you'll bleeding well let me finish,' snapped Barson. 'Now, as I said, it was the usual targets, only this time the bastard scored a direct hit on Boscawen block. It's just a heap of stone and rubble. What's bleeding worse, over eighty tradesmen were buried underneath. They're still digging the

17

poor bastards out after a week,' he said bitterly.

'The trouble with the navy is they haven't moved on since Nelson's day. I bet they're more comfortable in Dartmoor than here. Just look at this bloody dump. God knows what it's like when everyone's in at night. There's no space in the racks to stow hammocks let alone hooks to sling them. What do they expect me to do with this kitbag?'

The speaker was Ordinary Seaman Mick Shaw who was moving in to Exmouth block at the same time as Grainger.

'Why don't you try shoving it up your arse?' suggested the petty officer standing nearby who was in no mood to put up with Shaw's complaints. 'If you use your eyes there's room up there. The trouble with you fucking civvies is that you think you've come for a fucking holiday at Butlins. Now stow your gear and report at the divisional office in five minutes sharp.'

He stared at Shaw. 'You need to get some weight off, Tubby. I'll introduce you to Manuel.'

Shaw walked right into it. 'Manuel who, petty officer?'

'Manual fucking labour,' replied the petty officer striding away with a loud guffaw.

'Three badges red, bloody near dead; three badges gold, too bloody old!' muttered Mick at the departing back of the petty officer.

'Careful he doesn't hear you,' laughed Grainger. 'He'll have your guts for garters.'

'He's too thick to know what I'm talking about,' replied Mick. 'After twenty years in this outfit he's bomb happy. He's got a bloody lot to thank Hitler for. If it hadn't been for the Führer that silly bastard would be selling matches in civvy street.'

Mick Shaw was a born rebel against all forms of authority. He looked as if he had been in the navy most of his life. His stocky, rounded figure waddled from side to side as he walked with the rolling gait of a sailor stepping on to dry land after a long spell at sea. The illusion was completed by a pointed beard, sunburnt face and balding head. His light blue eyes roamed restlessly like a ship's lookout continuously scanning the horizon.

Mick was in his late twenties. Before call-up he had been a crime reporter on a provincial newspaper. His previous nautical experience had been an occasional trip on a pleasure boat including a memorable voyage in an open boat from Tenby to Caldy Island. A storm had blown up when they were on the island and Mick and the other passengers had eventually landed back in Tenby soaking wet and looking like survivors from a ship wreck. The experience had prejudiced him against the sea and he could only think he had suffered some kind of stupid aberration when he opted for the navy after his medical.

'If we don't get duty watch tonight I think I'll go to the canteen and wash the cockroach soup down with a few pints,' said Mick as they walked towards the divisional office.

'Coming?'

'No,' replied Grainger, 'I'm looking for a billet outside the town and a good night's sleep. Sod being turned out every night into the air raid shelters.' He was referring to the guards who went round the barracks after air raid warnings prodding sleeping men out of their hammocks at bayonet point, if necessary.

'I wish you luck, old son,' said Mick. 'You and the ten thousand other matelots looking for the same thing.' He looked at Grainger speculatively. 'Unless you've got a bird lined up. Booze and crumpet are all you youngsters seem to think about.'

'Strictly in that order, Dad!' laughed Grainger.

4

'Devonport was built for war, it's main business has always been war ever since these dockyards have been here,' declared Tom Rawlings, Chief Torpedo Gunner's Mate.

'How long have they been here, Chief?' asked Grainger who was part of a fire-watching team in the Keyham Yard for the night.

'First ships were launched in 1694. There were two small 73 tonners described as advice boats – we'd call 'em communication vessels. Then the *Anglesey*, a fighting ship over 600 tons and 48 guns. Navy ships have been built here since then, right up to the *Trinidad* last year.'

Rawlings was in charge of the team which was stationed in look-out positions above one of the workshops. It was still daylight as Grainger looked down on the massive complex of buildings known as the factory, consisting of foundries, machine shops, rigging houses, workshops, offices and store houses. Beyond the buildings he could see the vast system of docks, wharves and basins. Some of the buildings were scarred with damage from the incendiaries but the docksides and the ships secured to them appeared to have escaped damage from high explosive bombs.

'Not much damage here, Chief,' he said.

'It was the South Yard that caught it last week – you can't see it from here. Lot of modernisation work done there just before the war started,' replied Rawlings 'New tower cranes, big transit shed, plus a whole lot of other re-development. Gerry must have known about it. He's flattened the lot by all accounts.'

There were two dockyards, one at Keyham and the other at South Yard with the town of Devonport between. Less than 100 years ago a connecting tunnel was built and subsequently, a railway was constructed through the tunnel to serve both dockyards. The railway extended past the barracks to join the main

20

line routes.

'Why did they pick this place for a naval base,' asked one of the other naval ratings.

'I believe the Frogs had a lot to do with it, lad. You see they had their own set-up at Cherbourg and Brest where they could repair and victual their ships. They were good at making raids on our shipping in the Western Approaches then buggering off home before the Navy could tan their arses.'

'The Navy stopped their game then, Chief?'

'Not only that, lad, so many French prizes were taken afterwards that the number of prisoners became an embarrassment. They were kept in prison hulks on that stretch of water over there. They even had Napoleon Bonaparte himself as a prisoner on board the old *Bellerophon* while she was anchored in the Sound.'

'What's that ship over there, Chief?' asked Grainger pointing to the large grey mass of a battleship in one of the docks.

Rawlings laughed. 'That's what I call bullshit baffling brains. It's the old *Centurion* camouflaged as the *Anson*. Those guns and turrets are made of wood and canvas, strictly for decoration and to fool the Luftwaffe. They say Churchill's very pleased with it.'

'What's that big sub over there?' asked another rating.

'She's real enough,' replied Rawlings. 'Free French sub-cruiser – biggest in the world I reckon. It's the *Surcouf* in for a re-fit. She came here last year after France packed in – been on convoy escort since.

'There was a clapped-out battleship called the *Paris* came in with her, bringing those French matelots you've seen round the town. Refugees came with them bringing their belongings and pets – a right bloody crowd. They had a lot of 'em in the drill shed until they could be sorted out. They weren't used to bogs so they shit all over the floor.'

Grainger stared at the giant submarine with its two 8 inch guns in a twin turret for'ard of the conning tower. Abaft the conning tower was a seaplane suspended from a derrick-type crane above its hangar which was below decks. A sentry, rifle in the slope position, stood at the gangway.

Grainger was remembering the story he had heard about the *Surcouf*. It was said that last July, armed parties of British sailors boarded the French ships at Devonport to disarm and remove their crews. An ugly situation had developed on *Surcouf* where

21

three of the boarding party and a French sailor were shot dead. He looked at the Free French flag fluttering from the quarter deck. If the story was true then there was a score to settle and the *Surcouf* might play a double game, perhaps during the course of a convoy. The sirens wailed their regular warning before midnight and soon afterwards the drone of aircraft could be heard in the distance.

'On time, as usual,' said the gunnery rating from Liverpool who was standing with Grainger staring up at the night sky. Ack-ack fire split the darkness with searchlight beams criss-crossing the sky as they tried to pinpoint the aircraft.

'We're like Aunt Sallies stuck up here waiting to be knocked down,' said another man with a Birmingham accent.

Grainger made no comment. He knew that some of the men in Boscawen block had crippled themselves when they jumped from the roof to escape the inferno after the bombing. For his part Grainger would never forget the sight of the land mine slipping down the side of the building in Plymouth.He fingered the chin strap of his steel helmet as he fought against the fear which was urging him to escape from the roof before the bombs fell. He looked down. A drop of sixty feet on to a concrete yard below was no escape. The Liverpool man interrupted his thoughts.

'My old man was in France when they fired the first shot in 1914. When they fired the second one he was back in Bootle!'

'Got his bleeding priorities right,' said Brum. 'Not like us silly bastards up here.' The guns had stopped firing. Searchlight beams still probed the sky but there was no sound of aircraft.

'Some other poor sods getting it tonight, I expect,' said Scouse.

Rawlings' muffled voice came from the other side of the roof. 'Keep your eyes peeled and not so much bloody talking. There's been no all-clear yet.' As if to contradict him the searchlights were suddenly extinguished and the all-clear sounded in final confirmation that the skies were empty of aircraft.

During the night the sirens sounded again. The guns fired as aircraft droned overhead and searchlights probed again. A ball of fire erupted in the sky and fell earthwards marking a success for the ack-ack guns. Relief followed for the fire-watchers as the all-clear sounded. The Luftwaffe had returned to France minus at least one aircraft but they had dropped their load of destruction somewhere else – not Plymouth or Devonport tonight –

thank God, thought Grainger.

'That's the old Yank destroyer *Velperton* over there your mate's on
– and the best of luck to him!' Tom Rawlings pointed towards the
sturdy four-funnelled destroyer secured to the dockside. It was
early morning and the fire-watchers, sitting in an open truck,
were on their way to barracks through the dockyard. Grainger
looked down at the narrow flush decks of the destroyer and
wondered how the crew would manage to keep their feet at sea.
Even in calm weather it would be like walking a tight rope. Men
were mustering amidships and he leaned forward to see if Joe
Myers was amongst them but he didn't appear to be there.

'Wouldn't fancy being on that crate in a rough sea,' said
Scouse, 'I expect you heard that the bridge of one of them broke
away and another overturned on the way over.'

'World's worst ships to handle at sea,' replied Rawlings. 'That
tub would roll on wet grass.'

'A mate of mine is on one of them,' said Brum. 'He said the
Yanks had cleaned 'em up spotless and victualled them as well.'

Scouse was unimpressed. 'They can afford to, can't they, after
the deal they've made and they get 'em back afterwards for scrap
– they're only on loan.'

'I don't think there'll be many of 'em left to go back,' said
Rawlings grimly.

5

The barracks' cinema was full for the E N S A show. The lights from the stage were reflected on the gold braid of the officers' uniforms and the jewellery worn by their ladies as they sat in the front seats.

'Makes you laugh when you think about it,' said Mick Shaw as he and Grainger took their seats at the back. Grainger waited for him to continue, but Mick remained silent as he looked round at the audience.

'Go on then, I could do with a laugh. What's so funny?'

'That lot in front of us. Just look at 'em. Officers in front, then chief petty officers and then the also–rans behind.'

'What do you expect? They wouldn't let a scruffy bastard like you sit down there. If they see you in that rig you'll be up front alright – before the Officer of the Day.'

'What's wrong with these overalls– good enough to sit with that shower. Class distinction – that's what it is. They're really enjoying this war. They get all the perks while such as us have to do the real fighting.'

Grainger laughed. ' They've squeezed more salt water out of their socks than you've seen, Mick. Come off it.'

'Not all of them. Look at that geezer in the middle of the front row. Well fed and prosperous – just like my editor. It's alright for some. A few weeks eating the same crap as we get in Jago's mansion would get some of that fat off.'

'That geezer happens to be the commodore and if you want to see the show I should keep quiet. That guard on the door keeps eyeing you.'

'Sod him,' said Mick and settled back to watch the show.

The artist on stage was the Great Fernando, a magician specialising in sleight of hand tricks, who usually invited a member of the audience to assist with the act. When he had

24

discussed his routine with the commodore's secretary, he was requested not to invite officers or senior ranks to participate because of the indignity of being jeered at by the lower ranks. Any assistance needed could be obtained from the audience in the rear seats.

'Ladies and gentlemen, may I have a volunteer to assist with my next trick?'

There was no response, so Fernando came down from the stage and walked up the aisle to seek out a potential assistant. Recollecting the secretary's words he walked towards the rear seats and decided on the man in the aisle seat wearing overalls. He could only be from the lowest ranks.

'How about you, sir?'

Mick Shaw looked up in horror and vigorously shook his head. 'Not me, mate.'

The magician, assuming that Mick's reluctance was due to shyness, literally dragged him to his feet and pushed him forward to the stage. Mick made determined protests until they reached the front when he gave a resigned shrug of his shoulders and climbed the steps at the side of stage, closely followed by the Great Fernando. As the audience recognised the 'volunteer' emerging from the darkness on to the well–lit stage, there was a roar of laughter which threatened to lift the roof off its supports. Mick, in dirty overalls and once–white plimsolls, peered into the darkness beyond the footlights and fervently wished he could drop through the trap door. The laughter was now accompanied by thunderous applause and catcalls. Mick smiled sheepishly until he saw the commodore on the front row staring at him with a furious expression and bulging eyes.

The Great Fernando, unaware of the repercussions that would follow Mick's appearance in overalls, imagined that the applause and laughter reflected the popularity of the volunteer and congratulated himself on an excellent choice. Laughter increased again when Mick was invited to take a seat. One knee was exposed through a large hole in the left leg of his overalls and as he tried to cover it with his hand there were cries of 'Get 'em off! Give us a treat, Jack!' The laughter had now spread to the ladies and their escorts in the front seats. The commodore was the only one not amused and the look on his face did not bode well for Mick's future. The Great Fernando finished his act amidst loud applause and acknowledged Mick's assistance by leading the clapping as Mick left the stage. The audience quickly forgot Mick as the dancing girls came on stage, but Mick had not been forgotten by others. He had barely regained his seat when two guards appeared from nowhere and escorted him out of the cinema.

The following morning Grainger saw Mick queuing outside the canteen during the stand–easy break.

'Great show, Mick, you were right, it was a good laugh especially when you were on stage.'

'It's not funny – I've just seen the divisional officer. Told me I was a disgrace to the navy and that I'd caused the commodore a lot of embarrassment in front of his guests. I tried to explain but ...'

'Don't tell me you gave him that guff about your uniform not fitting?'

'I did mention that the pants were too small.They're like Blackpool Tower – not enough ball room.'

'Bet he didn't swallow that..'

'Well I thought I was going to get away with it when he said he'd decided to take a lenient view on this occasion. Not what I'd call bloody lenient. Kit inspection every evening until further notice. If it hadn't have been for interrupting my training he said he'd have made it during the day as well. Trouble is I haven't got much kit to inspect. It's not bloody fair.'

'It's your fault. You were on spud bashing duty in the kitchen and you sneaked into the cinema through a side door. You didn't get away with it this time,' accused Grainger.

'Would have done if it hadn't been for that berk of a magician. I should have asked him to produce a full kit out of his hat instead of that bloody rabbit,' said Mick with a grin.

Petty Officer Bell with six members of a naval patrol was watching the crowd in the amusement arcade on the opposite side of the road. The arcade, known locally as the Snake Pit, still undamaged from the bombing, stood in the ruined centre of Plymouth. The arcade was shaped like a keyhole with a long narrow entrance from the main road opening into a semi–circular space

26

at the back. On this particular evening it was crowded with servicemen looking for amusement after the pubs had closed. The patrol weren't the only ones eyeing the crowd. Two hard faced tarts, their tight skirts straining at the seams over bulging thighs, posed on either side of the Snake Pit's entrance as they sought to attract potential clients. Grainger, because of his height, had been included in the patrol for this particular night's duty. He reflected gloomily that even if there was no trouble it would be midnight before they returned to barracks.

'Don't seem right,' said Petty Officer Bell. 'All these buildings blown to bits and that effing den of iniquity hasn't even been scratched. Talk about the devil looking after his own. At least we know where the trouble–makers drift to at this time of night,' he added as an afterthought.

'They'll certainly be in trouble if they do business with those two cows over there,' laughed the thickset man next to Grainger.

'That's as may be, Taffy,' replied Bell, 'We're only concerned with the rough–necks. If jack–me–hearty wants to risk a dose, that's up to him. Now, lads, first sign of trouble I want you to follow me in there and we'll sort the bastards out.'

'He's balmy,' muttered Grainger. 'Once we go in there we'll be targets for a knife in the back.'

Taffy nodded in agreement. 'You don't know Ding Dong like I do. His one ambition in life is to collect a posthumous gong. He was on my last ship – I should know.'

Bell spotted the whispered conversation. 'If you two have anything to say that's relevant, speak up and let's all hear it.'

Grainger saw his chance. 'Petty officer, wouldn't it be better if we waited for reinforcements before moving in? Then the side and rear could be covered.'

'I don't think we'll need any help,' said Bell confidently. 'You've got your batons, swing 'em if necessary. If any of our lads are involved in there we'll have 'em carted off to barracks – and that's an order – savvy?'

Grainger nodded. Didn't Bell realise you wouldn't be able to swing a cat in there let alone a baton. Still, the order had been given and the navy had never been tolerant of disobedience – even if Nelson had turned a blind eye on at least one occasion. The confused din from the Snake Pit suddenly erupted into an ear–splitting roar. The two tarts glanced across at the patrol and then moved several yards up the road to comparative safety in the doorway of a derelict building.

'Right lads,follow me.' Petty Officer Bell, assuming that his order would have an immediate response, strode across to the Snake Pit's entrance and disappeared from view amidst a seething mass of bodies. The patrol moved cautiously to the spot where Bell had disappeared. On Grainger's suggestion they formed a square, backs to each other, and pushed forward into the crowd. As they moved in, Grainger wondered if Bell was still on his feet. A man could be suffocated or trampled to death in this mob if he lost his footing. As if in answer, the solid mass of people opened up to allow the dishevelled figure of the Petty Officer to be deposited on the pavement. His peaked cap was missing, his jacket was ripped at the shoulder and the knot of his tie had been dragged round to the back of his neck. He appeared to have escaped injury as he lay gasping like a stranded fish. Grainger and the others helped him to his feet.

'Do we go in or wait?' he asked Bell.

Bell did not answer. He was convinced now that more men were needed but he had no wish to admit he'd been wrong. At that moment a Free French Naval Patrol came on the scene and solved Bell's dilemma. The two patrols combined to cover sides and rear then moved forward as the jeers and abuse from the crowd deafened their ears. They reached the rear of the Snake Pit and found that the crowd had formed a ring round two free French sailors who were menacing each other with open cut–throat razors. Blood was pouring down the slashed face of one of them, while dark red stains soaked through the sleeve of the other's jacket. The two patrols, urged on by commands from their respective leaders, laid about the two combatants with their batons. The blood–stained razors were knocked to the ground closely followed by the two men under a barrage of blows. The men were handcuffed and escorted out of the arcade. The French patrol left with their prisoners while Bell's patrol lined up awaiting his orders.

'Excuse me, Jack, is this yours?'

Bell turned and the faces of his men creased into grins. One of the two tarts was wearing Bell's cap at a rakish angle. The hard peak of the cap had been forced upwards and the crown crushed under many feet.

'Bloody cheek!' Bell exclaimed loudly and grabbed the cap.

'Naughty!' said the tart wagging her finger.

'Piss off!' said Bell.

He turned to the patrol and looked hard at their faces, but the grins had disappeared. The crowd had dispersed from the Snake Pit and the entrance doors were being closed. The patrol moved away led by Petty Officer Bell, battered cap in hand.

6

May 1941 had seen the sinking of the battle cruiser *Hood*, the pride of the Royal Navy, with only three survivors from the crew of fourteen hundred. The battleship *Prince of Wales*, gained some consolation when her guns damaged the *Bismark's* fuel tanks, leading to the sinking of the brand new German battleship with nearly two thousand of the ship's company lost and only one hundred and ten survivors. The 38,000 ton *Prince of Wales* was now secured in Devonport dockyard after its mauling from the guns of the *Bismark* and the German heavy cruiser *Prinz Eugen*.

Joe Myers, on his way out of the dockyard on night leave, paused to look up at the massive superstructure of the battleship. He counted six forward 14 inch guns supplemented by a powerful secondary armament of 5.25 inch guns and a bristling array of anti-aircraft cannon backed by a huge quadruple turret of 14 inch guns aft. The ship looked impregnable against any attack and yet its first encounter with the enemy had nearly ended in total disaster.

'She didn't stand much chance, did she?' Myers turned to see Tug Wilson, the gunner's mate from *Velperton*.'She was unlucky, by all accounts,' replied Myers.

Wilson continued. 'Aye, she wasn't ready for action — mechanical trouble with the big guns. An oppo of mine said she still had dockies on board when she sailed with the *Hood*. Apart from the hits she got from the *Prinz Eugen*, a 15 inch shell from *Bismark* creased her bridge. Everyone on the bridge was killed or badly wounded except the skipper. One of the for'ard guns packed up and if that wasn't enough, the rear 14 inch gun turret jammed.'

'Christ!' said Myers, 'What happened then?'

'Inside twenty minutes, after the enemy was sighted, *Hood* was blown to pieces and the 'Prince' here broke off the action under cover of smoke,'replied Wilson.

Myers looked at the buckled superstructure of the bridge and wondered how anybody on there could have survived a hit by a high velocity 15 inch shell weighing a ton.

'She seems to be an unlucky ship,' said Wilson as they walked past the grey mass of the battleship. 'Like the *Exeter.*'

'Myers recalled the light cruiser *Exeter*, built at Devonport, returning to her home port in February 1940 after her gallant action with *Achilles* and *Ajax* in the battle of the River Plate against the *Graf Spee.* She had suffered terrible casualties after being struck by seven 11 inch shells from the German pocket battleship.

'Strange thing about the *Exeter*,' said Wilson. 'It was the near misses which forced the skipper to break off the action — not the direct hits. Her side was like a pepperpot with all the splinter holes. Water flooded in and put paid to the power supply and the only gun turret that was firing.'

'Have you heard anything about the *Velperton's* sailing?' asked Myer, changing the subject.

'No, but there's a buzz going the rounds that her boilers need replacing — that could take some time seeing she's obsolete.'

'Can't be bad,' said Myers. 'More time in dock — more shore leave.'

Wilson laughed. 'Between you and me — most of the ship's company will be paid off into barracks. They won't be there long— crews for escort vessels are in great demand these days.'

The pub opposite the barracks had received a facelift. The rubble had been cleared and a concrete frontage with small opaque windows near the top was an unattractive replacement for the original. Grainger, standing at the bar, had not yet decided where to spend the evening. He had thought of following the example of the locals who made for the outlying areas at night. Men, women and children could be seen every evening walking alongside or pushing carts and prams piled high with mattresses, blankets and cooking equipment. The milder weather was welcomed by everyone. If accommodation could not be found indoors, some would sleep on the moors, returning the following morning to their homes — or what was left of them. Grainger had no intention of sleeping outdoors if he could help it. He raised his pint glass then nearly spilt the contents as a hard hand came down heavily on his shoulder. He turned angrily and saw the grinning face of Joe Myers.

'Sup before spill,' laughed Joe. 'So this is where you spend your time? Is it the first and last stop then?'

'I don't think so — what about you?'

'I'm off to Ashdown shortly. Having another?' He pointed to the half-empty glass in Grainger's hand.

'No thanks. I didn't see you the other day when I was passing the Yank.'

'You wouldn't. I've been on a course at Whale Island for a couple of weeks. Came back this morning.'

'Glad to be back, I expect.' Grainger had heard about the tough discipline in the gunnery school at Whale Island.

'You might say that. But the alternative isn't all that bright either.'

'What's the attraction at Ashdown? Uphomers with a bird there?'

'Not at the moment — but you never know.'

'I'm looking for somewhere quiet and the chance of a decent night's sleep,' said Grainger.

'Why don't you give Ashdown a try then?' asked Joe, reaching over the shoulders of the customers for his pint.

'There's a chance of sleeping on the deck at the church hall. Sometimes the police station has an address were you can get a bed for the night. The dockyard bus picks up about six in the morning, so getting back isn't a problem.'

'Sounds alright to me..'

Joe gulped the remainder of his pint and grimaced as he set the empty glass down on a nearby table. 'Come on then — we'll see if the beer's any better at Ashdown.'

Grainger stared at the wall of the air raid shelter as his thoughts went back over the events of the previous night. He looked round the dimly lit brick-walled passage of the parade ground shelter. Ratings were lolling uncomfortably on wooden benches trying to snatch some sleep. It was early June and the wailing air raid sirens were still sounding their warning each night with unfailing regularity. Strategic targets like the dockyard and barracks had not suffered further damage. The mass attacks of March and April were directed elsewhere. but the enemy was obviously determined to continue with terror tactics designed to break morale. Isolated attacks by enemy bombers, sometimes acting singly, still brought death and destruction to the streets when they succeeded in penetrating the town's defences.

Grainger's thoughts returned to Ashdown where he and Joe had gone the previous night.

Ashdown had seemed like a place on another planet to Grainger after the devastation of Plymouth and Devonport. Fresh green foliage on the trees and hedges lined both sides of the narrow road which sloped down to the main street of the village. The sky was cloudless, and sunset coloured the surrounding hills with shades of red and gold. The main street was quiet and almost deserted, but strips of brown adhesive paper criss-crossed over the window panes to prevent flying glass, and the black-out curtains were grim reminders that there was a war on. A long, low building with a deep, thatched roof and dark cream cemented walls stood back from the road. Small mullioned windows revealed nothing of the interior and the front door, latched back against the wall,was in two sections like a stable door. A sign above the door in gold lettering on a black background proclaimed that this was the Seven Stars Inn.

'Black as hell's kitchen in there,' said Myers trying to peer through the windows.

'Let's try the other side,' suggested Grainger, looking across the road at the Black Bull — a large, square building with a subdued grey stone exterior.

'No, I think it's best if we look for a billet first and then come back here. It sounds more matey in the Seven Stars.'

The minister at the church hall was apologetic. 'We're absolutely full up tonight, but you might be able to find space on the floor to sleep if you can't find anywhere else. Why don't you ask at the police station. They usually have a few addresses. Sorry I can't be more helpful.'

The constable had nothing to offer apart from the church hall.

'I'm not going back to Plymouth tonight — and that's a cert. I vote we give the church hall a try later. Better than nothing,'said Myers as they left the police station.

'Let's see what the Seven Stars has to offer. All this trailing about has given me a thirst,' said Grainger.

The inside of the Seven Stars was as dark and dingy as it appeared from the outside. The reek of stale beer and tobacco smoke filled the low-ceilinged rooms. It seemed to both of them that the visit to Ashdown would turn out to be as flat as the beer until they spotted a notice behind the bar advertising a dance in the village hall that evening.

'What's your footwork like?' asked Joe .

'Good enough to get by, I suppose.'

'Right then, let's go. I should leave that, ' said Joe as Grainger prepared to drain his glass. 'There's a bar laid on at the dance according to the notice — we might do better there.'

There had been more than a bar laid on, recollected Grainger with a smile. Julie Johnson had been there — the girl he had noticed on the train at Newton Abbot; what's more, he had a date to see her again this coming Saturday. His luck must be changing. Joe had done alright too, with Ruth Mason, Julie's friend. An attractive brunette in her early twenties with a well-rounded figure. Because there was no room at the church hall, not even on the floor, Myers and Grainger thumbed a lift back to Saltash after the dance and were lucky to find some space in the Sunday schoolroom at the local church. Joe chose to sleep on the floor, while Grainger had stretched out on a table on the stage. He rubbed his shoulder which still hurt from falling off the table during the night.

'Good run ashore last night, Ted?' asked Mick Shaw, trying to make himself comfortable on the narrow bench in the shelter.

'Could have been worse,' replied Grainger.

'Could have been worse,' echoed Mick sarcastically.

'You look knackered, mate. Did you find that bird you were hoping to meet.'

'What bird would that be?'

'Please yourself,' grunted Mick as he sat upright and fumbled for a packet of cigarettes. Putting one in his mouth he was about to strike a match when the sentry's voice boomed from the far end of the passage. 'No smoking — can't you read the bloody notice?'

'Charming,' sneered Mick. 'Give some blokes a rifle and bayonet and they turn into right bloody Hitlers!'

He looked across at Grainger. 'Did you hear about the panto-mime we had down here last night when you were making it with the local talent?'

'No, but I expect you're going to tell me.'

'One of the new entries — a bloke called Simmonds — blew his top.'

'What happened?'

'Well,' said Mick, warming to his story as he noted that others nearby were showing interest. 'It seems that this Simmonds was like me — up to his eyes with Navy bullshit, and couldn't get back to civvy street quick enough. A sensitive sort of bloke who can't stand confined spaces — claustrophobic they call it.'

'Not like you.'

'Last night,' continued Mick, ignoring the sarcasm. 'It seems that Simmonds reached the end of his tether. He was sitting there where you are now, when all of a sudden he jumps up and starts arguing with the sentry on duty. Seems he wanted to go outside for a slash and the sentry told him to use the bucket. Simmonds tried to push his way out and the sentry grabbed him but dropped his rifle and bayonet. Next thing Simmonds picked up the rifle and tried to ram the bayonet into the sentry's throat. Fortunately, the sentry ducked and the bayonet went over his head and struck the wall.'

'I suppose you all just sat and watched?' said Grainger.

'It all happened so quickly we couldn't believe what we were seeing. Then Simmonds dropped the rifle and ran past us hoping to find another way out, but came up against a bleeding brick wall that seals the other end of the passage. Another bloody death trap for us poor sods.'

'Get on with it, Mick,' said Grainger irritably.

'Well, Simmonds tried to claw his way through the wall with his bare hands. You should have seen his hands— nails broken and skin hanging off — a right old mess I can tell you.'

'Didn't somebody try to stop him?' asked one of the listeners. 'What about the sentry?'

'He was whistling up the barracks guard outside, so I jumped on Simmonds to try to stop him doing any more damage to himself. His mouth was covered with saliva and he was screaming all the curses he could lay his tongue to. Then he suddenly collapsed and his face went white as a corpse.'

'With your weight on him I'm not surprised,' said Grainger.

'I thought he'd had it,' admitted Mick, 'but thank God he was still breathing. They whipped him up to the hospital. I think he'll get his ticket — lucky bastard!'

'Not while the war lasts — if he's warm, he's in for the duration,' declared Leading Cook Watts, one of the listeners.

'A bloke I know, a Petty Officer chef by the name of Hopkins, decided to opt out last year. He'd done twelve years and was hoping to set up his own business in civvy street when that bloody Hitler put an end to all that, didn't he?'

'After twelve years in this lot he must have been ready for blowing his top.' sympathised Mick.

'Anyway,' continued Watts, 'Hoppy told the quack that he thought he was suffering from depression. He was sent into hospital and given more tests than soft Mick.'

'Back to you again Mick,' chuckled Grainger.

Watts continued. 'The upshot was that the quack said Hoppy needed a change. He recommended a transfer to the seaman branch but the snag was that he would lose his petty officer rate and revert to ordinary seaman.'

'They couldn't do that, surely?' asked Grainger.

'Whether they could or not, Hoppy went white and assured the quack that the treatment had done him a power of good and he didn't think he'd have any more problems with his duties as petty officer. The quack seemed reluctant to change his recommendation and Hoppy nearly went down on bended knees to convince him. The only discharge Hoppy got was from skiving in hospital — reckon this bloke Simmonds will finish up the same way.'

'I don't think so — from what I saw of Simmonds he was in a bad way,' said Mick.

The 'all-clear' sounded as Grainger checked his watch and saw that it was 0130 hours. He rubbed the back of his neck which ached from being at an awkward angle as he had dozed intermittently. Most of the others were moving, glad of the chance to leave the shelter and return to their hammocks for the few remaining hours before the bugler sounded reveille. One exception was Mick Shaw who was snoring loudly. Grainger shook his shoulder. 'Come on, jack-me-hearty, get the hell out of here!'

Outside, the illumination of a full moon had turned night into day, clearly outlining the barracks, the adjoining docks and the warships berthed alongside. The parade ground was full of men walking slowly back to the main buildings. Grainger and Shaw were within twenty yards of clearing the parade ground when their ears were deafened by the sound of a powerful engine being revved under full throttle, then a Junkers 88 screamed out of the sky in a shallow dive towards the parade ground. The plane came down like a silver flash and the black crosses on the wings were easy to identify as the reflection of the moonlight glinted from the perspex forming the cockpit canopy. The clatter of heavy machine guns was accompanied by the explosion of cannon fire as bullets and shells tore holes in the surface of the parade ground.

'Underneath the huts,' shouted Grainger as he and Shaw rolled into a gap between the stacks of bricks supporting the huts and waited tensely for the dive bomber to make a return run. Spasmodic ack-ack fire could be heard, then, as abruptly as it started, the gunfire ceased and the sound of the plane's engines gradually faded away. They looked up at the night sky, cloudless and empty again except for the full moon and its revealing light.

'That bastard was on target alright,' said Watts, 'Look at that for a bullseye.'

They looked at the parade ground expecting to see casualties but there was nothing there except a line of ruts stitched by bullets and cannon shell across the central area of the parade ground.

'Would you Adam and Eve it.' said Mick, 'All those blokes around and he's missed the bleeding lot!'

'Better than a dose of salts for making you run when that bugger started firing.' commented Watts as they crawled out from the cover of the huts.

'Murderous bastard — he had everybody fooled by switching his engines off and diving under the barrage balloons,' said Mick.

'Not murderous,' replied Watts. 'In peacetime, yes. Now he's entitled to shoot up cannon fodder like us and get an Iron Cross from the Führer for being such a bloody good Nazi!'

'You're right there, chef,' said Mick. 'Murder a bloke for pinching your wife and you'll swing for it. But if it's war or an act of terrorism then it's patriotism and you become a hero. You get a gong instead of a rope. Our Government is as bad as the rest. Samuel Johnson said 'Patriotism is the last refuge of the scoundrel — he was bleeding right, too.!'

The three of them walked slowly back towards Exmouth block. Mick stopped and looked upwards. 'You know something — I reckon Gerry must have dropped his load of shit somewhere else tonight, otherwise he'd have come back and given us the full treatment.'

'He'd have been on his way back home and couldn't resist a final fling.'yawned Grainger. ' One thing's certain, he'll know where the shelters are and he'll have back up next time — unless the ack-ack lads get their fingers out.'

7

Ted Grainger checked his watch with the church clock for the umpteenth time. He was in Marlston, a small market town on the outskirts of Plymouth, where he should have met Julie Johnson half an hour earlier. He looked up and down the street willing her to appear but she was nowhere to be seen. The bus on which she would normally have travelled had arrived some time ago, discharging all its passengers before pulling into the nearby terminus.

His earlier anticipation of meeting Julie again was waning as he became convinced that she had stood him up.

But why? Alright, he had gone the wrong way in the progressive barn dance and trod on her toes, but she'd laughed about it. He'd apologised and said that he didn't think the trio of piano, guitar and accordion were keeping the right tempo. Later on she'd accepted his suggestion that they join Ruth Mason and Joe at the refreshment tables. Contrary to what the notice had said, there was no alcohol being served and the sandwiches of spam, spam and cress, dried egg, or dried egg and cress, were as uninviting as the posters on the walls which urged the public to join the A F S, grow more food and refrain from careless talk. But they'd all laughed and talked together as if they'd known each other for years. It seemed the most natural thing in the world at the end of the dance to arrange another meeting. Still, you never knew with women — they could change their minds. But they could let you know beforehand to save all this hanging around. But how could she let him know? He'd hadn't told her where he was based. He hoped Joe was having more luck with his date.

He looked up at the clock again. Another fifteen minutes and that's it, he decided. There'd still be time to see the Argyle match. Twenty minutes later he decided to catch the bus back into Plymouth. So much for women — he might see her again in

Ashdown and she'd explain everything. On the other hand, why bother? Let's get on with the bloody war and forget about it.

He was half way across the road when a big army lorry pulled up in front of the church with a squeal of brakes. A girl's voice shouted 'Ted, over here!' He turned to see Julie struggling to climb down from the high cab of the lorry. He ran across the road to help her down to the pavement. The lance corporal driving the lorry leaned across with a grin on his face as he saw Grainger. 'Special delivery,mate. Some buggers have all the luck!'

Julie looked up at him and smiled. 'Thanks for the lift, I'm very grateful.'

'All part of the service, luv, as long as the sarge doesn't know. He'd have me court martialled if he did.' He winked. 'Don't do anything I wouldn't do — that should leave you plenty of scope — cheers.' He moved back behind the steering wheel and the lorry roared off down the main street.

'I'm sorry I'm late — the Ashdown bus broke down and I missed the connection. I was lucky to get a lift. Were you leaving?'

Grainger thought quickly. 'No, I was on my way over there to report you as a missing person.' He laughed as he pointed to the sand-bagged frontage of the police station on the opposite side of the old market place. She looked as pretty as a picture in the pale blue outfit which outlined her slim figure.

'Is anything wrong?' she asked anxiously as she noticed the way he was eyeing her up and down.

'Nothing at all — just admiring the scenery. You look smashing — I'm glad you came.'

Julie smiled. 'Of course I came, whatever made you think I wouldn't?'

He glanced up at the cloudless sky. 'We're lucky with the weather. It's too nice to go indoors just yet. Any ideas?'

'Yes, I wanted you to see this place on a fine day. There's a lovely walk nearby which gives a good view of the coast. Come on, I'll show you.'

They were soon out of the town and walking down a lane skirted by woods and fields. After a few minutes the lane narrowed to a winding path which pushed its way round grass — covered slopes. From below came the dull roar of the sea as the receding tide left golden sands glistening in the sunshine.

'Pity we can't go down there,' said Grainger observing the Ministry of Defence notices warning that the beach was mined.

'Yes, it's a beautiful beach. We used to swim here before the war.' She paused then continued. 'Before the war — was there ever a time before the war? It seems more like a dream with each passing week.' Her face brightened. 'Never mind, it's bound to end one day and we'll have all the good times back again.' Grainger smiled but did not reply. After his recent experiences the future was something he didn't care to dwell on. Today was something to enjoy.

'Shall we sit down over there?' Julie pointed to a wooden seat which had been placed on a flagged area some distance from the path. 'Ruth said she was meeting Joe in Plymouth today,' said Julie as they sat down. 'Ruth and I are neighbours. She works in the local council offices. I'm a secretary for a firm of solicitors in Plymouth. Our respective mothers work in the W.V.S.'

'Better watch my step then,' laughed Grainger, 'otherwise I'll be looking for another port.'

'I'll take good care that you behave yourself when you're with me, young man,' replied Julie with a mischievous grin.

Time passed quickly that glorious afternoon as they sat overlooking the sea, sharing an animated conversation about themselves and life in general.

Grainger learned that Julie's father had been killed in an accident five years earlier in the dockyard where he had worked. There was an older sister, Margaret, who was married to a stoker petty officer and lived in Gosport. Julie was nineteen; she and Ruth, who was two years older, had volunteered for the Wrens and were hoping they would be called up together.

'You work in Plymouth then? You're lucky to have an office standing. I'd have thought your firm would have moved out of the town.'

'We're not in the centre where the worst damage is, but there are plans to move out as soon as possible.'

Julie studied Grainger without making it too obvious as he sat facing the sun with half-closed eyes. He was tall, fair-haired with good shoulders. He had a firm chin and regular features and she had already noted his frank blue eyes. What Ruth would describe as handsome or, more tritely, smashing.

Normally she refused dates with casual acquaintances on principle. She had only seen Grainger twice before. The first time from the opposite end of a packed railway compartment and then at the dance. But she felt happy and relaxed in his company. When he'd asked for a date she had been surprised to hear herself suggesting impulsively that they meet in Marlston. It was a place which held happy memories from childhood and she could think of no better place to meet him. If she hadn't seen him before he left she would never have forgiven herself for being late.

'That's enough about me, what about you and your family?'

'Not much to tell,' he replied. My father runs a haulage business and my mother works in a milliners. I was in the textile trade in Yorkshire. It was a small business which folded with the death of the owner shortly after the war started. Instead of looking for another job I volunteered for the navy. If I come out of this lot in one piece I'd like to go back into textiles — on my own account this time. I think there's plenty of brass to be made in that line, as they say in Yorkshire.'

'I suppose you've got girl friends back home?' asked Julie

'No-one special — but there are compensations.'

'Such as?'

'This afternoon for instance — glorious weather, wonderful view and kissing a beautiful girl.'

'But you haven't kissed anyone ....' She realised her mistake too late.

'Thanks for reminding me — we'll soon put that right.'

He kissed her cheek then her lips as she turned her face towards him. Briefly he felt his kiss being returned as she pressed against him then she moved away quickly and looked at him with mock indignation.

'That was taking an unfair advantage,' she protested.

'Sorry,' he grinned. 'I couldn't resist the temptation.'

He stood up. 'Come on, we'll have some tea and I promise to behave.'

She smiled. 'Alright, you're forgiven this time, I'll take you somewhere nice.'

Later that evening they were walking down Plymouth Hoe to the Barbican where Julie would catch her bus. They paused and looked across at Drake's Island.

'I'll see you home,' said Grainger. He grinned.

'The army might pick you up again'.

'I'll be alright, but you won't if you find yourself at Ashdown without transport.' She smiled. 'Thanks for a marvellous day. It's been wonderful.'

'Same for me,' he replied, then stared silently at the destroyer which was nosing its way from the mouth of the Tamar into the Sound. On its way to join another Atalantic Convoy, he thought, any time now and I'll be going the same way. He wondered if he would ever see Julie again. There was a slight movement and he turned to see her gazing at him intently. 'A penny for them.'

'They're not worth as much as that.'

'I was wondering if there is such a thing as love at first sight or is it just the war? she said.

'Why the war?'

'Emotional attachments are formed in a hurry because every day could be the last. Does that sound silly?'

'Not when you say it. It does when I think about it.'

She looked at the destroyer receding into the distance as it approached the breakwater to enter the Channel.

'I expect there are men on that ship with the same unanswered questions in their minds, hoping they'll be spared to come back for the answers.'

'They'll also hope that they don't get the wrong ones.'

'But if they're the right ones it makes everything worthwhile, doesn't it?'

She moved towards him and impulsively put her arms round his neck and gave him a long, lingering kiss. She moved away but he drew her close to him and as they kissed again he could feel the soft curves of her body as she pressed against him. She withdrew from his embrace and stood back to face him.

'Let's not rush our questions and answers, Ted.'

She gave a soft laugh and snuggled against him. 'I do have a bus to catch.'

To Ted's surprise he was pleased at what she said. He laughed. 'Come on, then,' and arm in arm they walked happily into the town.

8

Hopes that the *Velperton's* sea trials could start at an early date were dashed when, after a series of tests, the dockyard authorities reported to the Admiralty that replacement boilers were needed if the ship was to become an effective escort vessel. Repairs on existing boilers would only be a stop-gap measure; they could not avoid the risk of a complete breakdown without prior warning. The delay in fitting new boilers would be longer than usual because *Velperton* was an obsolete class of ship. As Tug Wilson, the gunner's mate, had predicted, most of the seamen originally drafted to *Velperton* were to return to barracks and would be drafted to other ships. A number of stokers, seamen petty officers and leading hands were to remain with the ship. Joe Myers was amongst those who remained and Grainger guessed from the expression on his face that he wasn't entirely pleased at the prospect. They had met in the barracks' canteen and were discussing their proposed visit to Ashdown the following evening.

'There's another dance at Ashdown tomorrow night,' said Joe. 'I saw Ruth last night and she and Julie are in favour of making it a foursome if that's okay with you. You're not duty watch are you?'

'No, that's fine by me,' said Grainger. ' I hear most of the lads from the *Velperton* have already been drafted.'

'That's right,' said Joe. ' In one sense I wish I was going with them.'

'Come on, Joe, ashore every night seeing Ruth. You two are still lovey dovey, aren't you?'

'That's the best part of it,' replied Joe. She's a grand lass is Ruth and we get on fine.'

'Then why do you want another ship when you can stay here to the end of the war? From what you tell me about the *Velperton* she's not likely to be going anywhere before then.'

'Don't believe it. It won't be all that long before she's ready for escort duties and those old four-stackers are the world's worst ships to handle at sea. I wouldn't mind the draft to one of the new frigates that those lucky buggers have got who came in here from the *Velperton.*'

'Can I quote you on that to Ruth tomorrow night?'

'You do and I'll tell Julie that you've been pestering the drafting office to get away from Devonport. By the way, Ruth invited me home last week to meet her folks — they're nice people. Got your feet under the table yet?'

'Yes, last Sunday — made a nice change from this dump.'

Grainger had found Julie's mother to be a pleasant, attractive woman in her early fifties. She had welcomed Ted more like one of the family than a stranger. Over a substantial meal which Ted suspected must have reduced considerably the Johnson's rations, the conversation tended to centre round their respective family backgrounds. It transpired that Mrs Johnson worked part-time in the village post office in addition to her voluntary W.V.S. duties. She was also a staunch member of the local Methodist church. When he and Julie decided to go for a drink at the Black Bull later on Mrs Johnson had refused to go with them. He hadn't thought about the Methodist views on alcohol at the time and when he mentioned this to Julie she'd laughed and told him not to worry.

'You must have made a good impression — mother's going to ask her sister if you can stay overnight next time you come. She lives about half a mile away and ran a small guest house before the war. With rationing and other restrictions she had to close down.'

'That would be great. Can we book a double room? Save you going home Julie.'

'I don't think mother or auntie would approve of that.'

'It's you I would be asking, not them — what do you say?'

She smiled 'I'd say don't push your luck sailor!'

Joe's voice brought him back to the present. 'Ruth says that Julie's aunt can put us up for the night. Should be an improvement on the floor at the church hall.'

'Just the job,' replied Grainger. Better still, he thought wistfully, if it had been Julie instead of Joe.

'See you tomorrow then — six o' clock main gates,' said Joe.

But fate was unkind and Grainger was unable to keep the appointment. On the following afternoon he heard his name being called over the tannoy system along with a list of other names which included Mick Shaw and Leading Cook Watts. An order to report to the drafting office followed where they were informed that they were to join a destroyer HMS *Hedron* at Immingham.

In the course of their drafting routine Grainger discovered that a good many of the ratings amongst those who waited with him to pass doctor and dentist were also destined for the destroyer. He learned from one of them that the *Hedron* was a comparatively new ship originally built for the Brazilian Navy but subsequently requisitioned by the Admiralty at the outbreak of war. It seemed that the ship had recently completed a re-fit at Immingham Docks.

'Just our bleeding luck — too late for any leave — and I've heard that we're likely to go on the North Atlantic run,' groaned Mick.

'Think yourself lucky it's not on the *Velperton*.' said Watts.

'We haven't seen what the *Hedron's* like yet,' replied Mick pessimistically. He turned to Grainger. 'No chance of letting that bird of yours know anything — they say we're leaving tonight, Ted.'

Grainger nodded but did not reply. Several weeks ago he would have had no qualms about leaving Plymouth. Shore-based in the bomb damaged barracks was not an attractive existence, but meeting Julie had given him warm glimpses of domesticity without which values became blurred, language coarsened and mentality became rigid with routine. Now he was on his way again to a life on the ocean wave. Some life that would be... Week after week of heaving green sea, bitter cold winds and stinging rain, debilitating fatigue, poor food and cramped quarters interrupted by periods of intense excitement when the jarring of alarm bells summoned the crew to action stations. Pity about the dance tonight at Ashdown — he'd ask one of the lads to pass the word to Joe at the main gates. He didn't suppose Julie would be short of partners. He'd write a letter to her at the first opportunity and in the meantime Joe would tell her what had happened. She'd probably meet someone else and forget about him. Bloody rotten war! Just when things were beginning to improve. Chances were that he'd never get to know her true feelings now. He knew

46

how he felt about her. Perhaps she would answer his letter.

Darkness had fallen when Grainger, along with the other ratings, humped their kit bags and hammocks into the baggage van of a special train standing in the siding at HMS *Drake*. The noisy slamming of doors finally gave way to the blast of a whistle and the darkened train slid furtively out of Plymouth to join the main line and then speed northwards throughout the night.

So that's what they call an ocean greyhound, thought Grainger as he stared at HMS *Hedron* resplendent in her white, black and grey dazzle paint. The outward sweep of her bows towered over the crew as they lined the dockside prior to divisions and Captain's inspection. There was something sleek and stream-lined about this two-funnelled destroyer despite its upper decks being littered with debris from the fitting-out work and the compressed air pipes which writhed like black snakes from one end of the ship to the other. His gaze took in the superstructure of the bridge overlooking the two 4.7 inch guns, one on B gun deck immediately below the bridge and the other on A gun deck on the lower level of the fo'c'sle. Abaft the bridge, hoisted on their respective davit heads, was a motor boat on the starboard side and a whaler on the port side. The two funnels were set at a rakish angle sloping towards the stern the forward funnel in grey, the rear painted with two black bands. Amidships, behind the first funnel was a gun deck with a two-pounder pom pom.

Grainger's eyes moved further astern to the four 21 inch torpedo tubes and to the next gun deck with its 3 inch high-angle gun abaft a search light platform. X gun deck lay further aft sup-porting another 4.7 inch gun and below the square cut stern pro-vided space for two racks of depth charges with replacements secured nearby. Twin depth charge throwers sloped outboard on either side of the ship immediately forward of the quarter deck with empty concave holders waiting to be loaded with their drums of destruction. With a displacement of 1,400 tons and a length of 320 feet the *Hedron* looked larger and much more formidable as a convoy escort than the *Velperton*, thought Grain-ger.

When she sailed from Immingham the following week ru-mours of their destination were rife throughout the ship. Arctic convoys to Murmansk, North Atlantic convoys, the Gibraltar run were all mentioned as possibilities.

'No chance of this ship going on the Murmansk run— she's not fitted out for it,' said Bungy Edwards, a big bearded Leading Hand who ruled his mess with iron discipline and language which threatened to sear the paintwork. His words were spoken confidently in reply to the Arctic convoy prediction of Stripey Jarvis who was a pessimist by nature.

It was six o' clock in the evening and the *Hedron* was facing a North Sea swell as she sailed northwards. Grainger and Mick Shaw, now members of the mess presided over by Leading Seaman Edwards, sat listening with interest to his conversation with Jarvis.

The forward lower mess deck was split into two triangular compartments, each about thirty-three feet by ten feet at the greatest width, and this comprised the living quarters for about forty men. A cushioned bench fixed round the outside perimeter of each mess housed separate lockers for the clothing of each man. A ditty box or attache case held their personal effects in a rack above. The portholes — open in harbour — were dogged down and blanked over. Air blown through shafts helped to disperse the stuffy atmosphere. Most of the mess deck space was taken up with scrubbed deal tables and long bench seats where the crew would eat. sleep, read, write or play interminable games of cards. Forward and in the middle of the mess deck was a hatch cover leading down to another mess deck fitted out in a similar fashion.

The music of a Forces' Favourites programme being played over the broadcast system was suddenly interrupted by an announcement from Commander MacDonald, captain of the *Hedron*. In measured tones he informed crew off-watch that the ship could not be an efficient unit until all her complement, no matter how skilled they may be as individuals, had learned to work together both as a whole and in the smaller teams in which they would be organised to work and fight the ship. For this purpose a series of working-up exercises would be carried out at Scapa Flow and Tobermory during the next two weeks before sailing to join the escort vessels based at Liverpool.

'Scapa bleeding Flow,' groaned Jarvis, 'Bare and bleak as an elephant's arse. More working-up, turning the fucking ship inside out and then back again.'

'What did I tell you,' roared Edwards triumphantly, looking round at the other members of the mess. 'It's the Atlantic run — pound to a penny!'

'We haven't finished with Scapa yet and the Murmansk runs start from there,' said Jarvis obstinately. 'Fitting the ship out for the run won't matter to them if they decide they want us to go at the last minute. We'll be the poor bastards who'll suffer,' he added gloomily.

At that moment two members of the mess, Sandy Wheeler and Scouse Harrison who were acting as cooks, came lurching in as they balanced trays of food against the roll of the ship. Knives and forks were hurriedly passed down each table while Edwards was engaged in dividing portions of fried sausage and tinned tomatoes from the trays. The filled plates were passed from hand to hand, and Edwards smiled maliciously as he noticed Mick Shaw's face was turning a delicate shade of green at the sight of food.

'Some bangers and red lead, Tubby?' he asked Shaw, 'It's the grease that makes them tasty.'

Mick jumped up and prepared to run, hoping he could make the guard rails in time. At that moment a head appeared through the hatch of the lower mess deck. The white face belonged to Signalman Shepherd who was obviously racing against time to reach the upper deck. Edwards grinned when he saw Shepherd rushing past.

'Alright, Brum?' he said alluding to Shepherd's home town of Birmingham, 'Getting our sea legs are we, boyo?'

Shepherd turned his face towards Edwards and while attempting to reply he vomited with great accuracy on to Edwards's plate. Amidst the roar of laughter from the members of the mess Shepherd made a quick exit. A look of shocked disbelief had replaced the grin on Edwards's face as Mick Shaw bumped into him on his way out. Edwards, quick to assess the situation, emptied his plate into the gash bucket and called for Mick's unattended plate to be passed to him.

'Reckon Tubby wouldn't like to see his supper go to waste,' he said philosophically and tucked into the food as if nothing had happened.

9

Scapa Flow had gained the unenviable reputation of being the most detested Royal Naval base of them all. Capable of holding the entire navies of the world and surrounded by barren hills, the land-locked anchorage stretches fifteen miles from north to south and eight from east to west. Strategically placed to enable the navy to control shipping between the Atlantic and northern waters, the defences of the base against enemy action had been badly neglected in peacetime. Six weeks after the war had started, the battleship *Royal Oak*, moored a mile off-shore in Scapa Bay, was torpedoed by a U-boat which slipped undetected in and out of Kirk Sound and escaped unscathed. The sinking of the battleship with the loss of 800 men, indirectly caused by the complacency of the Admiralty, was a humiliating disaster for the Royal Navy.

After encountering the usual rough passage through Pentland Firth where the Atlantic Ocean clashes with the North Sea between the land masses of Scotland and the Orkneys, the *Hedron* steamed towards Holm Sound and the entrance to the Flow. ' Hands fall in for entering harbour' was piped and the crew dressed in number 3's lined the fo'c'sle and quarterdeck. The defence vessels with bows resembling a crab's pincers began to swing open the boom and make a passage through the torpedo nets. As the *Hedron* went through, Grainger, standing on the fo'c'sle glanced to starboard at Kirk Sound which the U-boat had penetrated. The sky was dotted with barrage balloons and the muzzles of ack-ack guns could be seen on some of the headlands. When Grainger had been there the previous year the anchorage had been cleared of the big ships. While the defences were being improved and the loopholes plugged, the Fleet had left Scapa to operate from Loch Ewe and Rosyth. The Luftwaffe correctly anticipated this move by dropping magnetic mines at both places causing extensive damage to the battleship *Nelson* at Loch Ewe and breaking the back of the cruiser *Belfast* at Rosyth. Part of the Fleet was back again at Scapa as evidenced by several menacing warships comprising of battle ships, cruisers and flat-topped carriers. Drifters carrying stores, men and mail scuttled across the stretch of sea. A signal lamp winked from a tower ashore and the *Hedron* steamed towards the lines of Home Fleet destroyers swinging at their buoys in Gutta Sound. As they steamed slowly between Flotta and Fara the vast bulk of the *Iron Duke,* Jellicoe's old flagship at Jutland, came into view.

'Looks bloody pathetic, doesn't it?' said Edwards who was standing beside Grainger. He pointed at the old battle ship bombed, overturned and now beached on a sand bank in Longhope Sound. ' You been here before?'

Grainger nodded. ' Last year - Hunt class destroyer.'

'Good, we might need a buoy jumper later on —fancy the job?'

'Is there a choice?' asked Grainger. He was not enthusiastic about taking a swim in the chilly waters of the Flow. This was likely to happen when a man tried to retain his precarious position on the slimy tilting surface of the buoy after shackling on the ship's cable and the ship going astern to take up the slack. The whaler was there to pick him up but it didn't stop him receiving a ducking beforehand if he lost his balance.

'Good. I'd like a volunteer,' grinned Edwards. ' You'll know about the *Royal Oak* then over there?' Grainger nodded.

Edwards scowled. 'The stupid bastards sunk a block ship across the entrance of Kirk Sound the day after the U-boat had been and gone. Twenty four hours too bleeding late — talk about locking the stable door!' he said bitterly as he strode away.

Sandy Wheeler, a tough regular from Manchester, nodded in the direction of Edwards. ' Lost one of his oppos on the *Royal Oak,*' he explained.

After much shrilling of bosun's pipes as courtesy calls were exchanged with passing ships. the *Hedron* fuelled then secured against the massive HMS *Maidstone,* a depot ship, whose sides towered some twenty feet above the destroyer's upper deck. A gangway placed amidships on the *Hedron* entered the depot ship's loading bay some nine feet above the depot ship's Plimsoll line.

'Don't do it, Ted, no woman's worth it,' advised Mick Shaw as he saw Grainger standing near the guard rails on the upper deck looking out into the dusk of the summer evening.

Grainger turned. 'You won't see Scapa like this very often, enjoy it while you can.' He turned back to look at the water spread out as flat as a mirror in which the silhouettes of the motionless ships at anchor were perfectly reproduced. Sounds carried for miles. A Royal Marine bugler could be heard clearing his throat in the flagship a quarter of a mile away. When the bugler's notes floated out over the silent Flow every ship lowered her jack and ensign, taking her time from the flagship and being careful not to complete the lowering before the flagship.

'Fancy the cinema on the *Maidstone*?' asked Mick.

Grainger nodded his head in agreement and they made their way to the gangway.

'You lads enjoying life on the *Hedron* then?'

Jim Plowden, Leading Hand of the starboard mess was sitting at a table in the *Maidstone's* canteen.

He beckoned them to come and sit at his table. They purchased the non-alcoholic fizzy fruit drinks and came across.

'Not bad,' said Mick. ' It's the four meals a day I don't like.'

'Four meals a day lad?' queried Jim who was only about the same age as Mick. 'Don't tell me that Bungy Edwards has been overfeeding you lot.'

'Not exactly,' replied Mick. ' It was two down and two up as far as I was concerned.'

'Can't understand why that should be. Compared with the last trip the sea was like a bleeding mill pond.' said Plowden.

'Was that the one to Argentia?' asked Grainger.

'Correct. I've never seen seas like it and that's God's truth. We were escorting a battlewagon with Churchill on board — on his way to meet Roosevelt at Argentia. The battlewagon dived under the heavy seas instead of riding them like the smaller ships. Some of the crew were talking to us afterwards — said it was like being in a submarine most of the time. Gives you some idea what it was like aboard the destroyers and corvettes.'

Jim warmed to his tale knowing instinctively that he was getting the full attention of his audience.

'Weight of water crumpled the shield of A and B guns like matchwood. Officers stayed up for'ard to keep watch — walking back to the quarterdeck would have been suicide.'

'Anybody lost overboard?' asked Mick.

'No,' replied Jim. 'Two racks of depth charges were washed off the quarterdeck, though. Some genius in the depth charge party had left some of the charges on a shallow setting instead of putting them to 'safe' when the storm blew up. We were lucky not to get our stern blown off. Skipper damn near shaved off when he heard.'

Jim looked round and saw the *Hedron's* coxswain, Chief Petty Officer Pearson, passing the entrance of the canteen.

'I'll see you lads later. I want a word with the coxswain afore he disappears.'

They watched Plowden hurrying after the coxswain.

'Time for the flicks' said Grainger.

Mick nodded his head in agreement and finished his drink. He pointed to the empty glass. 'Listening to Plowden and drinking that stuff is enough to put the wind up anybody.'

The next two weeks of working-up exercises rigorously tested the *Hedron* and its crew, closely watched by the Vice Admiral responsible for the training of escort ships in the Western Approaches Command. Each night the ship returned to harbour but was moored to a buoy in midstream instead of going alongside the *Maidstone.* After twice being toppled in the sea Grainger became skilled at balancing on the buoy until the whaler's crew picked him up.

Guns were fired at air and surface targets, torpedoes with dummy heads filled with salt water hit the sea with a snake-like hiss and sped towards practice targets over 15,000 yards away. The working-up period was concluded with two days of anti-submarine exercises in the sheltered waters at Tobermory. Asdic and radar teams, look-outs, depth charge parties and boat crews all came under constant pressure.

Grainger's look-out position on the bridge was next to the asdic cabinet in which the operators took their turn in attempting to locate the friendly submarine involved in the exercises.

The monotonous *ping* of the asdic relayed through the bridge speaker would occasionally be answered by the *pong* of a submarine contact. When this happened the bridge became a hive of activity. A warning bell from the asdic cabinet was followed by the officer of the watch sounding the alarm throughout the ship for anti-submarine action stations. Orders to the wheelhouse and chartroom were shouted down voice pipes; the ship's position in relation to the target was shown on the bridge repeater, relayed from the plot in the chartroom, during the chase. The *Hedron* would swing round in response to those orders, laying over on its side and shuddering with the sudden impact of engines responding to a full head of steam. Depth charge drill followed, controlled by a string of orders from the gunnery torpedo officer. During a break in the exercises an argument developed between Scouse Harrison and Sandy Wheeler about the efficiency of the asdic.

'Can't be all that effective,' argued Wheeler. 'One time on my last ship we steamed down every column of the convoy then round the outside and the asdic never picked up a thing.'

'I expect there was nothing there,' said Scouse.

'Nothing there, my arse! Only a bloody great *Unter-see-boten* lying doggo which shoved its tin fish into two of the merchant men then scarpered.'

Harrison turned to Curtis, the senior asdic operator.

'What you got to say about that, Terry, then?'

'Could be several reasons. Noise of the ship's propellers, as Sandy says, masking the U-boat. We know that Gerry found out that if a U-boat can get below a layer of cold water the asdic *ping* won't penetrate.'

'I didn't know that,' said a disillusioned Scouse.

Curtis continued. 'Also if the hunting ship is going at any speed its asdic can't operate because the dome's got to be lifted. Otherwise, it'll tear the bloody thing off.'

'Well, aren't the back room boys working on improvements?' asked Grainger.

'Yes, but it takes time. The Admiralty thought submarines were obsolete so they didn't bother much about asdic before the war started. C-in-C thought it would be settled with the big ships.'

'Here,' said Scouse. 'Anybody seen my lifebelt? — I've got a feeling I'm going to need the bloody thing in the near future.'

The vice admiral in charge of destroyer working-up exercises must have decided that the crew had become a competent team. Before the end of the second day at Tobermory orders were received for the ship to oil and sail for Liverpool.

10

The *Hedron* entered Gladstone Dock early the following morning. Hopes of a run ashore in Liverpool faded when orders were received for the ship to stand-by for leaving harbour. Bungy Edwards, who acted as postman for the destroyer, was back on board with a backlog of mail within half an hour of the ship entering harbour. There was one letter for Grainger and a small parcel – both from home. He smiled as he read his mother's letter giving the latest news from the home front. Both she and his father seemed to be keeping well and busy. She referred to the parcel containing cigarettes and sweets despite him telling her that he could get both a lot easier and cheaper than she could in civvy street.

Funny thing, when he'd been on leave he never talked much about life aboard ship to the people at home. Their world was entirely different. His father, as an ex-army man, could understand to some extent, but the other members of the family would nod sympathetically without realising what he was on about. He didn't blame them. There were more tangible things to think about like rationing, bus queues and the blackout.

How could they understand the subconscious fear of mutilation or death, of being so cold and tired you could hardly find your mouth with a fork, or the murderous hate and gloating when an enemy submarine was smashed to its death in a depth charge attack. Sailors on leave appeared easy going and carefree with stories of a girl in every port. Better to spin a yarn about joining the navy to see the world – it was the only thing they would understand.

'Grainger!' He looked up from the letter as he heard Edwards call his name. Edwards tossed two letters to him. He recognised Julie's writing on one of the letters and opened it eagerly. She thanked him for his letter and expressed her disappointment that they had not been able to see each other again before he left. Yes, Joe had explained the circumstances. No, she hadn't enjoyed the dance as much as before – how could she when Ted wasn't there? Then followed details of the local news in Ashdown. The firm she worked for was moving to premises outside Plymouth during the following week. The new office was nearer her home but she didn't think she'd be there long as she was expecting her call-up for the Wrens at any time. The letter ended 'I am hoping to see you soon, so look after yourself, Love Julie.' The date of the letter was over a fortnight ago and he had written two letters to her since. Must be the post, he decided. The other letter might be a more recent one from her. He picked up the bulky envelope and noted almost subconsciously that the writing was unfamiliar.

The letter was from Mrs Johnson and he read the contents without realising its tragic significance. He read the first few lines again which explained that Julie had been killed in an air raid on Plymouth; she had been on her way home from work. A mass funeral of the victims had taken place and a memorial service would be held the following week at the church in Ashdown which Julie had attended.

He saw from the postscript that his last two letters were enclosed. Mrs Johnson expressed her sorrow that she had to send him such terrible news. The letters had arrived after Julie's death and they had been discreetly re-sealed. He looked at the date of Mrs Johnson's letter – a week ago. His tortured mind realised with shock that Julie had been dead when he wrote those last two letters.

'Love at first sight or is it just the war? Emotional attachments formed in a hurry because every day could be the last.' He remembered Julie's words and tears of anguish came to his eyes. The war – it was always the same. They had been brought together by the war and now the bloody rotten war had separated them permanently.

'Pretty as a picture'. He remembered his thoughts when he saw her on their first date in Marlston. Now she was dead – blown to pieces in a murderous attack similar to the one from which he had been lucky to escape. Lucky to escape – and then to receive news like this?

He picked up the letter Julie had written and read it again. The words brought her back to life for him but the surge of happiness within him disappeared in black despair with the realisation that she was dead. God – what could he do? How could he talk about his sorrow and grief to anybody in these surroundings?

He looked round the mess at the other men reading their mail and making jokes. It was like living in quarantine – a close community from which there was no escape. No opportunity for a few moments of solitude. Nothing could be hidden – even his letters were scrutinised by one of the officers. He couldn't bring himself to express his true feelings when he wrote to Mrs Johnson knowing that his letter would probably be discussed elsewhere.

But there was something he could do bloody quick. He checked the date on Mrs Johnson's letter.

'What is it, Ted, bad news?' Mick Shaw asked.

Grainger was silent, his face strained and pale. He picked up the letters. 'A friend,' he blurted. His mind had been numbed by the shock and he couldn't think of any more words as he walked out of the mess deck.

Grainger looked with unseeing eyes at the bustle and activity in the docks as ships were prepared for sea. He suddenly turned and strode quickly away towards the *Hedron's* quarterdeck.

'Officer of the Day about?' Grainger's question was directed at the quartermaster.

'Ship's office,' replied the quartermaster, barely looking up from his desk as he studied the orders of the day. 'Better make it quick, mate, we're under sailing orders.'

'I'm sorry, Grainger, but there's no chance of compassionate leave in these circumstances.' Lieutenant Jones, *Hedron's* Navigating Officer and currently Officer of the Day, looked up sympathetically from reading Mrs Johnson's letter. 'Even if a blood relative had been involved, and besides...' He looked at the date of the letter. 'It's too late for you to attend the memorial service.'

He stood up and passed the letter back to Grainger. 'If you can write your reply and let me have it in the next half hour, I'll personally see that it is posted.'

He saw the desolate expression on Grainger's face and said 'I'm sorry, lad, that's all I can do.'

．　　．　　．

It was 0730 hours the following morning when the *Hedron* cast off from the quayside of Gladstone Dock and moved slowly in a curtain of mist and rain down the Mersey into Liverpool Bay. A south-westerly began to gust, driving the rain before it under a lowering sky. The destroyer steamed out into the open sea and her bows pointed south into St George's Channel.

As she left the shelter of land, *Hedron* began to pitch and roll in the seaway. The wind whipped the green sea into flurries of white-crested waves matched by the white foam flung from her axe-like bow as she smashed through the sea.

Before sailing, Commander MacDonald had informed the ship's company that they were bound for the Gibraltar run where convoy casualties had mounted alarmingly during recent months. They were to meet a convoy of thirty merchant ships, and the escort vessels, including the *Hedron* as senior ship, would consist of two destroyers, two sloops and five corvettes. *Hedron* was to be relieved eventually and would join Force H based at Gibraltar while the convoy sailed on to Freetown.

There was an unmistakable sense of purpose about the convoy as it forged relentlessly forward, its vast bulk covering over fourteen square miles of the lumpy grey sea. The ships were in six ordered ranks and the columns five ships deep with approximately half a mile between ships. Tankers and ammunition ships occupied the innermost columns and leading the centre column was a 10,000-ton refrigerated cargo ship carrying the Convoy Commodore. Disposed in a close screen round the convoy some three to four miles distant, so that each ship's radar and visual range overlapped, were the escort vessels. Two days out of Milford Haven the convoy left its westerly course to turn south and move well to the west of the Bay of Biscay and its nearby U-boat bases at Brest, Lorient, St Nazaire and Bordeaux.

'Aircraft bearing red 160!' Grainger shouted his report on the *Hedron's* bridge during the afternoon watch causing Lieutenant Manson to swing his binoculars round to the reported bearing and see the black dot in the sky. The captain was already on the bridge, having been summoned from his sea cabin directly below when radar contact had been previously reported.

Commander MacDonald muttered a curse, 'Focke-Wulf Condor – pound to a penny – we could do without that bastard's company. Sound 'action stations' Number one.'

Manson identified the aircraft simultaneously with Grainger's further shout of 'Focke-Wulf, sir!' The aircraft was alone and it soon became evident that it had no intention of venturing within range of the *Hedron's* guns. It circled leisurely just below cloud base droning tauntingly and was followed around the horizon by the high-angle three-inch gun and the two-pounder pom pom which were the only guns that would bear. After thirty minutes of slow circling the Focke-Wulf climbed into the cloud and disappeared towards the south-east. Two hours later an identical Focke-Wulf materialised and the same procedure followed as before.

Grainger, closed up at his action station on B gundeck, stared at the aircraft and tried to visualise what was happening in the cabin of the circling plane. It was difficult to believe that there would be a navigator making calculations of course, speed and position of the convoy; a radio operator tapping a morse key while gunners fingered the triggers of their guns, and the pilot anticipated the destruction of the convoy.

'They're keeping us on ice until they're good and ready,' said Bungy Edwards, who was Captain of B gun's crew. 'Every couple of hours until his pals in the U-boat are within range. We can expect trouble tonight alright.'

'Expect he'll piss off before it gets dark,' muttered Jarvis. He adjusted the anti-flash hood round his face. 'One thing's fucking certain – he won't attack.'

'How can you be so certain, Stripey?' asked Grainger.

'They can't carry bombs, mate – they've got long-range fuel tanks instead. They'll tick tack to their bloody *Kamaraden* in the U-boats – just wait and see.'

'We've no alternative to wait and see, have we, you miserable pillock?' was the dispassionate response from Edwards.

Another Focke-Wulf relieved the second plane which wheeled in a circle and then disappeared over the horizon like a huge black vulture reluctant to leave its prey. The aircraft left the convoy when dusk interfered with visibility and a change of course followed shortly afterwards. The convoy was too slow and cumbersome to zig-zag effectively but each escort vessel zig-zagged independently for its own protection and also to distract any U-boat seeking to attack undetected. No hammocks were slung that night and although the strident clanging of action station bells and the explosion of torpedoes were expected at any moment, it remained quiet.

In the grey light of dawn the bridge lookouts stared through their binoculars searching for U-boats surfaced on the white-flecked sea or the trail of a periscope from a submerged enemy closing in to attack. The *Hedron* had now moved well ahead of the convoy and was making wide sweeps out to both bows. The speed of the ship did not exceed eighteen knots to allow the asdic to operate.

Commander MacDonald had returned to the bridge after a short break and was leaning with his head in the asdic hut watching the bearing of a contact previously reported by the operator.

'Contact moving nearer, sir,' reported the operator and the commander suddenly withdrew his head from the asdic hut and urgently instructed the officer of the watch to sound 'action stations'. The asdic operator jerked upright in his seat as his headphones were filled with a sound he had rarely heard since his training in the anti-submarine school at Portland – a chilling sibilant roar that had only one possible meaning.

'Asdic to bridge. Torpedoes running!' he shouted.

Hedron was turning to port. The forward starboard lookout shouted – 'Torpedo tracks – two dead ahead!'

Calmly the captain gave the helm orders for midships – 'Starboard ten, midships – and meet her – steady!'

The thin parallel streaks of tell-tale bubbles sped towards the ship almost head on. There was nothing anyone could do now except stare with thumping heartbeats as the *Hedron's* bow swung into what seemed certain destruction.

Senses cringed as the bow covered the whitening tracks which vanished from view. Then the port forward lookout shouted 'Torpedoes running down portside, sir. The bastard's missed!'

The captain had the quarterdeck telephone in his hand. 'Depth charge crews stand by – stand by – fire pattern.'

The muffled thuds of the pattern's detonators were clearly audible, but even before the giant upheaval of whitened water had broken the surface there was the roar of another explosion. Half a mile astern a colossal mushroom of smoke climbed into the sky, bursting outward and spilling flaming debris.

A merchant ship in the outside starboard column of the convoy had disappeared under a thick cloud of swirling greasy smoke. It was incredible that a ship could disintegrate like a burst balloon immediately after being torpedoed.

'Hard a port. Half ahead both – we're going about – Stand by – full pattern – stern rails, port and starboard!' came the captain's orders.

Grainger on B gun deck grabbed hold of the top of a ready-use ammunition locker as he watched the ship's main mast lean fifty degrees to starboard. A sub-lieutenant was about to shout that there could be survivors from the torpedoed merchant ship in the path of the *Hedron's* bows, when he saw the captain's face twisted in a snarl and kept silent.

The amplified *ping* of the asdic silenced every voice then Curtis's voice sounded urgently from the asdic cabinet. 'Asdic to bridge. Target dead ahead – range two hundred and stationary.'

'Full ahead both!' came the captain's order. 'All guns prepare to engage port quarter. Independent control. Stand by – all guns for target port side astern. Fire when ready.'

'Instantaneous echo!' shouted Curtis.

'Stand by depth charges. Fire pattern!' ordered the Captain.

Three thousand pounds of amatol and TNT tore the sea open with a thunderous roar. Hundreds of tons of white water rose slowly in three mountainous geysers and seemed to hang motionless before gravity brought them back to the sea to subside in white foam.

'Submarine surfacing, sir, – port quarter!'

The U-boat broke surface where Commander MacDonald had calculated it might – astern to port as *Hedron* turned. From the heaving spume the dark grey bows thrust upwards exposing her forward length, knife end bows, jumping wire and the dark mouths of torpedo tubes. Around the cascading pressure hull the sea boiled. For the *Hedron's* after 4.7 inch gun, the midships 3 inch and the pom pom already bearing, loaded and ready, it was a target impossible to miss.

'Target U-boat. Red 140. Range two hundred. Shoot, shoot, shoot!'

The pom pom gun layers failed to allow for the ship's sudden roll and aimed short. The first salvo from the 4.7 inch was square on target followed by a 3 inch shell that ricocheted off the sea and burst at water level. Then the pom pom crew found their mark as the shells from the 4.7s smashed into the rearing pressure hull.

Covered in smoke and spray the helpless U-boat lurched

upwards in its final death throes, hesitated, then plunged. The sea whirlpooled and the U-boat was gone. There was complete silence as the eyes of the lookouts searched and *Hedron* circled and turned her bows towards the churning area where the U-boat had sunk. But there was no sign of survivors from either merchant ship or U-boat.

'Asdic to bridge. No contact, sir.'

'Thank you – and well done. Keep sweeping,' said Commander MacDonald. 'Alright, Number One. Bring us up with the convoy as fast as you like. Take station two cables ahead and we'd better keep our eyes open. I've a feeling that the Focke-Wulf has given chapter and verse to U-boat Command so we can look forward to some more fireworks from the Dönitz brigade.'

11

The *Hedron's* bow waves sparkled with phosphorescent lights as the destroyer plunged at full speed through the blackness of the night. It was past midnight and the ship's company, closed up at action stations for the last hour, were tense in anticipation of another clash with the enemy.

Shortly after 2300 hours one of the corvettes had picked up a radar contact which was thought to be a U-boat using its high surface speed to gain position well ahead of the convoy. Two of the Flower class corvettes had been detached to give chase but the contact had been lost to both radar and asdic sweeps. The two corvettes now resumed position in the convoy screen but the warning had been given – real or not – and the *Hedron's* captain was not disposed to relax the state of readiness amongst the escort vessels.

Grainger's action station was ammunition supply on B gun, if he was not on lookout duty when action stations was sounded. He was standing near the ready-use ammunition lockers on B gun deck ready to pass the brass cylindrical charges to the breech loader. In the dim illumination from the control dials on either side of the gun inside the shield he could make out the implacable face of the gunlayer, Johnny Snaith, a powerfully built red-haired man from Lancashire. On the opposite side of the gun sat the trainer, McTaggart, a burly Scot from the Outer Hebrides and probably the most capable seaman on board.

Bungy Edwards, the captain of B gun, had his back to the outside of the gun's shield as he stared through binoculars at the convoy ships astern. It was a misty, damp night with no moon and visibility was so poor that he could barely make out the silhouettes of the ships as they plunged ponderously forward some two miles away on the *Hedron's* port quarter. Ken Jarvis, the thin pessimistic man from Plymouth; Miller, a barrel-chested Geordie and Wheeler, the tough dry-humoured character from Manchester, made up the remainder of B gun's crew.

'Might be a U-boat,' said Edwards thoughtfully as he lowered his binoculars. 'If it was a U-boat he's been smart enough to escape so far and he could be capable of moving into an attacking position now.'

As if to confirm the truth of Edwards's words there was a tremendous explosion in the middle of the convoy as one of the ammunition ships disintegrated into a geyser of water, flames and debris.

At a height of several hundred feet the massive pillar of smoke spewed out a fiery mushroom against the black sky; the exploding cargo multiplying the torpedo's charge many times over. As the *Hedron's* crew looked on in horror, the column of fire collapsed and pieces of wreckage could be seen hurtling down into the sea. Tongues of red flame flickered along the entire length of the ship. Suddenly, there was a fireworks' display of blood red rockets which broke through the smoke screen and showered debris into the sea near the side of the *Hedron* as she sped after the U-boat which had penetrated the heart of the convoy. There was only part of the torpedoed ship above water now and through the smoke Grainger glimpsed a smoking deck, part of the crumpled superstructure and the stump of a derrick. But there was no sign of any of the crew.

Another ship disintegrated completely in flames and a vast cloud of smoke. Steel plates flew like sheets of paper. Before the *Hedron* reached the end of the convoy column there was another hit on a freighter which also exploded. From bows to bridge the ship was under water and heavy debris narrowly missed the destroyer as she heeled back through the convoy in pursuit of the killer.

Distress rockets were being fired from the convoy combining with the blazing inferno of the torpedoed ships to light up the scene like daylight. The ammunition ship suddenly disappeared with one last tremendous explosion throwing debris hundreds of feet into the air. The torpedoed freighter with its rusted sides was literally falling to pieces as rivets were forced away by the cargo. As the *Hedron* passed, figures on the tilting decks could be seen moving with frantic haste to lower lifeboats and drop scrambling nets over the side.

'That's adding insult to injury,' said Sub Lieutenant Napier, officer in charge of B gun, to Edwards. 'Fritz was waiting for us to pass over him before he tin-fished those two ships.'

'Might not be as smart as he thinks,' commented Edwards as the destroyer gathered speed. 'Looks as if we've got a contact.'

The *Hedron* emerged ahead of the convoy which was swinging away from the sinking freighter; the other two vessels had already sunk. She turned and rushed back to the target area like a hound which has sensed the destruction of its prey.

Aboard the U-boat Kapitän Leutnant Manfred Preisser sat quietly in the control room near the periscope. Following his successful attack on this convoy he had hoped to add another piece of tin to the Knight's Cross – Second Class, which he already held. He glanced round at the officers and men who were sitting silently on any piece of equipment that was suitable to sit on. All non-essential machinery had been switched off – even the gyro compass which would have made a humming noise. The U-boat had been submerged for a considerable length of time and her batteries were in need of recharging. Potassium cartridges had been issued to reduce the amount of carbon dioxide but that only gave a short respite. There was no question of anyone using the heads for that could give away their position on the surface when they were flushed.

Preisser still felt that he could win the duel with the escort vessels. By keeping the engines at a slow, silent speed he could make alterations of course presenting the hunters with just a bow or stern on target which was difficult to pinpoint with accuracy. He was satisfied that his detecting equipment was superior to the hunter's and would give him time to take evading action against the next attack. Already the falling temperature and the salinity of the water through which the U-boat had dived was providing a solid barrier against the sound impulses of the enemy's asdic. The hydro-phone operator could hear the distant noise of propellers. Before reaching the present depth the probing fingers of the asdic contact against the steel hull had sounded eerily like handfuls of gravel being thrown into a tin pail. An encounter between submarine and surface warship was a lethal game of blind man's buff demanding considerable skills on both sides. An experienced commander seldom allowed his enemy to make a mistake and live to tell of it.

On the quarter deck of the *Hedron* depth charge crews stood by to launch an attack on the U-boat but the asdic contact disappeared as suddenly as it had been found. It was evident to Commander MacDonald that the U-boat captain was experienced in playing hide and seek with surface hunters. He paced up and down the bridge pausing frequently to enquire if the asdic had anything to report — but there was nothing The other destroyer and a sloop had joined the *Hedron* in the hunt and the three ships circled round and round, their asdic searching the depths and waiting for the sound which would confirm they had found their target.

MacDonald turned to his first lieutenant. 'He's waiting for his chance to break clear and surface. He'll run like hell then.' He turned to the yeoman. 'Send to our fellow searchers — Stop engines and await further instructions.'

MacDonald knew that he was gambling. The other two ships would be sitting targets but it was a risk worth taking. If the U-boat captain thought that two ships had been withdrawn he would fancy his chances of escape from the remaining ship. There would then be the possibility of regaining contact and MacDonald would launch an immediate depth charge attack.

The U-boat's hydro-phone operator reported that only the screws of one ship could be heard. The other two must have been withdrawn to protect the convoy, decided Preisser. He gave the order. 'Half ahead together' on the twin electric motors. Within minutes he knew he had made an error as depth charges exploded around the U-boat. Water was leaking through seams and pipe joints as the submarine was plunged into total darkness with the shattering of glass bulbs and gauges. Shock waves hit the hull and men cursed as they were thrown against machinery and metal fittings.

Preisser joined in the cursing. He realised that he should have stuck to his original plan and made a gradual alteration to his engine speed. The abrupt movement had given away his position. But he was still confident of escape as lighting was restored from the emergency circuit.

Depth charges were most effective when they exploded just below and abeam of a submarine, for along the keel were the weakest points of the pressure hull — the ballast tanks, vents, pump outlets, propeller shaft, rudder and hydroplane glands. The depth charges were nerve racking but still too far off to inflict a fatal blow. He gave orders to dive as deep as possible. When they were lower than the makers had ever envisaged, he resumed cruising speed. Once he could break clear and surface he was reasonably safe, for a surfaced submarine lying low in the water was difficult to locate. If it came to a surface battle he would use his armaments to good effect. The 88 mm deck gun, with its flat trajectory, had a successful record against surface vessels and aircraft. There were 20 mm cannons and, of course, the torpedoes in the tubes ready for firing at his command — four tubes for'ard and one astern.

On the bridge of the *Hedron* Curtis, in the asdic cabinet, reported a firm contact.

'Any time now,' said Sub Lieutenant Napier on B gun deck as the destroyer circled at speed. As he spoke, the dull thud of the *Hedron's* depth charge throwers could be heard. Depth charges were rolled off the stern then the sea erupted as great white columns of water were flung into the sky.

MacDonald signalled the other two ships to join in the attack. The three ships plastered the area with patterns of depth charges set for varying depths. Curtis reported the sound of metal being crushed, and soon afterwards a large patch of oil spread over the surface of the sea. But the ferocity of the attack was maintained.

In the U-boat there was considerable flooding and the damaged hydroplanes prevented it from diving. Priesser reluctantly gave the order to blow all tanks. Slowly the 750 tons of metal rose to the surface and Preisser prepared for the engagement he had wished to avoid

The blue-white beams of the searchlights blazed from the three ships, lancing into the oil-stained rollers as they centred on the U-boat. Grainger watched fascinated as two periscopes, one much shorter than the other, rose a few feet above the sea followed by the conning tower spilling water like an enormous over-filled saucepan. There was the deck gun emerging like a twisted sea monster with a long snout. Then, finally, the hull of the U-boat surfaced, lean and menacing, with streaks of rust like dried bloodstains.

A klaxon sounded on the U-boat and men tumbled out of the conning tower, then raced to take up their positions at the guns. Cannon fire from the three ships raked the U-boat stem to stern and men fell into the water before they could reach their gun positions, but there were others rushing to take their places. A shell from the U-boat's deck gun screamed a few feet above *Hedron's* B gun deck narrowly missing the bridge and making everyone duck.

Grainger heard the crackle of instructions through the headphones to the gun crew as A and B guns were trained and dipped to the port side. A gun, which had its muzzle trained immediately below B gun deck, was fractionally the first to fire. Momentarily blinded by the flash of the explosion of A gun below his feet and choking from the hot, acrid whiff of cordite, Grainger had little chance to recover before B gun added its contribution to the ear-splitting din. He moved quickly, carrying charges between the lockers and the gun; then clearing the expended brass cylinders as they were ejected with a ringing crash on to the deck when Edwards slammed open the breech of the gun.

The *Hedron* swung back into another attack. This time the port side depth charge throwers were used. One of the charges hit the casing of the U-boat and rolled into the sea. The subsequent explosion lifted the bows of the submarine leaving it to crash back into the sea. Huge sparks flew off the U-boat's deck casing and conning tower as it was raked by the destroyer's two-pounder pom pom. But the U-boat was being skilfully manoeuvred in a tight circle so that the *Hedron's* guns were now unable to bear. She swung away, then making a sharp turn bore down on the U-boat at full speed.

Some of the U-boat crew flung themselves into the sea while others still tried to keep their guns firing at the *Hedron* before she struck the U-boat at an angle for'ard of the conning tower. The destroyer's momentum carried her over the U-boat which disappeared beneath her with a water-muffled shriek of metal on metal. The U-boat bobbed up again and jerked away like a stick, still held in the intersection of the searchlights' beams from the three ships. The shrill whistle of the bosun's pipe sounded on the *Hedron* and the raucous shout of the bosun's mate echoed round the upper deck 'Clear lower deck — B gun's crew man the whaler!'

Grainger found himself following Edwards down the steel ladder without giving much thought to the likely consequences of the order. The whaler was being lowered from its davit heads by separate ropes attached to securing hooks in its bows and stern. The chief bosun's mate bellowed orders to the two columns of men on the upper deck who came forward or pulled back on the ropes as required.

'Put this on, lad, quick!' Grainger took the pistol in its canvas holder thrust at him by the gunner's mate and strapped it round his waist. He was then given two hand grenades which he clipped to the holster belt. The rest of the whaler's crew were similarly armed.

Sub Lieutenant Napier turned to face them following his hurried discussion with the first lieutenant and spoke in a tense voice. 'Our objective is to board the U-boat and take her in tow. She has vital coding equipment which we need to secure. You will use the pistol and grenades when you're ordered to and not before. Understood?'

The men nodded and Edwards spoke quietly. 'Remember the pins and the safety catch, lads, or it could be nasty.'

As the full realisation of what confronted them became clear to Grainger he felt the same numbing fear he had experienced during the Plymouth air raid when he had faced violent death in the town. If the remaining crew on the U-boat could still fire the submarine's deck armament, it was going to be nasty anyway.

'Away you go then, lads,' said Edwards as the whaler splashed into the sea and its crew swung themselves down the ropes into the boat.

The swell of the sea between ship and whaler caused them to pitch against each other as Grainger grabbed a rope and kicked away from the ship's side. In his haste he took his full weight on his hands instead of locking his legs round the rope for additional support. The rope cut into his hands and it was a relief to loosen his grip when his feet touched the whaler's gunwhale. Stumbling into the bottom of the boat he was lucky to keep his balance. Edwards, sitting in the stroke-oar position, motioned Grainger to sit behind him.

'Give way together!' shouted Napier from his position at the tiller and the whaler surged towards the U-boat which was surfaced some five hundred yards off the *Hedron's* port bow. It was obvious that the U-boat had been so severely damaged that it could not dive but Grainger could see no sign of life on its upper deck.

The whaler had closed the distance to a hundred yards when suddenly the conning tower hatch swung open. A tall, bearded man in grey overalls and peaked cap with a white cover stepped on to the small bridge.

'That's the skipper — you can tell by his cap — there's German bullshit for you, boyo!' grunted Edwards, pulling back on his oar.

Commander MacDonald kept the *Hedron's* bows on to the U-boat to minimise the target and watched with mounting anxiety as the whaler pulled towards the U-boat. He called the yeoman over and told him to signal the U-boat that a boarding party was being sent and firing would resume at the first hint of retaliation against them.

Kapitän Leutnant Preisser curled his lips contemptuously at MacDonald's signal. His only response was to place the barrel of an ugly-looking machine gun on the forward side of the conning tower.

'That's a bleeding Schmeisser!' muttered Wheler who was behind Grainger. 'Fires more than a thousand rounds a minute.'

'That bearded bastard looks as if he's going to use it,' muttered Jarvis.

Grainger was surprised to find that his fear had been replaced by anger. Anger that this arrogant German who had dealt such devastating blows to the convoy now held them in this vulnerable position. As he pulled back on his oar he could feel the ring of the safety pin of the grenade on his belt. If he had the chance he would give that Nazi bastard something to remember them by — if he had a chance.

Napier steered the whaler on a course which would bring them round to the stern of the U-boat. The remainder of the U-boat's crew were now appearing beside the captain as they clambered down to the deck and Grainger glimpsed a rubber dinghy being inflated. The U-boat's bridge was now deserted except for the captain who continued to keep the barrel of the machine gun on the whaler's crew.

Preisser stared along the barrel of the Schmeisser and carefully aimed its muzzle at the men in the approaching whaler which was now within fifty yards of the U-boat. If the Tommies arrived before the scuttling charges were detonated they were dead men, he thought grimly. Under no circumstances was he going to allow his boat and its Enigma machine to fall into enemy hands. The engineer officer appeared from below and confirmed that the charges had been set.

Preisser turned back and addressed the whaler's crew through a megaphone. He introduced himself in impeccable English as the captain, then threatened to shoot any man who attempted to board. But Napier was no less determined as he brought the whaler round so that it was lying parallel to the U-boat. The whaler rolled less as the hull of the U-boat formed a breakwater to block the Atlantic swells.

As the tension mounted each side waited for the other to make the first move. The engineer officer touched Preisser's arm and confirmed that the detonators would explode within the next minute. Preisser shouted to the crew on deck and the rubber dinghy was thrown into the water. The non-swimmers jumped after it and after a nod from Preisser the engineer officer climbed down to the deck. With the remainder of the crew he jumped into the sea leaving the U-boat's deck empty and the captain still standing on the bridge.

Through the megaphone Preisser requested Napier not to approach any closer as scuttling charges were about to explode and he did not want the men in the water or the whaler to be drawn down by the suction.

As he spoke, a series of explosions echoed across the water and Napier ordered his crew to bring the whaler round and row quickly away from the sinking U-boat. Commander MacDonald would not thank him if he lost the whaler's crew.

Preisser gave a sardonic smile and threw the Schmeisser into the sea. He descended quickly on to the sloping deck and dived off the casing to follow his crew in the direction of the *Hedron*.

As he bent over his oar with back and arm muscles straining, Grainger saw the bows of the U-boat point skywards as it slid into its last dive. There was a roaring noise under the surface of the sea as the pressure hull and ballast tanks were smashed open, then the U-boat was gone, losing its air supply in a whirlpool of bubbles. The whaler rocked sideways and Grainger felt his oar flailing in the air then floundering in the sea as the whirlpool threatened to engulf the boat and send it with its crew to follow the shattered U-boat. But the whaler bounced back on its keel and one desperate concerted pull on the oars was enough to send the boat out of danger, and they moved swiftly back to the *Hedron*.

The whaler was soon alongside the swimmers and there was a shout of *Kamaraden* as a German grabbed the gunwhale, swaying the boat as he attempted to climb inboard. Grainger caught a glimpse of the oar behind him as it came crashing down on the German's hands. There was a scream of pain as the hands released their hold on the boat.

Following this incident, there was no further attempt to board the whaler. The boat moved round the swimmers like a sheepdog herding the flock into a pen. When the swimmers reached the destroyer the whaler remained some distance away as the Germans climbed up the scrambling net thrown over the *Hedron's* side. As the last man climbed inboard the whaler came alongside the destroyer and was hooked on to its ropes.

The whaler rose and fell with the swell of the sea and the gap between the boat and the ship's side looked tremendous as Grainger hesitantly put one foot on a thwart and grabbed the hoisting rope. Edwards remained in the whaler to secure it after it was hoisted. Sub Lieutenant Napier had already climbed upwards, lifting his considerable bulk with all the grace of a cart horse, but landing safely aboard. The other members of the whaler's crew had no problems, they were well practised and went up the ropes without any apparent effort.

Grainger hesitated for a few seconds, painfully aware that the ship's company were waiting to hoist up the boat and the U-boat prisoners would no doubt be amused if he was crushed between the ship's side and the boat. This last thought gave him the impetus to fling himself at the rope. His feet scraped against the *Hedron's* side but his arms carried him upwards. As he climbed level with the ship's deck he swung his legs up and kicked his feet inboard landing on the iron deck with a crash which shook every bone in his body. He scrambled to his feet in time to watch the ship's company run back with the hoist ropes bringing the whaler and Edwards up to the davit heads. Edwards heaved himself from the whaler down to the deck which had now started to vibrate with the increased engine revolutions as the ship sped to a forward position in the convoy screen.

'Pity we couldn't use 'em,' said Edwards as he handed his revolver and grenades to the gunner's mate who had been busy reclaiming them from the rest of the boarding party. He grinned and pointed forward in the direction of B gun.

'It all helps to pass the middle watch, but there's still some of it left — come on, you layabouts!'

'That bloody German skipper was making sure we didn't board his poxed-up U-boat,' said Jarvis the following day. 'What do you reckon Napier was on about when he talked of vital equipment?'

'Dunno — but the first lieutenant mentioned something unusual when he was speaking to Napier just before we manned the whaler,' replied Edwards. He looked down to the other end of the mess table at Mick Shaw.

'Hey, Tubby, you used to be a newspaper reporter. What's an Enigma?'

'It's a puzzle or a riddle — derived from a Greek word,' answered Mick.

'What's vital about a bleeding puzzle?' asked Jarvis.

'Hang on,' said Mick, his voice rising with excitement. 'I worked in Holland over ten years ago. I heard about a cypher machine called an Enigma. It was being sold by a German on the open market to any country who wanted to buy.'

'But that wouldn't make it vital equipment — not if it was up for sale to anybody,' argued Edwards.

'Depends on how the Germans have developed the idea since,' replied Mick. 'There's one other thought that occurs to me,' he continued. 'If you had been able to grab that up-to-date model with working instructions, I don't think the Navy would have wanted our friends from the U-boat to know about it in case word got back to their masters.'

Edwards nodded thoughtfully but did not reply.

Grainger who had been quietly listening to the conversation suddenly realised that if they had been successful in capturing the U-boat intact there might not have been any German survivors.

12

There were thirty prisoners from the U-boat; Preisser at twenty-six years of age was the oldest and a seventeen year old rating the youngest. Twenty of the crew had perished in gunfire from the escort vessels. The engineer was the only other officer to survive.

'Typical bloody Nazi!' was how Wheeler described him after a spell of guard duty.

Unlike the other Germans who appeared cheerful and friendly, the engineer officer's manner was arrogant, and to the British sailors he was an example of the fanatical Nazi portrayed by the Allied media. The prisoners were under armed guard — ratings in the lower forward mess deck and officers aft in the captain's day cabin.

'They seem a decent lot — you wouldn't think they were the murderous bastards who tin-fished those merchant ships,' said Mick Shaw.

It was the day following the early morning action against the enemy. A group of the *Hedron's* crew were scraping rust from paintwork, including Shaw, Grainger and Wheeler. On the other side of the torpedo tubes they saw the German prisoners taking their morning exercise under the surveillance of an armed guard. Some of the prisoners waved and smiled cheerfully at them as if they were old friends.

'Well, that's yer Gerry for you!' commented Wheeler. 'If he's at the wrong end of a gun he can be the nicest bloke in the world, but watch out if its the other way round, he'll blow yer head off as soon as look at you.'

'Do you know what that bastard of a bosun did last night after I'd been out dicing with death in the bleeding whaler to protect his rotten skin?'

Johnny Snaith had been listening to Wheeler and his broad Lancashire voice was now raised in anger.

'No idea, Johnny, but I think you're going to tell us,' said Mick Shaw with a grin.

'Nothing to laugh at, Tubby. He'd only given one of those Gerries my hammock to sleep in. When I come off watch there was this Kraut sleeping like a a new-born babe and some of his mates sat drinking tea below him. All nice and friendly — you wouldn't have thought they were the same murdering buggers from that U-boat.'

'What happened, Johnny?' asked Wheeler. 'I heard you were up on the bridge with your cap off.'

'Jimmy's report, would you believe it, for disobeying an order on the bosun's say so,' growled Johnny.

'What order?' asked Mick.

'When I saw the Kraut sleeping in my hammock I chucked him out. They moved 'em down to the lower mess deck later but the bosun heard about it and when I asked him which bleeding side he was on he put me on a charge,' said Johnny disgustedly.

'You'll be alright, Johnny,' said Wheeler confidently. 'Just remind "Jimmy the One" what they'd have done to us if they'd sunk us. There wouldn't have been any survivors. According to that Nazi bastard Dönitz he's ordered his U-boat heroes to make sure there's no survivors when they tin-fish a ship.'

'Serve the bastards right if they were caught below decks!' said Wheeler bitterly as he chipped away savagely at a patch of rust.

Grainger could imagine Wheeler attacking the Germans with the scraper the same way — given half a chance. He had heard that Wheeler's family had been killed in a blitz on Manchester only a few months ago. These thoughts brought the shock of Julie's death back to him, and also the sight of men in the convoy who had suffered such terrible deaths. Anguish and sadness blunted any feelings of hatred which he had towards the enemy.

'You reckon that's true about no survivors?' asked Johnny.

'They did it in the last war,' said Mick. 'A U-boat tin-fished a hospital ship, the *Llandovery Castle*, then went round machine-gunning the survivors in the life boats. I researched the story for an article a couple of years ago when they tin-fished the *Athenia* on the first day of the war.'

'Bastards,' growled Johnny, looking across at the German prisoners who appeared exceptionally cheerful. 'Anyway, it's not all bad news — we could be back in the UK before long.'

'How do you make that out, Johnny?' asked Grainger.

'After we've landed that lot in Gib.' Snaith jerked his arm in the direction of the Germans. 'The ship has to go into dry dock for the damage to be inspected.'

'What's that got to do with the UK?' asked Wheeler.

'We'll be going home if they can't do the repairs at Gib,' replied Snaith.

'I know we've dropped speed but the damage doesn't seem all that extensive,' said Mick. 'You're not just being a bloody optimist are you, Johnny?'

'Latest buzz from the stokers is that the port screw has been damaged and if it's a replacement job they can't do the work at Gib. I'm very optimistic, Tubby,' replied Snaith.

The *Hedron* was relieved during the following night and in company with a tanker from the convoy arrived at Gibraltar the next morning. The destroyer was secured to the dockside ahead of an armed trawler while divers went down to inspect the damage.

In addition to the damaged port screw the bows of the destroyer had been torn open by the ramming of the U-boat, causing flooding in the paint shop and anchor cable store. Further inspection was necessary and arrangements were made for the *Hedron* to be moved into dry dock. While the divers were carrying out their work, the Germans were marched ashore under escort on their way to a military prison.

Preisser and the engineer officer led the column of Germans who marched smartly on to the dockside. Lieutenant Manson who was standing by the gangway courteously said goodbye to Preisser, but the German ignored him as he passed with an expression of arrogance and contempt on his bearded face. The only reply came from the engineer officer following Preisser on to the gangway. 'This time you were lucky. Next time we sink you!'

They were filmed by a battery of newsreel cameramen who were dispersed shortly afterwards to make way for senior naval officers from Force H headquarters.

The vice-admiral in charge of destroyers congratulated the ship's company, assembled on the quarter deck, and finished his speech by warning them that the war was no longer confined to the sea. Acts of sabotage had become regular occurrences in the dockyard, aimed at killing personnel as well as damaging ships.

'Keep a sharp look out and report anything which appears unusual,' concluded the vice-admiral.

'It's those Spanish dockies,' declared Edwards when he came back on board after collecting the ship's mail. 'They cross the border in and out of La Linea every day.'

'Aren't they searched at the checkpoint?' asked Snaith.

'They are, but it is the easiest thing in the world to conceal parts of a bomb. The military have nabbed a few but the bastards keep having successes, so watch yourselves when you're ashore.'

Before moving into dry dock the *Hedron's* crew were required to de-ammunition the ship — a process involving a long spell of heavy lifting and carrying which would have to be repeated when the ship was re-floated. When the ship eventually moved into the dry dock the following day the water supply was cut off and the ship's company were required to use the toilet and washing facilities in the dockyard.

Grainger paused at the top of the dry dock that evening and looked down at the *Hedron*. She was supported either side by numerous timber beams which had been floated and fitted between the sides of the dock and the ship before the water was pumped away. The ship's keel was balanced neatly on a series of timber trestles and its sides below the water line were thick with green vegetation. The destroyer looked extremely vulnerable out of its environment — like a stranded whale, he thought, as he walked away.

He passed the armed trawler which had been astern before the *Hedron* had moved into dry dock. The brick-built wash house was some twenty yards away to his right and he was within five yards of the door when there was a terrific explosion.

Grainger felt his legs leave the ground as he was lifted like a shuttlecock and flung by a whirling blast of air against a wall. He had no knowledge of what happened next and eventually found himself stretched on his back looking up at a darkening sky. The acrid smell of cordite and the crackle of flames amongst dense, oily smoke gave him the incentive to stagger to his feet, relieved that he was still in one piece.

The trawler's stern was blown off and a mass of flames raged towards the fo'c'sle. The base of the trawler's mast was already enveloped in flames and the creaking of timber sounded its imminent collapse. A dockyard fire-fighting unit attempting to board the vessel was forced back when the mast finally collapsed across the trawler's deck with a resounding crash.

A seaman was lying on the dockside some distance from the stricken trawler, attended by two dockyard policemen. As Grainger moved nearer he could see that the man on the ground was badly injured, his clothes were torn and his face and chest were plastered with oil and dirt. Although still conscious, his head was so badly injured that the white bone of his skull showed through the skin and clots of blood had replaced his eyes in their sockets.

The two policemen looked up as Grainger approached. 'You look as if you've had an argument with a brick wall — you alright, Jack?' asked one of them.

Grainger nodded. 'Got caught in the blast — anything I can do to help?'

The policeman shook his head. 'An ambulance is on its way for this poor chap, and the alarm's been given about the depth charges which have just gone over the side.'

His colleague pointed down the dockside. 'They're here now.'

A truck with the letters RN painted on the side had pulled up some distance away and a team of divers in rubber suits jumped from the vehicle. Shortly afterwards the ambulance arrived for the injured seaman and one of the policemen accompanied him in the ambulance.

'What about the rest of the crew, are they still on board?' asked Grainger.

The remaining policeman shook his head. 'The injured man was the only one on board. He managed to tell us that. The rest of the crew are on shore leave. Would have been a lot worse otherwise.'

The policeman walked over to the team of divers who were assembling tackle for lifting the depth charges from the harbour. The fire on board the trawler appeared to be under control.

Grainger cleaned himself up in the wash house after finding his towel and soap yards away where they had been blown by the blast. As he returned to the *Hedron* he saw the policeman who had gone with the injured man to hospital.

'How is he?' Grainger asked.

'Died in the ambulance, poor devil,' said the policeman

grimly as he walked back to the smoking trawler.

Edwards brought the full story back next day when he returned with the mail. The cause of the explosion had been sabotage. A delayed-action bomb, hidden amongst the depth charges on the trawler's stern, but divers had succeeded in lifting the depth charges from the harbour without mishap.

'Lucky the rest of the crew were ashore. If we'd been there a couple of hours longer the bastards could have blown us up as well,' said Edwards.

'What do you mean *could have?*' asked Grainger. 'I was blown off my feet. That's the second time the buggers have had a go at me.'

'Do you think they're trying to tell you something, boyo?' asked Edwards with a malicious grin.

Examination of the *Hedron's* damaged screw and bows confirmed that only temporary repairs could be done at Gibraltar. The ship's company were naturally delighted with the prospect of returning home, but the good news was offset by the information that the *Hedron* was to escort a troopship carrying sick and wounded personnel from North Africa.

'It'll be a nice leave if we make it,' said Jarvis in his usual pessimistic way. 'Talk about the crippled leading the sick — we're sitting ducks if Gerry spots us.'

'You can always stay in Gib and get blown up — right, Lofty?' remarked Edwards as he winked at Grainger.

Grainger did not reply to the gibe. His initial anticipation of home leave had cooled down when he thought of the odds against them reaching the UK. Enemy aircraft, surface ships and U-boats would threaten, but the Atlantic was a big place and he brightened at the thought that with anything like luck they would make it. The cheerful trend of Grainger's thoughts was immediately depressed by Jarvis's further prediction that 'those Nazi bastards in Algeciras and La Linea were certain to inform their chums in France when they see us leaving Gib.'

The *Hedron* and the troopship lay well to the west of the Bay of

Biscay, both ships pitching headlong into the turbulence of green, white-crested rollers. There had been no sign of the enemy since leaving Gibraltar but now the two ships were entering the critical stage of their voyage.

Radar, asdic and lookouts combined to provide a screen which would give early warning of attack from above, on, or under the rolling expanse of ocean. U-boats would be leaving or returning to their bases in France and their maximum speed on the surface was well in excess of that which could be achieved by the damaged destroyer.

There was a constant expectancy of sighting Focke-Wulf patrols. Grainger commenced his morning watch on lookout duty feeling more secure than previously as he watched the visibility being curtailed by dense fog which swept over both ships. The fog was so impenetrable that the bows of the *Hedron* quickly disappeared from the view of the bridge personnel and gave them the impression of floating above the surface of the sea in an isolated vacuum.

Two hours later visibility had not improved and the world of silence and unreality was suddenly shattered by the jarring sound of action stations bells. Word came from the transmitting station to the gun positions that German warships had put to sea from Brest, their course and destination unknown.

Grainger, closed up at his action station on B gun deck stared into the rolling clouds of fog which enveloped the fo'c'sle. He could hear the sound of A gun's crew moving below. Their muffled voices reflected their apprehension which had replaced the feeling of security given by the fog. If the German warships turned south on a raiding expedition against convoys, *Hedron* and the troopship could be in serious trouble, he thought.

He remembered the sinking of the *Hood* in the previous May. The presence of fog would not have affected that situation when the accuracy of the *Bismark's* opening salvoes had scored a direct hit on the *Hood's* magazines. His mind was taken off the possibility of 15 inch shells zooming inboard like express trains when news came through that the asdic operator had picked up a strong submarine contact.

'Only needs the fog to clear and we'd have the bleeding Luftwaffe round to complete the hat trick,' grumbled Jarvis.

But within a few minutes the asdic contact had disappeared and as the Hedron's main objective was to get the troopship and herself home safely, pursuit was impractical.

'Probably a U-boat returning to base without torpedoes, Number One,' was the opinion of Commander MacDonald when speaking to the first lieutenant.

The hours passed and still the fog remained. No further news had been received concerning the whereabouts of the German surface raiders and the crew were fallen out from 'action stations'. Watch keeping was now a system of 'one-on and one-off' while the deadly game of blind man's buff continued. There would be no reprieve for *Hedron* or the troopship if the luck they had enjoyed so far deserted them.

The following morning revealed that the fog had gone with the darkness of the night. To complement the improvement in the weather, news was received that the enemy warships had returned to Brest.

'Heard that we were about, I expect,' was Edwards's comment when he heard this news.

It was all over bar the shouting and destroyer and troopship moved confidently towards the Clyde and a well-earned leave.

13

The *Hedron* left the troopship at the mouth of the Clyde then headed south for Liverpool and Gladstone Dock. Before they arrived the ship's company were informed by the captain that while the ship was being repaired and fitted out with the latest anti-submarine weapons there would be leave for the first ten days of the work.

Grainger used part of his leave to return to Plymouth where he stayed at a services' hostel. Subsequent months of comparative peace from the holocaust of March and April has seen some normality return to the everyday life of the town. Building repairs were progressing; streets and roads were mainly cleared of debris; gas, electricity and water supplies were restored to most areas.

His visit to Ashdown was a sad experience. Mrs Johnson looked much older and it was obvious that Julie's death had affected her badly, although she managed to smile when she saw him.

'Come in, Ted, what a nice surprise! I'll make some tea.'

Grainger followed her into the cottage.

'Sit down, it won't take a minute.' She disappeared into the kitchen.

Grainger looked round the cosy room and half-expected Julie to come in at any moment, smiling happily as she had done each time they had met.

There was a rattle of cups and saucers and Mrs Johnson came in carrying a tray which she placed on a side table.

'Julie said she was going to write to you that evening when . .

Her voice faltered and she looked away as her eyes filled with tears. She busied herself with the tea cups and Grainger heard himself mumbling his condolences.

Later Mrs Johnson invited him to stay for a meal but he had no appetite and excused himself saying that he had to return to Plymouth.

Mrs Johnson forced a smile. 'You're welcome here, Ted, any time you want to call. Go with God, my dear, and come back safely.'

Grainger returned to Plymouth and saw the crater in the street where Julie must have been when the land mine exploded, killing her and twenty others. The office block nearby where she had worked was still standing but had been evacuated while a check on its structure was completed.

I expect the bastards have moved out now it's happened. Bungy Edwards's remarks about closing the stable door came to his mind. If only they'd moved out before, she'd be safe and well — it was so bloody obvious it would happen sooner or later. But they hadn't, had they? Like everything else in this country — lives lost needlessly because successive governments were too bleeding thick to recognise the Nazis for what they were.

As he turned to walk away a girl in a white raincoat was crossing the road towards him. he felt his heart beat furiously.

'Julie . . .'

He stopped and black despair returned as he realised that the girl was a stranger. She stared at him without recognition then moved on as he turned away with a muttered apology.

The visit to the cemetery left him more embittered.

There had been a mass burial and her remains were interred with those of the other victims; there was not even the consolation of being able to pay his respects at her separate grave.

He placed a bunch of red roses near the now faded wreaths.

As he walked away a faint breeze moved the card on the roses so that the message showed more clearly.

'Goodbye Julie — Love Ted.'

14

It was a chilly winter's evening when the *Hedron* sailed from Liverpool into a calm Irish sea, then sped through the North Channel at a speed exceeding twenty knots. Her repairs completed, she sparkled in a fresh coat of paint. Strange-looking aerials and radar scanners sprouted from her main mast and new asdic equipment had been fitted. Her fo'c'sle has been strengthened and A gun removed to accommodate a new anti-submarine weapon called the Hedgehog. Unlike its namesake the weapon bristled with metal tubes instead of spines and was capable of launching 24 anti-submarine bombs simultaneously 250 yards ahead.

Once asdic contact was established any U-boat lurking ahead, expecting the usual onslaught of depth charge patterns from the ship's stern, would be in for a nasty if not fatal surprise. The bombs exploded on impact only, but a single hit on a submarine's hull would be enough to sink her. The depth charge had a wide area of destruction without a direct hit being made, but the Hedgehog made it possible for an attack to be delivered while the ship was still in asdic contact. With a depth charge attack, where it was necessary to run over the submarine, contact was lost as the ship closed and there was a blind period during which the submarine could move away from its forecast position.

Leaving harbour following a break of several weeks was a nostalgic moment for the crew after spending their leave with family and friends, but many of them were not averse to a change; there would be some relaxation at sea from the formalities of harbour routine and the pubs ashore were too crowded for comfort.

During the middle watch the *Hedron* arrived off Northern Ireland and proceeded to an oiling berth at Moville near the entrance to Lough Foyle. The brilliantly-illuminated Eire shore made a mockery of the black-out regulations in force on the opposite shore of Northern Ireland.

Shortly after 05.00 hours the destroyer slipped its moorings and moved into the Atlantic. The weather remained calm and she joined the convoy and its other escorts in the choppy seas off the north west coast of Ireland.

Grainger stared through binoculars at the rust-streaked, battered sides of the forty ships as the *Hedron* moved up and down between the five columns of the convoy. It looked to him as if anything that could carry cargo and remain afloat had been assembled. The other escort vessels, consisting of a V and W class destroyer and three Flower class corvettes, flanked the outside of the convoy. The shape of the corvettes reminded Grainger of the pictures he had seen of the old whale-catching ships. He knew from experience that the corvettes were useful in keeping U-boats submerged away from a convoy, but their maximum speed of sixteen knots was too slow to catch a U-boat on the surface.

Bungy Edwards, who had served on corvettes, reckoned that the Flowers with their broad beams were more seaworthy against rough seas than destroyers.

'Destroyers are made for speed, see,' Bungy had declared one night in the mess when the subject had cropped up. 'You just watch the next time we hit a rough sea. We'll have to steer head-on into it to escape capsizing. The corvettes ride the seas easy enough anyway they want. They've got a vicious roll, though, you need a strong stomach to put up with 'em.'

'What about this bastard on the last trip to Argentia?' asked Jarvis. 'Worse than the Big Dipper and sodding wet on the mess decks with it'. .

'Like I said before I was interrupted', continued Edwards, glaring at Jarvis. 'A destroyer cuts through the waves, corkscrewing and crashing her bows and when her arse comes out of the water you think she's broken her bleeding back.'

'In other words' said Mick Shaw, 'destroyers aren't the best ships for this job.'

'You've hit the nail on the head, lad,' said Jim Plowden who had crossed over from his mess-deck to join in the conversation. 'They're neither efficient nor economical for convoy work. The tin-fish are useless — the 4·7s can't elevate against aircraft and those bleeding engines take up too much space and need all those tiffys to look after them.'

'But destroyers have got the speed,' argued Mick.

'Quite right, lad,' replied Plowden. 'When they can use it — which isn't very often. With a slow convoy like this we spend our time running round in circles. Reckon we cover twice or three times the distance of the merchant ships. Afore long most of the escort vessels will be sloops and corvettes — built faster, cheaper to run and as Bungy says, more seaworthy than destroyers, you mark my words.'

On the bridge Commander MacDonald was livid with rage. An old tramp steamer was sending up dense clouds of smoke through a solitary long narrow funnel. The pall of smoke was making a useful marker for any U-boat which might be within a radius of fifty miles.

Some of the convoys carrying food and armaments to Britain and eastern war theatres sailed at only five knots because the convoy's speed was that of the slowest ship. U-boats were capable of nineteen knots on the surface which gave them an obvious advantage.

MacDonald was fully aware of why these convoys were so slow; the fast ones varied but ten to twelve knots was normal. In peace-time the shipowners wanted a ship of the lowest possible net tonnage to keep down the cost of harbour and canal dues and the highest possible gross tonnage to carry as much cargo as possible. Neither tonnage bore any relation to a ton as a weight. Net and gross tons were based on a ton comprising one hundred cubic feet. Into the largest practical cargo-carrying hull the shipowners put the smallest and most economical engine that would propel the ship at the lowest speed acceptable to the shipper and produce in peace-time the largest profit to the shareholders.

In war-time, crossing the Atlantic at the equivalent of a walking pace meant that a U-boat could attack a convoy, use all her torpedoes then race back on the surface to her French base. On the last 200 miles home the U-boat would be forced to dive at daylight because of the risk of air attacks. After re-fuelling and re-arming it could then race back to make another attack on the same convoy.

MacDonald knew that the smaller shipowners regarded the war as a good thing; they were carrying insured cargoes at high rates — which was their first consideration. If the old ships, whose depreciation had been written down years ago in the companies' books, were sunk by the enemy, the government replaced them with new ships, and crews were drawn from the pool of seamen organised by the Ministry of War Transport.

Some of the old ships were little better than floating coffins in MacDonald's opinion and most of them sailed under the Greek flag. He was sure that there must be a special corner of hell reserved for shipowners who sent men to sea in such ships, especially in the North Atlantic during winter.

MacDonald gave helm orders which swung the destroyer round the stern of the convoy and inside the port flanking column of ships. As the *Hedron* came alongside the coal burner — still making clouds of smoke — MacDonald could see the captain standing behind the wheel in the glass-enclosed wheelhouse. He was a big man, even bigger than the tall, solidly built MacDonald, and his shirt sleeves rolled to the elbow revealed massive hairy forearms straining against the wheel to hold his ship on course. He opened the side window of the wheelhouse to answer the commander's terse warning over the bridge loudhailer.

'How do you think I can keep bloody moving without clearing out clinkers and stoking up. You navy blokes don't know you're bloody born with your oil fuel.' He shouted through a megaphone.

MacDonald didn't mince his words. 'There's no need for all that smoke. You're a bloody menace to the convoy. If you don't cut it down I'll make sure you drop out on your own!'

The captain of the tramp steamer pushed his flat cap to the back of his head and waved a fist like a sledge hammer at MacDonald. 'I was sailing these waters afore you was a twinkle in your mother's eye. I can bloody well manage without you coming round like a blue-arsed fly every few minutes.'

MacDonald's face took on a reddish tinge at the captain's reply, but he refrained from replying in front of the *Hedron's* bridge personnel, particularly as the smoke had thinned out considerably.

MacDonald ordered increased revolutions and the destroyer surged away through the convoy, continuing its sweep past each column of ships. The convoy steered on a north westerly course towards Iceland to keep within range of Coastal Command Liberators and Sunderlands, based in Northern Ireland and Iceland, for as long as possible.

As Grainger continued to search the forward port quarter through binoculars he could see the V and W destroyer taking station some three miles ahead. The V and Ws were veterans in the business of escorting convoys. Launched in 1917 to counter the escalating successes of the U-boats during the first World War, they had a displacement of 1100 tons and were something like 300 feet in length. They carried a crew of 125 but because of the removal of the forward boiler to increase fuel capacity the maximum speed was reduced to 25 knots. The modified number of guns comprised two 4 inch and one 3 inch high angle, two 2-pounder pom poms and storage space had been made for 118 depth charges.

The *Hedron's* crew numbered 160 men and, like the other navy ships of the time, the hard core consisted of peace-time regulars serving seven to twelve or twenty-one-year engagements. Grainger knew from working with them that they were well trained and experienced. Some, like Jarvis, who had enlisted to escape the hopelessness of unemployment during the early thirties had become quickly disillusioned and their discharge couldn't come soon enough.

For them the war had imposed an unjust extension of a prison-like existence Others like Bungy Edwards, Wheeler, Miller and Snaith were younger men and adapted more philosophically; they had signed on again after completing their initial engagements. All of them referred to themselves as active service ratings and like Joe Myers they had little time for the 'hostilities only' men. The regulars were supplemented by recalled reservists like Jim Plowden. Many of these were middle-aged men who had hoped their sea-going days were over but now had to resume a spartan environment for which they were often physically unfitted. Some of the crew were RNR, like McTaggart, ex-trawlermen and merchant seamen with a dislike of naval discipline but contributing valuable experience and skilled seamanship.

The crews were then made up from the 'hostilities only' ratings supplied by national conscription and these men provided the biggest re-inforcement in man power. They came from every conceivable background, from poverty to the middle and upper classes, from industrial towns and the green shires. For most of them the navy was the last career they would have chosen — and they had not chosen it. They could not guess what was expected of them and life on the mess deck proved to be a shattering experience. Soldiers and airmen, whose locations may have been remote and their duties arduous, usually had the consolation of a NAAFI canteen and other off-duty distractions. They were seldom long separated from civilian influences.

The sailor was a member of a small quarantined all-male community and whether or not he liked his mates, he could never escape from them. He could never enjoy a few moments of solitude, never be free of noise and motion; for every minute of his night and day the ship's engines throbbed, generators hummed and the deck under his feet was never still.

He performed his personal ablutions without privacy and his most intimate possessions were revealed to common gaze. For the newcomer the familiarity of naval life was punishing, but mercifully the more sensitive instincts became blunted and after a while he cared progressively less.

Eleven weeks of bullying by petty officers could not make seamen of clerks, labourers and bus drivers and most of them would never become seamen however long they served. But the new 'hostilities only' men were bringing a new logic and differ-ent perspective to a navy which could only justify many of its procedures by the fact that they had always been done that way. Mick Shaw was never tired of saying that the long-serving stripeys belonged to Nelson's navy.

If the time-serving men were the skilled seamen, the 'hostili-ties only' men were making invaluable contributions in the technical branches. Since the First World War there had emerged a range of new weapons — radar, acoustic mines, long range aircraft and the submarine wolf pack — each one of them making sea warfare infinitely more complex and more diaboli-cally scientific. But the nature of the men of the lower deck from whatever background — active service or hostilities only — had changed little over the years. They experienced the same emo-tions, fear, love, hate, home-sickness, happiness and despair.

Sometimes they got drunk on a run ashore, brawled, blas-phemed, often they laughed, occasionally they cried.

15

'Panic stations!' shouted Miller as he and some of the off-watch members of the crew were working on the *Hedron's* upper deck. It was the second day of the voyage and a merchant ship in the outside port column had developed steering trouble.

The ship started to veer towards a ship in the inside column which immediately steered to starboard, setting up a series of evading actions between ships in the remaining columns. The shutter of a signalman's Aldis lamp clattered on the *Hedron's* bridge as changes of course were signalled to separate the convoy from the ship in trouble. A corvette had left its position at the rear of the convoy to screen the unfortunate merchantman as it wallowed helplessly in the Atlantic swell.

'God help them if they don't get the steering fixed before dark,' said McTaggart grimly, as he looked up from his splicing of a manila rope.

Fortunately, the weather remained calm and the trouble was cleared in time for the merchant ship to resume its position in the convoy before nightfall.

'It's been too quiet so far – I've got a feeling in my water that it's the lull before the storm.' Edwards was forecasting to the crew of B gun during the afternoon watch of the fourth day.

The convoy was moving towards the southerly entrance of the Denmark Strait with Iceland on its starboard side. McTaggart looked at the wall of black clouds which lay across the horizon. As he watched, the clouds rose higher and higher into the sky and then disintegrated into puffs of yellowish haze in the watery rays of the sun.

'Aye, storm is right – and afore the day's out,' he agreed.

His opinion was shared by the Officer of the Watch as he consulted the barometer and noted the ominous fall of the needle. Orders were given for the ship to be secured against the expected storm. The convoy had been recording an average speed of seven knots since leaving Ireland and with a clear run and good weather it would take the best part of twelve days before they reached their destination.

The light began to fade as the suction and friction of gusting wind ruffled the water. To Grainger's ears, in his position of forward starboard lookout on the bridge, the roar of the sea was gaining in volume until it became one single vibrating sound. The wind began to howl on a steady high-pitched note, sometimes breaking shrilly then reverting to its former noise. The *Hedron* was staggering – shaken and wrenched by the white-crested, grey greenish breakers which came rushing past. Squalls of heavy rain driven by gale force winds swept the decks of the ships as they ploughed their way towards the south-east coast of Greenland. The rain was flung at the convoy as if the forces of nature had been marshalled against the ships to warn the men who had the temerity to sail through this vast wilderness of water. The ships rolled heavily as they were pounded by sea and wind and it was inevitable that the convoy columns should begin to lose their formation.

Night fell, adding its darkness to that of the storm. Sheets of spray from the heavy seas and intense cold made conditions miserable on the open bridge and lookout positions. During the first watch the winds reached hurricane force, blotting out all visibility as the *Hedron* was buried by green water crashing inboard. The night was pitch black and thick clouds rolled overhead but the ocean surface, beaten white by the storm, was clearly visible. The convoy was heading directly into the storm and ahead loomed great rolling mountains of water, each threatening to break the ships into pieces.

Grainger, back on lookout, gripped the corner of the bridge with one hand as he pressed his eyes to the binoculars in a vain attempt to see through the mass of water. The bridge was some forty feet above the *Hedron's* waterline yet the seas were towering up to forty-five degrees above the bridge. As each wave loomed up, the destroyer rose to meet it, climbing steeply up the front as the sea slid past her bows and she was left hanging in the air before dropping into the next trough. The ship was then buried with a resounding impact which sent shock waves throughout its length to add to the vibration of the screws racing madly as they came out of the water. At times, it seemed to the men on the *Hedron's* bridge that the bows of the ship were permanently trapped in the waves, then somehow she managed to dig herself out, poise for a few seconds, before rushing downwards again.

He came off watch at midnight and began the dangerous descent down three flights of steel ladders which led to the forward mess deck and found it to be a place of concentrated misery.

Dim emergency lights provided the only illumination as one watch tried vainly to catch a few hours of oblivion. Hammocks, which would normally have been slung between stanchions about eighteen inches beneath the deck head, remained stowed in the hammock netting. There was moisture everywhere, two inches of water swirled from one side of the deck to the other, water on the steel of the ship's sides oozed from countless deck welds and rivets where it was forced in by the wind outside. Plunging into the head sea the noise was deafening, a constant roar of turbulent wind and water punctuated by a massive thud as the bows hit another great sea. The ship was lifted then came crashing down as it plunged to land with an impact which hurled Grainger from one side of the mess deck to the other. He stumbled through the sleeping bodies and swishing water until he found a space on the lockers.

He turned on his side and gripped the rack fixed above the lockers in a vain attempt to sleep before the bosun's mate called the next watch in just under four hours' time. With a rolling corkscrew motion the nightmare world of the forward mess deck started to climb again. The twin anchor cables rattled in the hawse pipes and cranked at each movement adding a jarring note to the endless din. Grainger gripped the rack with both hands to stop himself falling on to the deck. As he lay in wet clothes, cold and bruised, it suddenly occurred to him that the storm had occupied his attention to such an extent that all thoughts of a cunning, brutal enemy waiting for an opportunity to sink the ship had been pushed out of his mind.

As he stared at the heaving deck he forced himself to think about the eventual arrival of the ship in port when the bucking, rolling and misery would end and he could sleep without interruption. To endure the crossing was the chief aim and to hell with the U-boats, he thought, as his mind impelled the ship forward to its appointed destination.

Hopes that the storm would run itself out after the first night faded. Gale after gale shrieked down from the north; fierce winds snatched the tops off waves and sent them flying to the mast head, stinging the faces of the crew and blinding their eyes. Life below deck continued to be a hell of wet clothes, fitful sleep and constant bruising motion.

On the second morning Grainger was standing by as messenger at the back of the bridge when he saw the sky blotted out and in a moment of mind-numbing panic he realised that the wall of blackness was an enormous sea. The *Hedron's* bow rose and there was a thunderous roar as everything was submerged. Miraculously, the wave passed and they emerged soaked but unscathed. The gaps between the ships in the convoy had increased as they sought greater sea room. As Grainger looked at the convoy, now on the destroyer's port beam, he could make out the big tankers rising like whales with water streaming from their rusting decks.

Suddenly, a great bulk carrier ahead slewed out of line and collided with a freighter in the adjoining column. He heard the screech of fractured metal above the howling of the gale. The collision had amounted to only a glancing blow but the starboard bow of the freighter showed a gaping hole.

The speed of the convoy was now reduced to four knots and at this speed some ships were finding it difficult to maintain a proper course. As the day passed, more and more ships fell out of line.

By the fourth day of the storm the convoy was scattered over miles of ocean, its shattered ranks had long since been broken into shapeless huddles of storm-lashed ships.

Commander MacDonald, wedged in a corner between the base of the gunnery director control tower and the hatchway leading down to the signals office under the bridge, huddled down against the prolonged ferocity of the weather. The wind had risen steadily to hurricane force since the outbreak of the storm, throwing up mountainous seas into terrifying rollers which had towered high above the ships with their tops streaming downwind in spray.

But, far from intimidating him, the storm had only served to stoke up MacDonald's anger and frustration. His ambition from the outbreak of the war had been to fight against the U-boat menace. When it was evident that the Atlantic was to be chosen by the Germans to wage their murderous campaign, he had welcomed the chance of taking the *Hedron* into the thick of the fray. In his opinion, the stalking and final killing of a U-boat was all about getting to the enemy at close quarters – a personal combat in which good seamanship would usually decide the issue. Not for him the anonymity of a fleet destroyer screening battleships and aircraft carriers, always at their beck and call. But the present position was that the *Hedron*, like the other escort vessels, had spent most of the last four days hove-to in appalling weather while reports streamed through of U-boat attacks on other convoys to the South.

The destroyer's engines were just turning enough to maintain steerage way which was a problem, for any forward motion meant that each gigantic wave struck the ship much harder and the bow buried itself that much deeper into the waves, hurling tons of water on deck from bows to stern crushing any movable object in the way.

To walk along the upper deck was impossible without being swept overboard and it had been necessary to divide the crew into two sections, aft and for'ard.

MacDonald and Lieutenant Knight had held the fort on the bridge for the last three days and nights, snatching food and sleep when they could. The terrible shaking every time the ship had slammed down into the trough of a wave had put the gyro compass out of action and the magnetic compass veered wildly from side to side. Hour after hour the ship had to be conned by orders from the bridge to the man at the wheel below as the two officers tried desperately to keep her from falling away and getting beam-on to the seas. But the rudder alone was insufficient, and only by calling on the engines for short bursts of power could MacDonald keep the ship heading up into the seas.

During that afternoon the wind showed signs of easing and by the evening it was no more than a fresh breeze; by nightfall the enormous seas began to subside. Normal watch keeping was resumed and men were able to move along the battered upper deck where the wreckages of both the whaler and motor boat hung from their respective davit heads.

The storm had left MacDonald with more problems. The corvettes were running low on fuel with a thousand miles of stormy Atlantic ahead and the U-boat gauntlet to run. The cold grey light of the following morning revealed that apart from the commodore's ship and the other escort vessels the convoy had vanished from the face of the ocean. One of the corvettes was screening the commodore's ship; the rest of the escort circled in different directions like sheepdogs anxious to regain control over a wayward flock.

For much of the forenoon watch the escort vessels searched an ocean empty of ships. The weather now was the blue calm of the southern latitudes and crystal clear. A cry from the look-out in *Hedron's* crow's-nest brought confirmation to MacDonald that the search area he had chosen was accurate. Although well off course the faster ships in the convoy had been able to maintain approximate station with each other.

'Thank God we've found them, sir,' muttered Lieutenant Knight.

'None too soon,' said MacDonald, 'with this visibility and no escort, the U-boats would have had a field day if they'd got here first. We've still got to find those bloody coal burners – damn and blast 'em for their stupidity!'

Not their fault this time, thought Bogey Knight. The old man must be still smarting from his encounter with the skipper of the coal burner. Bogey was wise enough to keep his thoughts to himself. Mac was a good skipper but a bastard if you got on the wrong side of him.

Shortly after mid-day the black smoke of the coal burners was seen on the horizon. Miraculously, not a ship was lost and by late afternoon the convoy was re-formed into its original columns. The five-ship escort circled and swept round the convoy, occasionally going alongside to administer reprimands to the offenders who straggled or made too much smoke.

In theory, the escort commander was responsible only for the defence of the convoy against enemy attack. Commodores of ocean convoys came from the ranks of retired admirals and senior merchant navy officers and were given the rank of commodore RNR. They embarked with a small signal staff in the ship selected as their flagship for the voyage. Their duties were to ensure safe navigation and internal discipline of the convoy.

The dividing line of responsibility between escort commander and commodore was not clearly defined in convoy orders. A breach of internal convoy discipline would be an improperly darkened ship, excessive smoke, or the inevitable straggler who could not make the speed claimed at the conferences ashore. If strict protocol was followed the situation would be dealt with by a request from the commodore to escort commander for an escort to go alongside the offending ship and reprimand the captain as MacDonald had done with the coal burner. Reprimands so far on this convoy were being given without prior reference to the commodore because MacDonald considered the culprits were exposing the convoy to danger from attack and therefore it was within his jurisdiction as escort commander to deal with the breach of discipline.

He was well aware that the commodore was very much senior in rank to himself and had the commodore chosen to stand on his dignity and insist on the letter of the law regarding responsibilities, relations would have been difficult. In his dealings with commodores, including the present one, MacDonald had found them to be courteous and co-operative, particularly in accepting guidance and suggestions from the escort commander. They had appreciated, without exception, that the escort commander was better informed of the general situation by virtue of superior radio facilities. MacDonald reflected that if a difference of opinion arose with the commodore, which in his opinion involved the ultimate safety of the convoy, then he would have no hesitation in following his own course of action.

Before dusk MacDonald ordered the corvettes to drop back to fuel from the aftermost tanker in the centre column. On one occasion, as the *Hedron* swept past, Grainger who was on bridge look-out could see one of the corvettes moving alongside the tanker maintaining the 'U' in the bight of the fuel pipe which connected both ships. He remembered seeing a similar operation in the North Sea when a destroyer had been covered with thick black oil as a result of a hose breaking during the refuelling. The destroyer had increased speed in excess of the tanker by mistake and the broken end had swished about under great pressure, squirting tons of heavy bunker oil over everything.

He smiled to himself. What a bloody mess – pity the poor sods who had to clean that lot up. Then he thought about the corvettes in the recent storm. Life aboard the *Hedron* had been sheer misery; on the corvettes it must have been sheer hell.

'That's the position the U-boats like to be in before they attack,' commented Jim Plowden as he pointed through the wheelhouse window. 'Well ahead and either on the port or starboard bow of the convoy.'

A series of orders from the bridge came through the wheelhouse voice pipe and Plowden swung the steering wheel round with practised ease as he repeated the orders and then confirmed that they had been carried out. Grainger had brought Plowden a cup of tea from the adjoining signal office and he was now deputising for Wheeler on the telegraph position while that rating was attending first lieutenant's defaulters. He looked through the window in the direction Plowden had indicated. The sea was still rough after the storm but apart from the churning white-topped waves he could see no other movement.

'You're not likely to see anything out there in daylight,' said Plowden. 'The bastards like to maintain contact at visibility limit astern, either on the surface or at periscope depth, then after night fall they'll overtake at top speed.'

'We could be lucky and slip through without being spotted,' replied Grainger hopefully.

Plowden shook his head doubtfully. 'Hope you're right, mate, but we'll know better after tonight.'

'Why tonight?'

'We'll be steering south west for the run down to Newfoundland and we'll be in the air gap. If Gerry's spotted us he'll make his move there. If not, it could be on the last part of the run into Argentia where there's a bottleneck of convoy routes.'

'What do you mean by air gap, Jim?' asked Grainger.

'Well, you know we've come north instead of taking the direct course which is normal in peacetime. Before we reach the ice area off Greenland we'll turn on a south-westerly course. Up to that point there's always the chance of Coastal Command giving us some air cover. There's about 600 miles of ocean after that afore we're covered from the Newfoundland air bases.'

'Why can't the air gap be closed from the west if the RAF can come so far out from Northern Ireland and Iceland?'

'The Yanks have a long-range Liberator which could do the

job from Newfoundland but one of their bleeding admirals reckons they need all of them for the Pacific.'

'Not much consolation for the crews who get tin-fished in the air gap,' replied Grainger.

'Too bloody true, lad, especially as we might be among 'em.'

The next few days of the convoy's progress were filled with tension and on several occasions the jarring sound of bells sent the ship's crew to their submarine action stations. Asdic and radar contacts were received but there was no other sign of the enemy. Sheer weight of water had buckled the forward gun shields on the *Hedron*. The whaler had been stoved in; all the life rafts had been washed away and the motor boat was reduced to matchwood as it hung from its davit heads. The crew was still recovering from the mental and physical numbness caused by the incessant violence of the storm.

'Not much chance of anyone getting away from this ship if we get tin-fished.' said Mick Shaw as he surveyed the damage on the upper deck.

'It'll be quick, anyway,' replied Jarvis with his usual pessimism, 'Only prolongs the agony floating about in the 'oggin.'

'You miserable lot of moaners,' said Edwards, 'Has it ever occurred to you that the storm could have upset Gerry as well as us and put him off having a go?'

Edwards's optimism seemed justified for no enemy attacks took place and on the eighteenth day after leaving Liverpool the full convoy of forty ships was handed over to a Canadian escort group for the last stage of the voyage. As the UK escort altered course for Argentia Bay, Grainger, with the other off-watch crew, worked on the preliminary preparations for entering harbour.

'Wish I was going with them instead of the God-forsaken place we're bound for.'

Grainger turned to see Wheeler staring at the disappearing ships with a wistful expression on his face.

'Where do you reckon they're going?' he asked.

'New York, Boston – some of them, at any rate, – places where there's no bleeding rationing – they'll be filling their boots alright, lucky bastards.'

'Not just on the grub stakes, either,' commented the Captain of the Fo'c'sle, Petty Officer Dalton, who had heard Wheeler's remarks. 'Think of all that crumpet going to waste!'

'Maybe just as well,' replied Wheeler with a wink at Grainger,

'They do say that too much of it can send you blind.'

'Chance would be a fine thing.' muttered Dalton, who had a wife and four children in the UK.

Argentia was one of the bases leased to the Americans in exchange for fifty 1914-18 destroyers loaned to the Royal Navy. The *Velperton* was one of the destroyers remembered only too well by Grainger.

'Wonder how Joe and the rest of them are faring?' he thought as he looked round the harbour installations from the *Hedron's* fo'c'sle.

The surrounding hinterland was barren and desolate but the harbour was a deep natural one. This was the scene of the historic meeting on board the battleship *Prince of Wales* between President Roosevelt and Winston Churchill at which the Atlantic Charter was first formulated. The British and Allied escort groups were now based here for their turn-round between convoys as St John's, used by the Canadian groups, was too small to take any more of the escort ships. The Americans had taken Argentia over the previous year and created the base out of nothing. The dock facilities, repair shops, supply and re-fuelling arrangements of old-establishments like Liverpool or Greenock had been provided within a few months as well as a full-sized air station. Argentia itself was a tiny village, so small that the bay on which it stood was named after the larger village of Placentia nearby.

The *Hedron* was secured in an outside berth alongside two American destroyers and within the first hour, dockers were on board with welding equipment to patch up the ship's crumpled superstructure. ·

'Volunteers wanted for victualling party, you, you and you!'

Chief Bosun Baker walked down the line of the *Hedron's* crew standing amidships and detailed a dozen hands for the job including Grainger and Shaw.

The American supply ship lay further along the jetty from the destroyer and the party led by Petty Officer Dalton was halted at the gangway by the American quartermaster. Dalton showed his written orders and after a brief examination the quartermaster went in search of the Officer of the Day. A few minutes elapsed before the quartermaster returned with an officer whose uniform displayed the gold braid of a commander. The *Hedron's* victualling party were surprised to hear the quartermaster, a leading hand, address the officer by his first name.

'One big happy family,' muttered Shaw. 'It's time we introduced this happy note of informality to the *Hedron's* officers.'

'Keep quiet there!' ordered Dalton.

The American officer completed his inspection of Dalton's papers, handed them back and instructed the quartermaster to show the way.

'And who looks after the gangway?' grumbled the quartermaster.

'I'll see to things here, Jack,' replied the officer.

'You sure, Harry?'

'Sure, I'm sure.'

'Sure is one helluva set up,' laughed Mick Shaw as they followed the quartermaster below decks. The quartermaster pointed to a large area of deck filled with upholstered seats facing a large screen.

'Ship's cinema – change of programme three times a week – fancy changing navies?' he grinned.

The return journey to the upper deck, loaded with crates of vegetables, fruit and meat, was strenuous work. Mick Shaw, feeling the strain more than most, reached the upper deck carrying a large side of frozen meat, gasped as he dropped it on the deck then climbed after it through the hatchway. He bent down reluctantly to hoist the meat back on his shoulder when he heard a voice behind him.

'Here, let me show you how that should be lifted – a little guy like you could hurt himself.'

Shaw turned to see a young American officer smiling at him. He was a tall, thick-set man and Shaw, never a man to refuse assistance, let the meat drop to the deck. The officer hitched up his trousers at the belt, bent down and swung the meat to his shoulder with such impetus that he lost his balance, spun on his heel and fell to the deck with a resounding thud still clinging to the meat.

'Excuse me,' Shaw grunted as he lifted the meat from the officer's chest and staggered away with it down the gangway.

'God-damned Limey!' muttered the officer as he struggled to his feet.

101

'Get this deck cleaned up,' he yelled at the grinning quarter-master. 'It's as slippery as hell. Do I have to do everything myself around here?'

Leave was restricted to four hours daily and a special bus transported the liberty men to a services' canteen and stores. The canteen served canned beer and soft drinks but, having heard about the extensive range of unrationed goods on sale in the adjoining store, most of the *Hedron's* crew decided to make their purchases first and sample the beer later.

'Bloody hell!' remarked Mick Shaw as they entered the huge store. 'Talk about Aladdin's cave!'

Eyes were avidly cast over rows of open shelves which displayed without restriction, goods that were rationed or unobtainable at home. Laden with purchases from nylon stockings for wives and girl friends to cigarette lighters and chocolate, the men with money left in their pockets went into the bar.

There were no American servicemen in the canteen and Grainger asked the bartender about their absence.

'At first they came in with you Limeys but after drinks there were arguments then fights about who was winning the god-damned war. Now their leave is at a different time to you guys.'

The *Hedron* stayed at Argentia for three days which gave the crew a chance to relax and enabled the essential work of victualling, fuelling and repairs to be completed.

Early morning on the fourth day after arrival, the *Hedron* and the other escort vessels from the previous convoy slipped their moorings and moved out to meet the next convoy of loaded ships bound for the UK.

'A different looking convoy to the last one,' commented Able Seaman Bailey as he took over Grainger's lookout position on the bridge.

Grainger nodded in agreement. The low-decked single fun-nelled Liberty ships were prominent in the thirty-six ship convoy which was already averaging over ten knots.

While the *Hedron* had been moving through and round the convoy he had observed with interest the new type of prefabri-cated cargo ship which was being mass-produced by the Ameri-cans. They looked well-armed, judging by the number of gun positions.

Three tankers in the convoy lying low in the water, full to capacity, struck a note of disquiet in Grainger's thoughts. He recollected how a torpedo could transform a loaded tanker into a blazing pyre and leave the oil-soaked swimmers to meet a ghastly end. Engulfed in flames, choked by oil and suffocated by smoke, they faced a manifold death.

'Have you ever thought about what's underneath you on this ship?' Jarvis asked him one day when they had been talking about tanker crews.

'Two magazines filled with high explosives, two high pressure boilers filled with super-heated steam and a few thousand gallons of oil – to name but a few of the things which could give us a lift-off if we copped a tin-fish.'

'The only thing I want to know about the bleeding boilers is when they're going to be cleaned and how much leave I'm going to get,' yawned Edwards.

In contrast to the previous trip, the weather remained calm. It was as if the elements had been discouraged by the appearance of the newly-built ships, preferring to reserve their hostility for the rusty obsolete tramp steamers which presented easier targets for destruction and consignment to the bottom of the ocean. The enemy, like the weather, appeared to be selecting other targets in the convoy cycle which was continuously crossing the Atlantic in both directions.

Ten days later the *Hedron* had successfully discharged her duties as senior escort ship. With salt-caked, rust-streaked sides she returned to the River Mersey and the crew on deck were happy to see the Liver Building with dockyard installations and blocks of warehouses to the north and south. The week's boiler-cleaning leave passed quickly. All too soon the *Hedron* was leaving the Mersey on her way to keep an appointment off Londonderry as escort to another slow-moving convoy westward bound.

The cold and stormy Atlantic offered only boredom, discomfort and danger. Like all escorts, conditions on board the destroyer in winter were miserable. Water slopping about on the messdecks, condensation dripping from the deckhead and everywhere wringing wet. The continuous pitching and tossing placed a severe strain on all the crew, especially the 'hostilities only' men and there were a number of casualties with broken limbs and ribs.

Grainger had come to accept that for four weeks out of every five he was existing rather than living, on the Atlantic run. Just so long as the *Hedron* survived for her boiler cleaning was all he could reasonably hope for.

There was one consolation so far as the *Hedron* was concerned — over the next few months there were no U-boat attacks and her convoys arrived safely at their destinations.

16

'Those WC ratings give me a pain in the arse,' said Jarvis.

'You mean CW candidates,' replied Grainger.

The *Hedron* was back in Gladstone Dock in between convoys and both Jarvis and Grainger were watch on board. As cooks of the mess they were dishing out an appetising supper of fried liver, bacon, egg and chips, under the watchful eye of Leading Seaman Edwards.

'What does CW stand for anyway?' asked Jarvis.

'Wartime Commission,' said Grainger.

'Exactly what I said, WC's, only they've twisted the letters round so it doesn't sound so bad,' said Jarvis. 'We had one in the mess afore your time — as wet as a water closet.'

'Hetherington,' said Edwards slowly, and the name rolled off his tongue like an obscenity. 'He wouldn't do his turn as cook of the mess — reckoned it was beneath his dignity — him going through for an officer and all that. Bloody well told me that I couldn't stop him having his rations when I said there'd be no grub for him if he didn't do his share.'

Jarvis took up the story. 'He still refused and sat down for his dinner next day, waiting for his meat and two veg, and a sweet. When he didn't get anything he walked up to Bungy Edwards and started playing bloody hell. 'I know my rights,' he said. 'I'll report you to the Officer of the Day.'

Edwards grinned. 'Your grub's over there, I said.' He pointed to the metal shelves fixed to the outside of the ammunition hoist. 'Hetherington went over and saw the plate we'd left for him — an unpeeled spud, a piece of raw meat and a handful of dried peas.'

Jarvis laughed. 'We'd even left him some custard powder, and flour, lard and jam for his sweet. 'What do I do with this?' he asked.

Edwards broke in. 'I could have told him alright, but I kept it polite, see? I said that if he spoke nicely to the petty officer chef he might let him cook it in the galley.'

Grainger could imagine the menacing bulk of the perspiring chef as he finished the cleaning of the galley after the morning's cooking. 'He'd get a right roasting there,' he laughed.

'You're right,' chortled Jarvis. 'When Hetherington came back all flustered he said the chef wouldn't let him in the galley — he didn't tell us the rest of it.'

'I sympathised with him,' said Edwards, his mouth full of liver and bacon. 'I couldn't offer him any grub as this shower had scoffed the lot but, as I told him, there was always cook of the mess on the next day's team if he was interested.'

'What happened then?' asked Grainger.

'He fell in line — no choice,' said Edwards. 'Reckon he had me to thank for putting him right on one or two facts of life before he went to Brighton for the next part of his training.'

Later that evening a familiar voice echoed round the *Hedron*'s mess decks. 'Able Seaman Grainger report to the Officer of the Day with your cap.'

Grainger looked up, recognising the voice and saw Mick Shaw, closely followed by Joe Myers who was grinning all over his face.

'Joe, you old bugger, where've you sprung from?' shouted a delighted Grainger as he shook hands with his friend.

'He's taking a night off from chasing the camels down Lime Street,' laughed Mick Shaw.

Edwards interrupted. 'Just watch your mouth, Tubby, that's no way to speak to a leading hand.'

'It's alright,' said Joe, 'he doesn't know any better, anyway, they run too fast for me.' He turned to Grainger. 'The *Velperton's* tied up on the far side of the dock — came in a week ago. You're not the only one on the Atlantic run. Fancy a pint at the Flotilla Club?'

'You're on,' said Grainger, and introduced Joe to Edwards, Jarvis and Snaith who had been playing cards with him.

'You're on duty watch,' reminded Edwards, then he grinned, 'I reckon it's alright this once — get the pints in, boyo, I'll be across myself later on.'

Mick Shaw went with them and they walked through the dock towards a long single-storey wooden building faintly outlined by the subdued gangway lights of the various ships. They pushed their way through the door and blackout curtains into a room full of noise, tobacco smoke and sailors. Sandwiches and tea were offered at a counter near the entrance and there was a bar at the opposite end. Women – local volunteers – served on.

'Over there,' said Joe, pointing through the smoke-laden atmosphere towards a corner of the crowded bar.

'Three pints of bitter, love,' he called to the cheerful woman behind the bar. Pints in hand, they made their way across to a small table.

'Like to swap ships?' asked Joe as they sat down.

'As bad as that?' asked Grainger.

'Bloody sight worse,' replied Joe. 'The *Velperton's* got a mind of its own and its a vicious bastard for rolling. Anyhow, how's things with you two?'

'Could be worse, but not much,' said Grainger, then he and Mick gave Joe an account of the *Hedron*'s exploits.

'You've seen more than us,' said Joe. 'Even if we saw a U-boat on the surface, by the time that old tub changed course to attack, the U-boat would be miles away. Still, I reckon we might have persuaded Gerry to keep his head down more than once.'

He turned to Grainger with a more serious expression on his face. 'I was sorry to hear about Julie. We'd left Plymouth on trials before it happened. I heard when I called at Ashdown after we came back for a spell.'

Grainger nodded and told Joe about his visit to Ashdown.

Joe sympathised. 'Bloody rough on Mrs Johnson as well, I liked her — a nice woman.'

Grainger drained his pint. 'Same again?' he asked.

'Better make it four, Ted,' advised Mick, 'I've just seen that bloody man Edwards come in.'

At 0700 hours the following morning in a murky grey light, the V*elperton* sailed from Gladstone Dock leaving the *Hedron* to complete her boiler clean.

Shore leave in Liverpoool for the liberty men usually started at the Caradoc — a rough dockside pub outside Gladstone Dock.

It was here that McTaggart and his compatriot McLean, from the Outer Hebrides, made their first and last call ashore. After drinking steadily without speaking, except to order another round, they would leave quietly when their money ran out and return to the ship. It was said amongst the *Hedron*'s crew that the two Scots were capable of drinking over twenty pints each in a session, returning on board still apparently sober. They were both RNR, Royal Naval Reserve, and like most of the young men in the Outer Hebrides they had turned to the sea for a living.

'Just look at those two Jocks,' said Wheeler to Grainger on one occasion when they were standing at the bar of the Caradoc. Wheeler was pointing at McTaggart and McLean who were seated in a small room behind the bar. 'Some blokes get nasty after a few drinks but not those two — they've gone back to Lewis until closing time,' he said with a grin.

Grainger saw the complacement expressions on the Scots' faces and could readily believe they were back in their imagination on their beloved island of Lewis.

The overhead railway took the sailors into town and gave them an impressive bird's eye view of the line of docks on the way. When they left the railway in the town centre they went their separate ways. First, the locals, who wasted no time in going home. Some of the sailors, not so lucky, headed for the hurly burly atmosphere of the saloon bars, and afterwards became the targets of prostitutes soliciting in the vicinity of Lime Street.

Grainger, who would have welcomed female company of a different type, had to be content with a few quiet drinks and a visit to a stage show at the Empire Theatre. He found that he could book a clean, comfortable bed at the forces' hostel adjoining Lime Street station, and the nearby canteen supplied hot meals, day and night, including the luxury of a cooked breakfast the following morning.

Six hundred miles south east of Greenland the sun disappeared behind streaky rain clouds and the horizon was lost in a dark squall of rain. The UK bound convoy stubbornly held its northerly course towards Iceland against the surging white-veined slopes of the sea. A mile off the convoy's port beam the *Hedron* circled slowly, alert for any development, but there was nothing except the wailing squalls and the flying spray which drenched the lookouts to the skin.

Grainger swung his binoculars round as he scanned the starboard bow sector. He could barely make out the rain-smudged outline of the convoy and its escort plunging through the white-crested breakers. The rain turned to snow which fell lightly on the deserted upper deck and dusted the surface of the sea before it melted. Grainger cheered himself up with the thought that five more days should see them back in Liverpool and there would be a week's leave for his watch. One again, they had been lucky with a slow but uneventful outward trip and if their luck held this homeward-bound convoy of fully-loaded ships would also have a clear run. The bad weather reduced the risk of a U-boat attack, but the convoy would be delayed and if the column of ships was scattered by storm the U-boat packs would be in a strong position. One thing was certain, thought Grainger, they had reached the critical period of the trip when the life or death of the convoy and its escort would be decided.

The weather improved and the night was clear. A full moon put the convoy at further risk by giving almost daylight visibility over a range of ten miles.

Inevitably, the jarring sound of the alarm bells sounded midway through the middle watch and as the *Hedron* surged forward the sickening thud of an explosion was heard from the front of the convoy.

From his position on B gun deck, Grainger saw that a motor ship at the head of the starboard column had been hit. To his horror, the stricken ship was sinking so quickly that it was soon standing vertically on end and as the *Hedron* swung round the front of the convoy he could hear loud, metallic noises.

'Bulkheads breaking loose,' said Edwards grimly.

There was a rapid corkscrew motion and the ship disappeared into the swirling mass of ocean as if it had never existed. Red lights bobbing in the water, accompanied by the flares of the distress signals, directed the convoy rescue ship to the survivors while the *Hedron* moved away in its search for the attacker. Radar and asdic contacts indicated the presence of several U-boats but there were no further attacks during the next hour. Nerves remained on edge and ears strained in anticipation of further explosions at any moment.

'I can just see some dirty big U-boat lining us up in its

periscope while we're moving around like Sisters of Mercy,' said Jarvis with more than a trace of tension in his voice.

'They'll be using the 3 inch for star shell any time if radar's got a contact,' predicted Edwards.

He had hardly finished speaking when there were three tremendous explosions — this time from the direction of the convoy's port column. Two large cargo ships and a tanker had been hit.

'Bloody hell, where's the rescue ship on that line going to?' Miller pointed to the last ship in the convoy's port column. This was the designated rescue ship but it was veering away from the stricken ships.

'That one's not going to make itself a sitting target — but the other one doesn't mind,' said Edwards, pointing to a ship from the next column which had detached itself after exchanging signals with the commodore's ship.

Grainger saw that the crew of the volunteer rescue ship had already lowered rope ladders and cargo nets over its lee side and lines were being thrown to the life boats which were making their way alongside. A corvette made for one of the cargo ships and began to pick up survivors from the freezing water. A destroyer in the escort must have obtained a contact because it heeled round and sped towards the stern of the convoy. *Hedron* and the remainder of the escort, consisting of two sloops and four corvettes, maintained their screening positions while the other destroyer pursued its lone hunt for the enemy.

'You'd think the skipper would help out with the chase,' said Snaith.

'He's senior escort officer. His priority is to protect the convoy,' replied Sub Lieutenant Napier. 'He hasn't got enough escort for forty-five ships, in my opinion,' he added.

'Forty-one now, sir,' corrected Jarvis.

Snaith was about to reply when a message came through his headphones. After a brief moment of concentration he repeated. 'Ammunition supply crew required to remove star shell and charges to 3 inch from forward magazines.'

'Right — Dusty and Lofty — away you go,' said Edwards, and Miller with Grainger following began the task of carrying ammunition aft to the 3 inch high-angle gun.

The dull thud of depth charges exploding could be heard from the stern of the convoy and the other escort vessels were illuminating their sectors with star shell. As Grainger reached the 3 inch gun deck he heard the sound of the gun's breech being slammed shut, and then came a blinding flash followed by a deafening crack with the hot acrid smell of cordite as the gun fired.

It seemed like an age to him before the shell burst.

As the magnesium flare attached to its parachute drifted slowly down, night turned into day. The 3 inch fired again and again producing a curtain of star shell which hung over a wide arc of the sea. Now a human chain had been formed to pass the shells and charges from the forward magazine to the ready-use lockers on the gun deck.

'If there's a U-boat on the surface we should see it with all these bloody fireworks going up,' grunted Miller, as he carefully handed a cylindrical charge up to the gun deck.

'They'll see us as well,' replied Grainger. He looked astern and saw the other destroyer returning to its position in the rear of the convoy screen. Lost contact, he thought. He was about to comment to Miller about the destroyer when suddenly a corvette on the forward port side of the convoy, some two miles away from the *Hedron*'s port bow, exploded in a sheet of flame which quickly climbed to several hundred feet.

A further resounding explosion occurred and the huge flame was doused like a massive candle, leaving only a white cauldron of sea where the corvette had been seconds before.

'Bloody hell, look at that!' exclaimed Grainger.

'We're in trouble this time, mate,' said Miller as he and Grainger were ordered back to B gun deck. 'It's a bleeding wolf pack we're up against — they're having a go at the escort now.'

The *Hedron* was now turning at full speed and the transmitting station confirmed to the gun crews that the asdic had a contact. There was a smell of diesel fumes and Grainger turned as the other destroyer, now astern of the *Hedron*, commenced firing star shell.

'There's the bastard on the surface — stand by for ramming!' shouted Jarvis.

Grainger could now see the phosphorescent wake of the U-boat ahead. The *Hedron*'s decks vibrated as her engine revolutions increased and the ship smashed through the sea like an angry animal. The U-boat managed to crash dive before the *Hedron* ran over her to drop a full pattern of depth charges. The two destroyers, now abreast with a gap of a hundred yards between, followed the U-boat's every twist and turn and remorselessly dropped depth charges. They were depth charging simultaneously and it seemed to Grainger that there was no more than a few seconds interval between each drop.

'Deep setting,' decided Sub Lieutenant Napier after he had watched the charges being flung overboard and waited for the explosion of white spume.

'There she blows!' shouted Miller. He was pointing to the great spout of water which had burst round the black shark-like hull of the U-boat as it lifted above the surface.

This time the other destroyer was moving in for the kill.

As the *Hedron* circled round the two opponents, Grainger could see that the U-boat was turning continuously to starboard and just inside the destroyer's turning circle.

The other destroyer's A and B guns fired until they could no longer bear on the U-boat. Grainger could now see movement round the U-boat's conning tower as gun crews attempted to man the twin anti-aircraft cannon abaft the conning tower, while men on the U-boat's forward casing were swivelling the main gun in the direction of the attacking destroyer.

'When do we open fire for God's sake?' he muttered. As if in answer, the two-pounder pom-pom on the other destroyer took over from the 4·7s and the blood red line of shells quickly transformed the U-boat's conning tower and forward casing to a slaughter house.

The attacking destroyer clawed round then gained momentum as it bore down on the U-boat. Grainger heard the ominous shrieking of metal being torn apart as the destroyer's bows hit the U-boat abaft its conning tower. The U-boat hung for a few seconds on the destroyer's bows like a speared fish then it scraped away in the direction of the *Hedron*. This time it was the *Hedron*'s turn to attack. As she veered past the battered U-boat her stern flung out a ten-charge pattern with a shallow setting. Some of the charges were seen to be hitting the U-boat's casing before rolling into the sea and exploding. The *Hedron* sheered away at top speed and columns of water flung the U-boat out of the sea.

As Grainger watched, the U-boat was lifted into mid-air and blew up in a mass of red and yellow flame, spinning like some gigantic catherine wheel as it disintegrated.

Star shell continued to illuminate the area after the flame was extinguished but apart from the debris which now littered the surface of the sea there was no trace of the U-boat or its crew.

There was a lull in the firing of star shell and the clouds had mercifully covered the moon but the reddish glare from the burning tanker — now several miles astern — still outlined every ship. The *Hedron* circled round the other destroyer which was stopped while its damaged bows were being inspected. After the lapse of several minutes which seemed like an eternity to the crews of both ships, an Aldis lamp blinked from the damaged ship and she began to move forward.

'Thank God for that,' said Napier. 'The damage hasn't stopped her from getting under way.'

After a further exchange of signals, the *Hedron* swung round and headed for the front of the convoy.

17

Despite the victory over the U-boat it was obvious to the men in the convoy ships that the wolf packs were biding their time for another opportunity to attack, like sharks which had scented blood.

There would be no peace, day or night, until the convoy reached its UK destination. While the escort searched with asdic, a deadly acoustic torpedo could be homing on to the sound of their propellers.

Under these conditions men were under great strain and alertness was being impaired; lack of sleep was one factor with crews continuously closed up at action stations. Another factor was the knowledge that for sixty minutes of every hour and for twenty-four hours of each day there was never a moment that might not bring the shattering concussion of an exploding torpedo.

The torpedo struck the *Hedron* under the bridge as she was moving at full speed and reduced her to a shambles. A second torpedo struck and sent the after end of the ship up and then crashing down in the sea on top of some of the crew, forcing them under the water.

A series of explosions was heard deep inside the ship and lights went out causing wild confusion. Men were blinded and trapped like rats below decks as they struggled hopelessly to open water-tight doors which were buckled with the breaking up of the ship.

Outside, a black pall of smoke enveloped the centre of the ship and suddenly the collapsed stern was on fire. A blinding flame seared upwards and then went out almost immediately.

The twisted upper deck was a terrible sight with the dead, the dying and the wounded.

The air was filled with the acrid smell of cordite and fuel oil mingling with the stench of burnt flesh.

On B gun deck when the first torpedo struck, Grainger was temporarily blinded by the vivid flash of an explosion which flared over the bridge then up the main mast. Blast flung him over the side and he landed on his back thirty feet below in the sea. The impact twisted him round under the water and he was bounced back to the surface head first. The ice-cold water bit into his body like a knife as he floated vertically in the sea with head forced back gasping for breath. His blurred vision gradually cleared and he turned on his back to look for the ship. The horrific sight which met his eyes numbed his mind with despair.

The *Hedron*, some two hundred yards away, was broken in two; the fore and after parts had become completely separated. The fo'c'sle still floated with up to fifty feet of its length jutting out of the water. While he stared with disbelief, the fo'c'sle sank, followed by what was left of the after part of the ship. There was a series of muffled explosions and Grainger felt a surge of underwater pressure grip and then release his body. The ship had gone — but where were the crew? It was impossible for him to believe there were no survivors. Yet, as he looked round the surging, swelling surface of the sea which flung icy water up his nostrils and down his throat, he could not see any other movement in the dark troughs of the surface.

The night sky was red, still lit by the burning tanker. Where the *Hedron* had been, a long rolling swell shone under the cold light of the moon which had re-appeared through a break in the clouds like a curious onlooker.

On the horizon he saw flashes of gun fire and heard the thud of explosions. A mass of flame and smoke in the distance could only mean another ship was disintegrating. The convoy battle was still raging and he groaned as he realised that there would be no rescue ship looking for the *Hedron*'s survivors while the weakened escort was fighting off the wolf pack. If the U-boats penetrated the heart of the convoy they would pick off every ship as long as they had torpedoes left and his chances of survival would sink with the torpedoed ships.

His legs and arms were beginning to feel numb, despite the protection of heavy woollen underwear and a duffel coat which was hampering his movements. He loosened the coat and his hands touched the red bulb and battery fastened to his lifebelt. He switched on the light and the fact that it was still working gave him confidence against the fear which was now attacking his mind. He began to feel sleepy and there was a strong smell of fuel oil which was irritating his nose and throat. He thought of the ships sunk in previous convoys and the terrible cramp and retching of the men who had swallowed the oil. Now it was his turn to suffer from the poisonous filth which must be coming from the *Hedron*.

So this is what it was like to die for King and country. An inglorious end to the career of a never-was. Should he rejoice that he would not be withered by age or condemned by the years? He felt withered and old already; destined to be a name on a war memorial that people would look at with unseeing eyes — except the ones who had known him.

Was this what patriotism was all about, or was he just part of the cannon fodder which was necessary to cull the population within the requirements of nature?

The cold was crucifying, the sea restless as if it was waiting impatiently to snuff out his breath. He wondered if he would see Julie again when he died. Was there really life after death or would it be a trip into oblivion? No-one had come back to tell the tale, had they? He would soon know. It would break his mother's heart. His father would be more philosophical. He'd served in another war and seen it all before. He'd have it all in perspective — even if he hadn't, he'd never let anyone know his innermost feelings He'd probably come out with his usual 'These things happen'. Make a good poker player would the old man — never knew what he was thinking.

Why did he continue to hold his head back out of the water? There was no hope of survival now. Was there a God? Would he be waiting to check his name on a roll call?

He forced his mouth into an attempt at a grin. His mouth remained closed — his lips hardly moved. It would more likely be old Nick. It should be warmer than this lot.

Fifty years from now it wouldn't mean anything. The only names remembered would be Churchill, Roosevelt, Stalin and that bastard Hitler. They'd never forget him.

Funny the way the villains are always remembered.

Behave yourself, walk a straight line and nobody's interested.

Get yourself killed — that's what's expected.

Some day people will think Hitler was a hero and mugs like me were the cause of it all.

The surging water jerked him in another direction. His anger was extinguished by the terror of knowing that the preliminaries of this madness had been completed and the climax of death would have to be faced.

His determination to survive was being numbed out of existence by the intense cold. Even the fear of drowning was becoming secondary to the overwhelming desire to sleep.

How long did Edwards say you could stay alive in the 'oggin? Minutes, he'd said, less than five at that. God, I feel like I've been here for hours. Maybe I'm already dead and don't know it. Still, it doesn't seem so bad now. Somebody must have switched on the central heating down below. Davy Jones in his bloody locker or was it King Neptune? Think I'll have some shut-eye — doesn't look as if anyone's coming this way now. His eyes closed and his head fell forward but the force of water stung his mouth and nostrils and his instinctive spluttering and gasping for air forced him to lift his head and make a last desperate effort to fight off the sleep from which there would be no awakening.

He knew now that dying was not going to be easy. Nothing like he'd once heard his mother describe the death of an elderly lady up the street. She'd been making meals and helping out generally because the old girl was confined to bed. The doctor had just left and mother was telling her how pleased the doctor was about her progress. The old lady had been smiling as if she knew something no-one else did. Even as mother watched the old lady's eyes closed. She died with the smile still on her lips.

He'd never thought much about death before; where it would happen or when — why the hell should he? His life was in front of him with everything to live for. Hadn't he been told that more than once by his family and friends. Now he knew the where and when and how bloody useless everything had been and he couldn't do a thing about it. There was this blinding pain in his eyes now and his throat felt inflamed from swallowing the oily lapping water. He thought about the old lady's peaceful end and envied her.

Mick Shaw was passing the 3 inch gun deck on his way to relieve one of the bridge lookouts when the torpedo struck the *Hedron* on her starboard side He was thrown to the deck then, almost immediately, through a pall of thick smoke he heard a second shattering explosion near the ship's stern. Towering columns of flame parted the smoke over the quarterdeck and he glimpsed water shooting upwards in the midst of which could be seen depth charges, lumps of metal and human bodies.

The whole length of the ship whipped madly and now the siren on the for'ard funnel was going berserk with a continuous deafening shriek. Clouds of white smoke belched from the torn bulk of the *Hedron* where the stern had broken away.

Shaw scrambled to his feet, choking in the fumes, then shuffled his way with lowered head towards the windward side of the ship so that he could breathe. He could now see that most of the stern was missing. Hideously shattered corpses lay everywhere. He looked for'ard for some life but he saw only flames and black smoke split by flashes from exploding ammunition. His eyes searched desperately for other survivors. Was he the only one? Surely it was time to abandon ship. But who was left to give the order, for Chrissake?

The bridge was a mass of tangled wreckage — no chance of survivors there. Skipper and Jimmy had bought it — that was for sure. He'd seen them both up there with the navigator just before the first hit. Was there a boat or a Carley float that could be lowered? He wouldn't last five minutes in the sea without one. His heart skipped a beat when he saw the broken pieces of the whaler and motor boat. Why were the means of survival on a warship always placed in such a vulnerable position?

The deck under his feet was rolling sluggishly and it was obvious that the ship had lost stability and might sink very suddenly. He'd heard about men being dragged down with the suction of a sinking ship. But was there something he could hang on to in the sea? One of the Carley floats was still in position near the torpedo tubes amidships. Before he could move in that direction a sudden shuddering movement of the ship caused the deck to slope abruptly at a steep angle.

Shaw, losing his balance, was flung against a stanchion which he was unable to grasp before rebounding on to a deck now rapidly going into a vertical dive. He slithered helplessly against the torpedo tubes and was flung back with such force that he went over the top of broken guard rails and fell some twenty feet into a swirling sea stained red with the reflection of flames from the doomed *Hedron*. He had the sense to hold his breath and keep his eyes and mouth closed before hitting the water feet first. His descent below the water seemed never ending and the pressure in his lungs became unbearable. God, his sea boots and his duffel coat wouldn't help him, would they? They'd take him to the bottom like a lead weight. It was too late — he couldn't get rid of them now.

Although his eyes were tightly closed he was seeing bright lights like flashing stars and the pressure in his lungs was causing him to release the bottled-up air. Then the force of gravity finally spent itself and the displaced sea flung him to the surface. His immediate relief at being able to breathe again was soon replaced by fear as he saw the *Hedron* less than twenty yards away with her fo'c'sle veering skywards, separated from the rest of the ship. He must get away from the suction area before she sank. He struck out frantically with a crab-like side crawl, not daring to look back.

Suddenly, a great roar of escaping steam followed by the numbing pressure of an underwater explosion confirmed that the after part of the ship had gone to her grave. The underwater pull on his body began to weaken as if he was on the fringe of the whirlpool created by the sinking and then he was clear with his head out of the water, gulping in air gratefully.

What about the fo'c'sle? There was still the danger of that sucking him down. He couldn't see anything in the darkness. Where was it, for God's sake? Somewhere near hovering like some kind of Nemesis, ready to take him down into oblivion. There'd be no second chance if he went down again. The whirlpool would hold him until he drowned. Keep on swimming and hope it was in the right direction — wherever that might be. The cold was seeping into his body. Couldn't last much longer at this rate.

Was he the only survivor? Surely not — there must be others. Where's that bleeding life-belt? He'd inflated it before the ship had been torpedoed — always did before action stations. It felt flat — his fingers found a tear in the cloth of the belt. Wasn't that just the way of things? Like everything else connected with the navy — they just gave you a cheap life-belt to boost your confidence. When you needed it you found it as much use as a pain in the arse. Suppose they wanted you to go quick like Stripey

Jarvis had said.

Merciful, really, wasn't it? Better than freezing your balls off trying to swim home. God, what a way to go. Mick Shaw, doyen of the press, crime reporter extraordinaire. They'd miss him at the local boozer, even if his editor didn't.

He'd bought shares in that bloody place, hadn't he? Jesus, what was that? Somebody's voice — or was he starting to hear things — there was nothing he could make out in the darkness. He'd heard about people being lost in the desert. Dying of thirst, they sometimes saw an oasis in front of them — only it wasn't an oasis. What did they call it? A mirage — that was it — a bloody mirage, only he was hearing one instead of seeing it. there it goes again — sounds a bit like Plowden's voice. Can't be. Stripey's action station had been on the pom-pom. The gun had gone and the crew with it when he'd looked up there.

'Over here, Shaw, move yourself, lad.' That was Stripey's voice without a doubt — but from where? He narrowed his eyes as oily water splashed into his face. There was a curious red glare — that must be the tanker which had been tin-fished before the *Hedron* — and now a cluster of red lights — figures moving on the surface — there in front — like Jesus walking on the water.

His heart pounded with relief — some of the lads on a Carley float just a few yards away. The Carley float wouldn't be the final solution but it was better than nothing.

He summoned up his last reserves of strength and struck out with flailing arms. Hands reached out to hold him as he reached the float and held on to the rope round its side. Gasping for breath, he was able to heave himself on to the edge of the float.

'Where's that fo'c'sle?' he gasped.

'No need to worry about that,' replied Petty Officer Dalton over Plowden's shoulders. 'It went down just afore the after part. You were bleeding lucky, lad.'

18

The warmth from Grainger's blood was being slowly drained away by freezing cold; soon his blood would be solid ice. Before that happened his heart would have seized up and death would be a merciful end. It was strange how much warmer he felt; he had a vague feeling that there was something ominous about that. One last look round before his body gave up its instinctive struggle to survive.

The burning tanker had disappeared over the horizon but it was an eerie scene which met his eyes. The flames from the tanker still tinged the night sky with a reddish glow which was reflected in the swollen surface of the sea.

His mind was suddenly jolted by the vague hubbub of voices — men's voices! Turning his head slowly in the direction of the sound he glimpsed a cluster of red lights sprouting against the blackness of the sea. It could only be survivors from the *Hedron*. Grainger tried to attract attention by raising his arms, but the cold had paralysed his limbs. He opened his mouth to shout but there was only a croak which he could barely hear himself. His thoughts raced desperately, filled with frustration and anger, then cold fear when he realised that it was likely he would be left to drown with help so near.

'Is he alive?' shouted a voice nearby. Grainger's despair lifted. God, they must have seen him, and the sudden surge of hope gave him the strength to raise one numbed arm above his head.

Shadowy figures drifted towards him and he was now able to make out the shape of a Carley float beneath them. Hands reached out for him and he was rolled into the float.'Welcome aboard, Ted!'

A hand touched his shoulder and he saw Mick Shaw regarding him with a wry grin on his grey, haggard face. Someone thrust the neck of a flask into his mouth.

'Here, Lofty, take a swig — not too deep, mind, it's neaters.'
Another man snatched the flask away before Grainger could drink. He heard Dalton's voice. 'Here, give me that, do you want to kill the poor sod?'

'Only wanted to warm him — worked for us, didn't it?'

Grainger recognised the disgruntled voice of Conroy, one of the torpedo men.

'He's been in the 'oggin longer than us,' replied Dalton harshly. 'You'd thaw him out too quickly and stop his heart. We need to get his circulation moving gradually. Here, Shaw, and you, Conroy, work his arms up and down.'

Dalton and Plowden pummelled each leg.

'Come on, Ted,' grunted Mick as he and Conroy worked his arms. 'Don't give up now, old son, we're almost home and dry.'

There was nothing dry about being on a Carley float. It was only a balsa frame with a rope bottom. Hard rations, a small barrel of fresh water and two paddle oars, now in use, completed the float's facilities. The Carley float had never been designed for long-term survival and none of the men on that float had any delusions about surviving if there was no rescue ship within the next few hours.

Grainger was stretched out and held in position on the frame of the float by several pairs of hands. Gradually, the numbness in his limbs was replaced by excruciating pain as blood circulation increased.

'Here, lad, drink this. Got some feeling back now, have you?'

A tin cup was pushed to his lips and he gulped some of the liquid which it contained. It tasted of strong peppermint. Coughing and spluttering, he began to feel the benefit of the warmth which the liquid had produced. They'd already stopped working on his limbs and he was pushed up into a sitting position.

While he drank, Dalton was holding the cup. 'Wife's homemade recipe — always carry a drop in a flask when I'm on watch — warms the cockles of your heart, eh, lad? Won't harm you like spirit. Reckon you'll be okay now.'

Grainger looked round at the others. Apart from Dalton, Plowden, Shaw and Conroy, there were four other ratings.

'Where's the rest of the lads?' he gasped, struggling to keep his legs pressed against the side of the float as the muscles locked in the agony of cramp.

Plowden jerked his thumb to one side and Grainger saw another float containing huddled figures moving towards them. As they came alongside he looked eagerly for the faces of the men who had been on B gun deck — Sub Lieutenant Napier, Edwards, McTaggart, Snaith, Miller, Ken Jarvis and Wheeler — but they were missing.

He counted eleven men on the float including the *Hedron's* chief bosun and the engineer officer. He looked again but he could not see any other officer.

Plowden was watching his face grimly. 'There's nobody else — they're all here,' he said in a dejected voice.

'What about B gun's crew?' asked Grainger, knowing the answer as he asked the question but hoping that he was wrong.

'Went up with the bridge after the first tin fish blew up the for'ard magazine.' This time it was Dalton who answered. He continued. 'B gun deck shielded us on the fo'c'sle from the blast. How did you make out?'

Grainger told him what he remembered and Dalton nodded.

'Reckon your luck was still holding when you switched on your light, Lofty. We wouldn't have seen you otherwise.'

'Let's hope his luck continues,' intervened Plowden, 'We're not out of this by a bleeding long chalk.'

Grainger began to feel sleepy as the bitter night progressed. The two floats bobbed alongside each other and the survivors peered round anxiously into the darkness, tinged red with the flames of the burning tanker.

'Looks like the night sky over some bleeding big city,' observed Shaw.

They listened to the noise of the sea and the wind and there was always the smell of the oil.

'Wonder if there's any ships left afloat in the convoy?' asked one of the other ratings. 'They were getting a right bleeding pounding judging by the noise that was going on.'

'Could have been depth charges,' said another man hopefully.

'That wasn't depth charges half an hour ago when we saw all that flame and smoke — more like another ship being tinfished,' said the first man who then leaned across and spoke to Dalton.

'How far away do you think the convoy is, petty officer?'

'Could be over ten miles now — what's left of it,' replied

Dalton. 'God knows if they'll ever be able to send a ship back for us,' he added glumly.

'Christ, it's cold!' said Shaw.

'It'll get a bloody sight colder before dawn,' replied Dalton. He noticed Grainger's head slumping on his chest and shook him by the shoulder. 'Wakey, wakey. Everybody keep awake or you won't see bleeding daylight. Anybody know any filthy jokes,' he asked. 'We'll start with you, Shaw, tell us about some of the crap you used to write about.'

So they each told stories; then sang any song that came into their heads until the first grey streaks of light came creeping across the sea from the east.

A brisk wind had sprung up, whipping ice-cold waves over the edge of the floats. But there was nothing to see on the oil-stained surface except the other float and its occupants and, further away still, bodies of the *Hedron*'s crew rolled grotesquely amongst pieces of wreckage.

'And that's all that's left of one hundred and sixty men and one destroyer,' said Plowden. 'It's enough to make you bleeding well cry,' he said bitterly.

'They could be the lucky ones. At least their troubles are over — we've got ours to come,' remarked Dalton quietly as he stared at the rolling corpses.

The sea had become choppy and splashed over the sides of the floats, completely drenching the already soaked occupants. The two floats were keeping station with each other and those who were strong enough to row took turns on the paddle oars.

The last of the rum was diluted and mixed with half a cup of water rationed to each man by Dalton, with a piece of broken ship's biscuit.

They sat huddled on the sides of the float — legs and feet under water — chilled to the bone. The other float was drifting away as the sea swell became too strong for the short paddle oars to have much impact, either for making way or steering.

'Come on, lads,' said Plowden, taking over one of the oars. 'After me then,' and he began to croak a naval ditty and attempted to increase his stroke rate in time with his song. Dalton moved round pushing and slapping those who seemed ready to close their eyes, urging them to join in Plowden's song. The sound of their cracked, weary voices was almost drowned by the blustering wind. The words were defiant and blasphemous, yet they sounded an innermost optimism against the hopeless odds of survival.

'Roll on the *Rodney, Nelson, Renown,*
We can't say the *Hood* 'cos the bastard's gone down,
Side, side, *Hedron's* shipside
Jimmy looks on it with pride . . .'

Their voices petered out into silence, each man with his own thoughts and an image of the *Hedron's* sinking. Jimmy wouldn't mind now, would he? The poor bugger was dead — like the ship.

Grainger looked round in the grey light and saw faces drained of blood, blackened by oil, cheeks sunken with cold, more dead than alive. There's no way we'll see another day, he thought. If they weren't rescued before nightfall they were dead.

During the late afternoon when their hopes were fading with the daylight and several men had lapsed into comas, one of the sloops from the ill-fated convoy found them.

19

'Should be interesting, this course, make a change from 'lift those spuds, stow that gear' routine. Come on, Ted, show a bit of interest for chrissake!'

The speaker was Mick Shaw. He and Grainger were sitting in the beer canteen at HMS *Drake*. Grainger nodded absent-mindedly and stared at the group of sailors being served at the bar. The last time he'd been here was with Joe Myers over a year ago.

Things had been going well then, with the prospect of meeting the two girls at the dance in Ashdown the following night. Everything in the garden lovely, as you might say. Poor Julie — his eyes blinked back the tears. Although she was dead he was certain that she'd helped him to survive — kept his mind occupied thinking about her all that time in the sea. Maybe she'd known and somehow helped him to pull through and then afterwards in hospital — bless her.

Wonder where Joe is. Still trying to keep his feet aboard the *Velperton* — if she hadn't suffered the same fate as the *Hedron*. Christ, things would never be the same again, would they?

Shaw's eyes narrowed as he saw the desolation on Grainger's face. He'd seen depression before in others and knew the torment it could inflict from personal experience. Strange really, his own depression had been in civvy street.

Break-up of his marriage — no kids involved, thank God. His job hadn't helped. Too much time spent away from home working. Excessive drinking even for a newspaperman. He didn't really blame Jean now for having had that affair with her boss, who was also married She'd asked twice to come back when she found out that the mistress role didn't have any future for her. She should have known that slimy bastard was only using her. He'd played straight and wasn't having her back. Things would never have been the same between them again. He'd been lucky to hold on to his job before he got some sort of order back into his life. A bloody good editor who saw promise in his work had been responsible for that. He'd got back though, hadn't he? Writing was something he was good at. Before this lot started he'd had his own column. Going places — so he thought. Finishing up in the 'oggin hadn't been part of his plans. He still felt knackered and he was just glad to be alive. Must have been fitter than he thought.

He smiled to himself — more like the excess fat he had been carrying had been a protection against that terrible sea and the freezing cold. His smile faded as he remembered the eight men who had died from their injuries.

Poor old Stripey Plowden and Dalton, who'd done so much to keep everyone else alive on the float, died in hospital. Plowden, too old to cope with hyperthermia; Dalton, seemingly on the road to recovery, died in his sleep. Wives and kids left to fend for themselves on just a lousy navy pension that wouldn't keep them above the bread line.

Wonder how the Gerries behaved towards their bereaved families? Bloody sight better than this country which from time to time expressed its gratitude to its war casualties. Lip service, that was all it amounted to. If he survived this war he'd write about the hardships suffered by the bereaved and the wounded and put pressure on those two-faced politicians to do something about it in practical terms.

Who was he kidding? Successive British governments had a notorious track record for looking after everybody except their own. If we won the war he suspected that the Krauts would win the peace.

He shrugged his shoulders and stared at Grainger's haggard face. They'd both been passed fit for sea service by a snooty young surgeon-lieutenant who hadn't known one end of his stethoscope from the other. Still they'd get a breather ashore with this torpedoman's course.

Smart move on Ted's part — he'd seen the AFO on the notice board inviting applications from ratings with experience at sea. They'd both applied and been accepted to do the course on *Defiance*, the training ship tied to a buoy in the Tamar. But the admin. boys had slipped up. Typical navy; training facilities on the doorstep here in Plymouth and now they were on draft to HMS *Vernon* at Pompey for the same course. Expect it was to make numbers up. He'd heard there'd been heavy casualties in Pompey from recent bombing. Like HMS *Drake* — home from home.

He picked up their two empty pint glasses. 'Same again, Ted, and cheer up, mate, for God's sake.'

'Move your arse, Mick, it's just on closing time,' replied Grainger.

He stared after Mick who was now using his bulk to advantage in forcing his way to the bar for last orders. Grainger was only too well aware that he would have to fight off this mood of depression. The nervous tension remained as it did with the other survivors.

At first he couldn't accept that Jarvis, Edwards, McTaggart and the remainder of B gun's grew were dead. Watts, the leading cook, must have been killed in the same explosion. Good kid, Watts, with his cheeky lower deck sense of humour. Wouldn't have stood a chance at his action station in the for'ard magazine. Blown to hell — if he was lucky. Otherwise, slow suffocation from drowning which happened to some men when hatches and bulkhead doors were damaged or closed on the magazine crew to save the rest of the ship.

He remembered Watts telling Mick to think himself lucky that he was facing the Atlantic run on the *Hedron* and not the *Velperton*. As far as he knew *Velperton* was still afloat. Things never turned out the way you expected. Likely that Joe Myers would have second thoughts about the Yank when he heard about the *Hedron*. He had vivid recollections abut Stripey Plowden pointing to the other Carley float with eleven men on it, making twenty survivors in all. 'And that's all there's left of one hundred and sixty men and the *Hedron*.'

Not even twenty now. Four had died from their injuries on the other float before the sloop came. Another four died in hospital, including Stripey and Ken Dalton. God, it was unbelievable after all those two had done to keep up morale.

He'd nearly gone the same way. He must have been in the sea for something like twenty minutes before they'd got him on the float. Another day on that float had all but killed him. After two weeks on the critical list in hospital he'd begun to show signs of recovery. Evidently his number hadn't been drawn — probably reserved for another time. Shell, bullet or bomb instead of hyperthermia — take your pick, my jolly jack tar!

Scars on the memory, never to be erased, and more to come. Not surprising one of the lads had been transferred to a mental hospital after a nervous breakdown had reduced him to nothing more than a human cabbage.

'Thanks, Mick.' He took the proffered pint. 'Here's to fair ladies — bottoms up!' he said raising his glass and taking a deep gulp as if it was his first pint of the night.

Mick grinned and responded by raising his pint.

'That's more like it, mate. There's hope for you yet. Here's to the Pompey bar maids. May their looks improve with every pint!'

Mick replaced his glass on the table then turned to face Grainger with a serious expression. 'Look, Ted, it's none of my business, I know, but so far as Julie's death is concerned it's my opinion . . .'

'You're right, Mick,' said Grainger angrily, 'it's none of your damned business.'

'It's my opinion,' continued Mick stubbornly, 'that it's bad enough on a bloke if he loses his wife or girl friend through death. At least there's respect left and memories worth having. But if he loses her because she's been two-timing him and he has to find out the hard way from other people, I reckon it's a bloody sight worse.'

The anger had faded from Grainger's eyes and he suspected that Mick was speaking from personal experience For the first time he felt some relief from the sadness which had haunted him from the time he had learned of Julie's death.

'Sorry, Mick, flying off the handle like that. There's a lot in what you say, I can see that. Mind if I ask something?'

'Fire away, Ted, be my guest.'

'It sounded like the voice of experience. Was it?'

'You know what they say about fools, Ted, some of them become wise men from experience,' replied Mick, then he concentrated on draining his pint.

129

20

'Hold the grenade in the hand you use to wipe your arse, and keep your thumb against the spring — like so!'

Sergeant Boxall glared at the group of sailors who surrounded him. The Mills grenade which he held up in full view was a live one; the wooden imitation used for previous instruction had been discarded. Tense expressions on the faces of the listeners indicated that they were well aware of the devastation which this pineapple-shaped piece of metal would cause if it was dropped in the confined space.

There was a shuffling of feet as the group instinctively edged away from the sergeant, at the same time trying to maintain their concentration on what he was saying. Each man knew it would soon be his turn to stand in the nearby dugout and throw a grenade so it was important that they listen carefully to what this brown job was on about.

Normally it was a welcome diversion for the training class at HMS *Vernon* to receive small arms instruction from the army once a week. The purpose being to make them useful as a supplementary force to the local army and Home Guard units if there was an invasion.

Sergeant Boxall was a Dunkirk survivor who had seen most of his regiment killed or wounded in the hard-fought rearguard action through Belgium to the Channel. He had been picked up, half dead, by a destroyer which had risked a hail of bombs and bullets to come close in. Just when he'd given up hope of being evacuated, and death on the beach or being taken prisoner — if he was still in one piece — seemed certain.

Good old navy — he'd always be grateful. He owed 'em, didn't he? Nothing wrong with this lot in front of him as far as he could see. Bound to be nervous first time they hold a grenade in their hand. He felt some sympathy for them but he was careful not to show it. They'd soon get cocky if he did. What the hell, he smiled to himself, didn't sympathy come between shit and syphilis in the dictionary?

'Now, concentrate, you lot. Pull the pin out, but for Christ's sake keep your thumb on the spring until ready for release at the target,' continued Boxall as he stood with the pin in one hand and the grenade securely clasped in the other.

'Now, remember when you go into the dugout this is the position for release. Don't, repeat, *don't* let go of the spring beforehand or we'll have to scrape you off the sand bags and they're difficult to replace.'

Mick Shaw glanced at Grainger and gave a nervous grin, then looked back at the sergeant with what he hoped was an impassive expression belied by a twitching of his left cheek. The nervous twitch did not escape Boxall's notice and he added 'Don't think I'm trusting you lot in there on your own. For some reason or other the Navy wants you back in one piece, so I'll be in there with each of you to make sure you throw the bloody thing before it explodes. Now, you all know how a cricket ball is bowled — that's how you deliver this grenade — bowl it, don't throw it, then you'll get more accuracy. The grenade has a ten second fuse which gives you time to throw it after releasing the spring without it blowing up in your face.'

Boxall replaced the pin and his audience, relaxing slightly, moved nearer.

'Right, lads, who's first in?' he asked. Nobody seemed anxious to accept the invitation so Boxall pointed to Grainger. 'You'll do, lad, rest of you stand well back.'

The group dispersed to a position well behind the dugout while Grainger stepped reluctantly into the dugout with Boxall close on his heels. Once in the dugout Boxall handed him the grenade. 'Now's the chance to make a name for yourself, son,' he added soothingly. 'If it explodes in your hand, you won't feel a thing — but it won't if you keep the spring in like I've shown you — right, now pull the pin out.'

Grainger yanked at the ring attached to the pin, at the same time making sure that his thumb was pressed tightly against the spring.

'Brilliant,' said Boxall. 'Now, bowl it over there on that patch of waste ground.'

Grainger's arm moved in an arc and the grenade shot away as

131

he and the sergeant ducked behind the sand bags. After travelling some twenty yards the grenade hit the ground and exploded harmlessly with a dull thud.

'Good — next!'

A grenade was selected for the next man from a box some distance away from the dugout and the procedure was repeated. The last man in, Mick Shaw, stepped nervously into the dugout. He stared at the grenade in his hand as if he was in a hypnotic trance.

'Take it easy,' warned Boxall, 'now pull the pin out and keep your thumb on the spring — not too bleeding hard or you'll find it sticks in your hand.'

But Shaw's knuckles were white as he tightened his grip, determined not to release the spring.

One of the men, watching from a position of safety at the rear of the dugout, laughed, 'Just look at Mick trying to squeeze the juice out of that pineapple!'

'I wouldn't laugh if I was you,' said another man warily. 'If he does manage to throw the effing thing it's anybody's guess where it's going to land.'

The grins subsided into serious expressions as they realised that Mick had frozen with his hand wrapped tightly round a grenade minus its pin. They watched in silence as Boxall spoke to Mick, presumably telling him to get on with it.

Suddenly Mick's arm shot back like a ramrod then came forward with a sudden jerk. Instead of bringing his arm over and releasing the grenade in a forward position the grenade left his hand before his arm had reached the vertical position above his head.

The spectators looked on horrified as they saw the grenade travelling upwards directly above the two men in the dugout.

'Jump out!' roared Boxall, but Mick was standing transfixed staring at the falling grenade. In the fraction of a second which followed, Boxall hurled himself at Shaw and they both crashed over the top of the sandbags. The grenade exploded with a dull thumping sound and a red flash at the bottom of the dugout, hurling its segments of metal into the surrounding sandbags.

Boxall and Shaw, protected on the outside of the sandbagged perimeter stood up. Boxall gave the winded Shaw a withering look.

'Well, that's my debt paid to the navy. Whose side are you on for Chrissake? A few more like you, mate, and there'll be bugger all for Hitler and his pals to do.' he grunted, brushing the sand from his uniform.

The torpedo course which Grainger and Shaw were on at *Vernon* included basic maintenance of high and low power electrical systems aboard ship, in addition to Whitehead Torpedo work. In a previous class there had been a tragic accident when instruction was being given on the care necessary in the handling of the small glass tubes containing mercury amythol, an amber coloured liquid which was the detonator used to explode the 750lbs of TNT in a torpedo warhead.

The instructor had become so familiar with handling the detonators that he was in the habit of passing a tube from one hand to the other while talking to his class, instead of re-placing the tube in a box packed with cotton wool after display.

Inevitably, the instructor's hand missed the detonator which fell to the floor. He instinctively reached for the glass tube which broke, exploded and blew most of his right arm off. The class wasn't near enough to sustain any casualties but the instructor died from injuries and shock.

'Makes you wonder why that instructor didn't jump the opposite way,' remarked Mick Shaw to Grainger and Jock Anderson who was another member of the course.

'Like you did the other day with the grenade?' asked Grainger.

'Aye, if it hadn't been for yon sergeant, ye'd have been in the same boat,' added Jock.

'Happen so, but I wasn't tossing that bloody grenade from one hand to the other, was I?'

'No,' said Jock. 'Ye just forgot which direction to throw it. Could have killed us all if ye'd let it go our way instead of straight up.'

'Bollocks!' retorted Mick. 'I had it well under control.'

'Ye mean the sergeant had,' retorted Jock. 'Reminds me of a bloke on my last ship.'

'Who does — Mick?' asked Grainger.

'No — this instructor that was killed. The bloke I'm talking about was working on a storing ship party. He let a bag of spuds slip off his shoulders as he came over the gangway. Instead of letting the bag drop he tries to hold on — automatic reflex, see. Both he and the spuds finished up in the hogwash. Mind ye, he was lucky, he was fished out without a scratch.'

'The important thing was did they recover the spuds?'

The three men turned to see that the questioner was Chief Torpedo Gunner's Mate Jack Swann, one of the instructors.

'Oh, aye, chief, they got them back as well,' said Jock.

'Lucky for him — losing ship's stores can be a court martial offence,' added the chief.

'You serious, chief?' asked Mick incredulously.

'Too true, lad, and don't you forget it. How are you lot coping with the course? Not going in one ear and out of the other, I hope?'

'On the contrary,' said Mick. 'We're all as keen as mustard, aren't we, lads?'

The other two nodded vigorously in agreement.

'As a matter of fact,' continued Mick. 'It should come in useful back home — if we ever get there after the war. Might even pack up the newspaper lark and set up my own business — electric gear and radios for starters.'

'Mind you give a free screwdriver with every set,' said Swann.

'Why's that, chief?'

'A lot of people can't resist taking the back off a radio to see how it works — screw driver encourages them. Should keep the repair side ticking over very nicely,' grinned Swann as he walked away.

'That bloke's an exception to the rule,' said Mick staring after Swann.

'Why, because he gave you that crap about the screwdriver?' sneered Jock.

'No, you bleeding Heeland haggis, because unlike you and the general run of jack-me-hearties he's got brains and he uses 'em.'

'Ye'll apologise for that remark, ye bloody Sassenach, unless ye want filling in!' growled Anderson.

Mick smiled and winked at Grainger.

'Sorry, Jock, nothing personal intended.'

'We've got the *Rapier*, lad!'

Grainger had recently returned from leave following the

successful completion of his course when the news was given to him by Chief Torpedo Gunner's Mate Jack Swann. He looked across the barrack room at the slim fair-haired Swann who was one of the most knowledgeable and popular instructors at the school. Before he could ask the obvious questions, Swann supplied most of the answers.

'She's a brand-new destroyer and we leave here tomorrow for Birkenhead. There's two more from here — Shaw and Anderson — the remainder of the torpedo party and the ship's company join from Plymouth.'

'Did you say *we*, chief?' asked Grainger. 'I thought you were on the permanent staff here for the duration.'

Swann smiled. 'I put in a request some time ago for a move — before I became a barracks' stanchion.'

Grainger was surprised at Swann's keenness to return to sea after serving on destroyers for most of the war. Like Joe Myers, Swann had been a survivor of the ill-fated Norwegian campaign and later had experienced a hectic time against E-boats, air attacks and mines on east coast convoys. The chief had been at the school for less than six months which hardly supported his idea of becoming a barracks' stanchion.

Mick Shaw and Jock Anderson had qualified on the course with Grainger. When Mick heard that Swann was also joining the *Rapier* he shook his head in surprise.

'Doesn't know when he's well off — personally I was hoping for something bigger, like a battleship which doesn't sink as quickly as a destroyer.'

'Ever heard of the *Hood?*' asked Anderson drily.

It was an overnight journey from the south coast and when the four men arrived in Liverpool the next morning they welcomed the chance to wash and eat at the forces' hostel before continuing their journey to Birkenhead. As the truck transported them across the town centre of Liverpool, Grainger looked at the familiar streets and buildings which brought back memories of recent events.

'Weren't you and Shaw based at Liverpool on the *Hedron?*' Swann's question interrupted Grainger's thoughts. He saw that Swann was regarding him with a quizzical expression and Shaw and Anderson had stopped their conversation. It was an effort for him to speak.

'She was sunk,' he said lamely.

Swann nodded. 'Yes, I heard about it.' Grainger did not elaborate, he glanced across at Mick who made no comment.

21

'There she is, lads, our home for the next three years.'

Jack Swann's arm pointed up at the brand new destroyer moored alongside the wharf.

The *Rapier* looked impressive, from the outward sheer of her bows, along the sweep of the upper deck to the square-cut stern. The upper half of her bows and all the superstructure were painted light grey, while the remainder was covered in the dark bluish grey of the Home Fleet. The ship's pennant numbers were painted in black either side of the bow and her single funnel was marked in broad red and black bands.

'We'll have plenty of tin-fish to look after,' remarked Jock Anderson as they took note of the eight empty torpedo tubes divided into two quadruple mountings amidships — one for'ard and the other aft of a searchlight platform.

They could see four 4.7 inch guns — A and B for'ard, Y on the quarterdeck, with X gun on the deck above. A two-pounder pom pom was mounted abaft the funnel and two Oerlikon guns on single mountings were placed on either side of the searchlight's platform. There were two stern traps for depth charges and two sets of throwers had been fitted either side for'ard of the quarterdeck with racks for spare charges welded into the deck. Aft of the Oerlikon gun decks, a short mainmast had been fixed with a small yardarm for the W/T aerials, while a high-frequency direction-finder mast stood tall and solitary against the superstructure immediately for'ard of X gun deck. The foremast consisted of a tripod base carrying a topmast with two single yard arms and a crow's nest. A radar aerial topped the masthead and below, the bridge was dominated by the direction control tower and range-finder.

The ship looked almost ready for sea with her boats hoisted at their respective davit heads, a whaler on the port side and a motor boat on the starboard side. Underneath the motor boat and secured to the deck was a motor dinghy presumably for the captain's use. The *Rapier*, with a displacement of over 1,700 tons and a length of 360 feet — 40 feet longer than the *Hedron* looked every inch a Fleet destroyer.

Swann led his torpedo men on board, crossing the rough gangplank and stepping down on to a deck littered with empty packing cases and laced with snake-like compressed air pipes from the fitting-out work. They were met by the *Rapier's* coxswain, Chief Petty Officer Baines, the senior rating of the lower deck — equivalent to a regimental sergeant major without a warrant. A fleet reservist, he was elderly to be still at sea in wartime.

'A space has been cleared in the lower mess deck for'ard for you lads,' said Baines after Swann had made the introductions. 'Take your gear with you, the dockies have finished down there and the hammock nettings and lockers are ready for use. Take your pick.' He turned to Swann, 'Follow me, chief, I'll show you round the PO's mess.'

'Dump your gear, lads, and I'll see you back on deck in fifteen minutes. We've got plenty of work on before the others come,' said Swann.

'Aye, and when you come back I'll give details of ablutions and eating arrangements ashore, courtesy of the dockyard. There's no water laid on yet,' added Baines.

'Alright for some,' muttered Anderson as they humped their kit bags and hammocks for'ard. 'They might have given us shore billets while this bloody mess was cleared up by the dockies — hard-over bastards.'

'Main draft from *Drake* arrives in two days,' said Grainger. 'Gives us a chance of getting to know the layout and we've got overnight leave 'til then — according to Jack Swann.'

'Fair enough,' said Mick, 'we'll get fixed up with beds at the Lime Street Services Club tonight. A few pints, and I know a place which serves steak, egg and chips to special customers.'

'Black market, d'ye mean?' asked Jock Anderson suspiciously.

'I wouldn't know about black market, Jock. I said special customers. They happen to think there's something special about the navy and I'm in full agreement. Mind you, if you prefer powdered egg, spam and principles in the canteen that's your lookout.'

'I didna say I wouldna come,' protested Anderson.

'Big on ya, Jock, well keep your trap shut and be thankful for what you might receive.'

'The next move is to get back on deck and fix up leave with Swann. I think he mentioned something about work beforehand,' said Grainger.

'Jesus H Christ!, can't you two ever look on the bright side? Come on then, let's see what the bleeding score is,' grumbled Mick as he climbed the steel ladder leading to the upper deck.

Several days later, the rest of the ship's company arrived and Grainger was surprised and delighted to see a familiar figure coming over the gangway. Joe Myers, with kitbag and hammock on his thick set shoulders, was struggling on board, his vision blocked on either side by his burdens.

'Hey, mate, you're on the wrong ship!' shouted Grainger. 'This isn't the *Velperton.*'

Myers swung round in surprise and his kitbag and hammock crashed to the deck, narrowly missing the quartermaster's feet.

'Bloody hell', it can't be — Ted, how are you, lad? Good to see you again.'

They shook hands and clapped each other on the back.

'If this is the *Rapier,* it's the right ship,' grinned Myers.

'What's happened to the *Velperton,* then?' asked Grainger.

'Back on the Atlantic run as far as I know— left it when I got this.' Myers indicated the crossed anchors of a petty officer on his left sleeve.

'What about you, Ted? You seem to have got yourself a quiet number — torpedo party, eh?'

Myers pointed to the badge on Grainger's overall sleeve.

The conversation was interrupted by the voice of a harassed Chief Petty Officer Baines, the Rapier's coxswain. 'Would you two mind holding your re-union somewhere else — you're blocking the bleeding gangway.'

The hard, strenuous work of loading stores, ammunition and victualling began. Fuel tanks were filled, boilers flashed up and the *Rapier* commenced a series of acceptance trials in the Irish Sea. There were no complicated snags and the ship subsequently sailed from Liverpool towards the Orkneys and Scapa Flow. The *Rapier's* crew were informed by their captain, Commander Thompson, that the working-up period would be three weeks, with every hour counting.

For Grainger the time went more quickly than before on the *Hedron*. He was putting into practice the theory which had been taught at the torpedo school. The ship sailed each day to exercise every one of its various units from engine room to signals. The weather was rough and, as it was a new ship, the exercises were more exacting and comprehensive than they had been with the *Hedron*. There were several days and nights at sea in gale force winds steaming round the Orkneys and the shattering sound of alarm bells for day and night action stations became common-place Nobody on board escaped the rigorous exercises which had been devised for them by an enthusiastic and, for most of the time, impatient commanding officer.

On completion of the first part of the working-up period, the *Rapier* left Scapa Flow for torpedo trials off the Outer Hebrides. The weather improved and the torpedo party were kept busy as torpedoes were run, calibrated and subsequently hoisted in-board. As he helped to man-handle torpedoes weighing one and a half tons each, either with the sea boat's crew or on deck into the tubes, Grainger realised that the work of the torpedo party was not the quiet number that Joe had humourously referred to.

The days passed and the time taken for firing the guns, dropping a depth charge, lowering a boat or Carley float or sending a signal was reduced until the *Rapier* began to measure up to the vice-admiral's requirements. The repetitive grind of exercises from action stations to ship's general drill gradually changed an inexperienced ship's company into an effective fighting unit.

The *Hedron's* crew had been mainly composed of regulars. On the *Rapier* the efficiency of 'hostilities only' men was built up from the expertise of a small number of regulars amongst officers and senior ratings. The vice-admiral's report came through eventually confirming that he was satisfied. His permission for the *Rapier* to leave came with an abruptly-worded signal which ordered the ship to sail for Greenock and take on stores and ammunition.

'There's a buzz that port watch might get leave before we shove off to God knows where,' gasped Mick as he helped Grainger and the other torpedo men to lower depth charges with block and tackle through the after mess deck hatchways into the magazine below. The *Rapier* was secured alongside the ammunitioning wharf at Greenock.

Grainger nodded. 'We should be alright then — although the skipper seems dead keen to shove off.'

'Bugger him — leave should be given if he's anything like a Christian. Just imagine we won't have another chance of a run ashore in the UK for three years. He's got to give leave,' argued Mick.

'You'll only get drunk in the first pub you come to. Might as well be anywhere.'

'Not this time, Ted, it'll be different. There'll be booze alright but with anything like luck I'll have other fish to fry.'

'Female fish, is it?'

Mick smiled and tapped the side of his nose with his forefinger. 'Discretion is the better part of valour, mate — wait and see. If the old man gives leave you're in for a surprise, I can promise you.'

A few minutes later leave was confirmed by the shrill sound of the bosun's mate's pipe followed by a harsh voice announcing leave for the port watch until midnight to commence after completion of victualling and ammunition supplies were inboard.

Mick grinned, 'What did I tell you. Who said the old man's a bastard?'

'You did — several times,' retorted Grainger. Jack Swann's voice sounded from the magazine below, 'Keep those charges moving or nobody goes on leave.'

'His master's voice,' grunted Mick. Then he made sure Swann could hear by shouting, 'Come on, Grainger lad, move yourself if we're going ashore.'

'Thanks a bunch,' replied Grainger, 'now get your fat carcase on this rope and heave instead of talking about it.'

Finally, the last depth charge was swung over the open hatch, lowered carefully through the lower messdeck then guided into the magazine below.

The bosun's mate's raucous voice could be heard summoning fo'c's'le and quarterdeck crew to their stations and shortly afterwards the ship moved slowly downstream, eventually securing against the main dockyard jetty.

It was dark by the time the hands were fallen out, except for special duty men in harbour. Members of the port watch scrambled below to the mess decks to get themselves ready for the first call for liberty men. It was short of miraculous how quickly men could wash, shave and change into number ones from working clothes when shore leave was given. It was an even more remarkable performance how over seventy men could make do with the use of a small bathroom with perhaps half a dozen enamel washbowls. Yet within minutes they were lining the upper deck for inspection by the Officer of the Day; tiddly suits, gold badges and not a lanyard out of place.

'Handy for the main gate, anyway,' said Mick out of the side of his mouth as they hurried over the gangway. 'Come on, Ted, I've got to make some enquiries.'

Grainger stopped. 'Look Mick, if you've got a bird lined up I'll push off with some of the lads and see what the local brew's like.'

'Don't be so bloody daft — I want you to meet a relation of mine. Now let's see if that copper over there can tell us where the nearest phone is.'

They made their way towards the subdued lighting which outlined the main gates. There wasn't a phone and the burly policeman wasn't particularly good in explaining how to reach an address that Mick was enquiring about.

'Looks like the surprise is off,' said Mick sadly, 'unless someone else knows how we can get there — bloody disappointing — come on, let's find a decent boozer — if there is one.'

'What's so important about this surprise of yours?' asked Grainger as they walked through the dockyard gates.

'Well ...' began Mick then stopped as a girl's voice shouted his name from somewhere behind them.

'I don't believe it ... come on, Ted. Sounds as if things are going to plan after all.'

A mystified Grainger followed Mick back into the dockyard and he saw a girl running towards them. The shielded light from the gate revealed a glimpse of golden hair beneath her round cap. Mick flung his arms round the girl and kissed her cheek.

He turned. 'Let me introduce you, Ted. My cousin Leading

Wren Jill Davidson. Jill, meet my oppo Able Seaman Ted Grainger.'

Grainger shook hands with the girl.

'How did you know we were here, love,' asked Mick.

Jill smiled. 'I knew the *Rapier* was coming. I'm with the Clyde Escort Group now and I got permission to come on board to see my poor suffering little cousin on compassionate grounds before he leaves our part of the war.'

Mick laughed. 'I hope you didn't mention anything with the word passion in it to that lot on the ship. They're not to be trusted, eh, Ted?'

Grainger smiled at Jill and nodded in agreement. Mick had been right. She was a surprise alright. Just imagine the old son of a gun having such an attractive cousin.

Tall, slim, blonde and good-looking with it. Mick must have guessed his thoughts.

'You're beginning to stare, Ted,' he grinned.

Jill laughed. 'I asked a very handsome chief petty officer on the *Rapier* if he knew where you were. He told me that you'd just left and I might see you before you left the dockyard if I hurried. His name was Jack Swann and he said he'd be pleased to pass a message on if necessary. He also said that you were known to him.'

'And he's well known to us, eh, Ted?' said Mick.

'I'm glad you didn't have to go back to the ship, love, you might have suffered a fate worse than death.'

'He's alright is Swann,' said Grainger. 'He's our TGM — keeps Mick on his toes — me as well for that matter. Look, I'm pleased to have met you, Jill, but I dare say you two will want a private natter. I'll shove off now.'

'You'll do no such thing,' replied Jill firmly.

'You're both coming with me and there'll be a friend of mine to make up a foursome.'

She linked arms with both of them as they walked past the dockyard gates.

'Goodnight, enjoy yourselves,' said the policeman.

They walked through blacked-out streets away from the docks and after a few minutes they came to a row of gloomy Victorian terrace houses. Jill led the way up the front steps of one of them and inserted a key in the lock of the massive front door.

'It's a ground floor flat I share with two other girls,' she explained. 'Ann is on leave, but I'll introduce you to Joan, you'll like her.'

Joan Mitchell was in her mid-twenties; an attractive brunette with a generous mouth which gave a welcoming smile to Grainger and Shaw.

Her relaxed manner dispelled the hesitancy which so often follows an introduction and within minutes they were all chatting animatedly like friends of long standing.

Grainger was quietly amused to see the lively interest which Mick was showing in his conversation with Joan.

'Will you all have tea?' asked Jill.

'Yes please,' said Grainger.

Now that Jill had removed her cap he saw that her hair, which shone like spun gold, was pulled back to the nape of her neck emphasising a well shaped nose and chin, good bone structure and calm blue eyes. She looked neat and trim in her uniform; younger than Mick — early twenties he reckoned.

Jill laughed as she saw the expression on Mick's face 'Don't worry Mick, you can have something stronger later on. We've got a decent local round the corner.'

'Thank God for that. I was beginning to think my last run ashore in the UK was going to be a dry one. Wheel in the tea, girl, by all means and then we'll try this local of yours.'

They went to a cheerful little pub nearby and talked about everything except the war. The evening passed all too quickly and the two were invited back to the flat for supper.

Grainger had managed to buy a bottle of whisky from the pub landlord and he divided the remaining contents between the four glasses. He raised his glass.

'May we all meet again soon.'

'I'll drink to that,' said Jill.

'So will I. I'll look forward to that day,' said Joan.

'Can't come too soon,' said Mick as the four glasses clinked together. 'It's been a grand evening. I've enjoyed myself but it's back to the ship — worse luck— the war must go on.' Mick looked glum as he replaced his empty glass on the table.

'Never mind.' Joan smiled. 'The war could be over sooner than we think.'

'Pigs might fly,' Mick replied, then he grinned at the two girls. 'Don't you two do anything I wouldn't do.'

Jill smiled. 'That gives us plenty of scope, anyway.'

She led the way into the hall followed by Grainger and the other two. She unlatched the door.

'Take care, Ted, see you soon.'

Before he could reply she turned to face him and kissed him on the cheek. He was conscious of the old familiar stirring and the slight feeling of anger which went with it. Maybe it was the whisky. For Christ's sake, was this a replay of his meeting with Julie? Was this another moment of happiness doomed to end in despair? If so, he wasn't going through that again if he could help it.

A radio was switched on upstairs and a man's voice was singing the last lines of a popular song 'Tomorrow was made for some, tomorrow may never come — for all we know.'

Grainger smiled. 'There's no maybe. We all know tomorrow never comes. Bye, Jill, look after yourself.'

He turned to see Joan and Mick in a farewell embrace.'

'Time to go, Mick, midnight's near and our floating pumpkin awaits!'

Jill slipped a piece of paper into his hand, 'If you ever feel like writing, I'll be pleased to hear from you. That address will find me.'

At the gate they waved to the two girls and walked down the dark, empty street. Turning again, they saw that the door was closed.

'End of another chapter Mick?'

'Beginning of a new one, maybe. She's quite a girl is Joan. What do you think about Jill? Careful what you say, she's family.'

'Was that the surprise? You being related to a good looking girl like Jill.'

'Cheeky bugger — seemed to take a fancy to you. Can't think why.'

'Pity we're going away,' mused Grainger.

'Doesn't bear thinking about,' replied Mick glumly.

22

Grainger and Shaw were not given much time to brood on the way events had deprived them of further leave in the UK, for the *Rapier* sailed through the Clyde boom at 0600 hours the next morning. The ship waited off Arran, in company with three other destroyers, for the convoy, of six former passenger liners loaded with troops and equipment, to appear from their anchorage in the Clyde. Any doubt about the *Rapier*'s eventual destination had been dispelled by the previous issue of white tropical kit to the ship's company.

'At least it won't be the Murmansk run,' observed Mick Shaw, closed up at the torpedo tubes with Grainger. They were gloomily watching the convoy taking up their positions in three columns. *Rapier* moved ahead of the convoy while the other escort vessels swept round the flanks and stern of the huge ships as they rounded the Mull of Kintyre.

'We could still finish up in Russia — depends which course we take when we get clear of Ireland,' grumbled Jock Anderson.

Early the following morning the escort was strengthened by a County class cruiser and three fleet destroyers. The cruiser steamed ahead of the commodore's ship in the middle column, while *Rapier* and another Fleet destroyer covered the port and starboard bows of the convoy. A thin drizzle of rain heralded the deterioration of visibility as the convoy steered west and subsequently entered a blanket of fog which was to last over the next twenty four hours.

Jock Anderson's forecast of a Russian convoy was unfounded, for the ships eventually steered south and the weather cleared. The next few days saw the continuation of exercises in anticipation of U-boat, surface and air attacks. The ship's company worked a one-in-two sea watch system and they were kept at 'full alert' as action stations were closed up at dawn and dusk when

146

the enemy was most likely to attack.

During these exercises Grainger found himself working alternatively as part of a depth charge team and then on torpedo drill. Hoisting and manoeuvring depth charges from the ship's magazines into stern traps and throwers watched by the keen eyes of the Gunner T caused Grainger to reflect on the wisdom of his choice in volunteering for the torpedo branch. There were a few alarms when asdic contacts were reported but these were subsequently cleared as being non-submarine and the convoy approached the Azores without enemy interference.

The weather was clear and a blazing hot sun was beating down on a placid blue ocean when *Rapier* was detached from the convoy screen and ordered to re-fuel at the Azores. It was rumoured that the U-boats used the neutral fuelling base and Grainger half-expected an enemy attack at the Azores. It seemed that the enemy was elsewhere, as they had been during the voyage so far, and the operation and subsequent return to the convoy screen were completed without incident.

The following day the County class cruiser and the three Fleet destroyers left the convoy.

'Buggering off to Gibraltar, I shouldn't wonder,' said Lofty Jackson, one of the Leading Torpedo Operators, who was working with Grainger, Shaw and Anderson.

'Beats the Atlantic run,' said Mick Shaw.

Grainger nodded in agreement. The long days of hot sunshine meant their working dress of the day was a pair of shorts, plimsolls and cap. Wearing a shirt was necessary after half an hour at the most until the skin became acclimatised to the powerful rays of the sun. Anyone foolish enough to ignore this rule would not only suffer the agony of sunburn but find himself on a disciplinary charge at the end of the ordeal.

He looked up and saw Joe Myers in charge of a working party on X gun deck. Joe's action station was captain of X gun and at this particular moment the sweat was running in rivulets down his muscular arms and reddening back as he was showing one of the working party how he wanted the brass work on the breech of the gun to be cleaned.

Lofty Jackson also noticed the energy which Joe was expending. Jackson cupped his hand to his mouth and shouted. 'Don't wear yourself out on that polishing, petty officer, save your strength for Freetown.'

147

Myers looked down at Jackson as he handed the rag to the gun sweeper. 'What's so special about Freetown then — apart from the sharks?'

'Nude washer women — no hidden extras — free shows daily!' laughed Jackson.

'Makes a change from Scapa sheep,' replied Myers.

'No excuse here — too bloody hot for sheep or duffel coats for that matter,' replied Jackson with a grin.

Grainger laughed as Myers made a scathing remark about Jackson's warped sense of humour. He turned and saw porpoises and dolphins leaping out of the sea in front of the *Rapier*'s bows.

'Clever how they keep clear of the bows,' he remarked to Lofty.

'Too bloody fast, mate, they know where they're going, which is more than they do.' He pointed to the flying fish which were skimming across the surface of the sea from the ship's side. 'You'll usually find a few of those stranded on the deck in the mornings.'

Fourteen days after leaving Greenock the ships arrived safely at Freetown and the *Rapier* was now at anchor waiting for her sailing orders from the local commander-in-chief.

Grainger, standing near the guardrails, held a small circular piece of scrap metal concealed from the keen eyes of the man in the canoe which lay a few feet from the destroyer's starboard side.

'You'll have to be quick — he's got eyes like a hawk,' muttered Mick Shaw.

The man in the canoe, a magnificent physical specimen, was as black as ebony. The silk top hat he was wearing made a ludicrous contrast to his loincloth. His arm and shoulder muscles rippled and gleamed with beads of water in the glare of the sun as he waved his hands and shouted for the ship's crew to throw money into the water.

'You throw Liverpool tanner — Glasgow sixpence — I dive,' he said.

He looked up with supreme arrogance at the group of sailors lining the guard rails. So far the black man had distinguished between coins and other objects before they reached the water. If it was a coin he dived, holding it in his teeth when he broke the surface of the water. If he identified the object thrown as useless, he remained in the canoe with a look of contempt on his face.

'He can see what you throw as soon as it leaves your hand,' said Jock Anderson after unsuccessfully trying to deceive the man into diving for a metal washer.

'See if he'll fall for this,' said Grainger.

Shouting 'Liverpool tanner' he brought his right arm over quickly showing only the back of his hand to the man below. The piece of metal splashed into the water and the man sat staring at the point of entry with inscrutable eyes shaded by the brim of his hat.

For several seconds there was no movement, then he removed his hat and carefully placed it on the box by his knees. He uncoiled himself with the smooth action of a well-oiled spring and disappeared over the side of his canoe without a splash. The canoe, suddenly relieved of his weight, bobbed away from the *Rapier*'s side and the top hat gave the impression of being in charge during the absence of the owner.

'By the time he comes up the canoe will be out of sight,' laughed Mick Shaw as they watched it being pushed farther away by the eddying current.

'When he finds out what he dived for he'll do his nut — stand by to repel boarders, Ted,' grinned Anderson.

Almost a minute ticked by before the water erupted and the head and shoulders of the black man broke the surface. The piece of metal which Grainger had thrown was held between his teeth and his face was contorted with rage. His eyes rolled as he transferred the metal to one hand and shouted abuse which would have gained the respect of any gunnery school instructor. The noise brought the Officer of the Day to the scene and he became the new target for the flood of insults. It was only the sight of the disappearing canoe rather than the threat from the officer to have the hosepipe turned on him that silenced the black man, and he turned to swim after the canoe with an effortless crawl stroke.

The black man's rage was short-lived for the following morning saw him alongside the *Rapier*'s mess deck portholes bartering fruit for woollen garments.

As Grainger looked over the fo'c'sle guard rails the man looked up and grinned 'You like pineapples? Pair of woollen socks for one pineapple — no bum tanners this time, man!'

· · ·

The convoy from Greenock with its escort sailed south for the Cape but the *Rapier* was left anchored in Freetown roads, much to the chagrin of the crew.

'It'll be up awnings and down bloody awnings all the time we're in this hole, you mark my words.'

The speaker was Leading Torpedo Operator, Bob Carson, who was responsible for the low power circuits of the ship. Bob had been on a V and W destroyer at Freetown during the previous year.

'Every bleeding night we put to sea chasing our tails as Gerry picked off another convoy. When we came back the C-in-C would send us out again as soon as the awnings had been rigged — not before, mind you!'

It was not surprising that escort vessels were urgently needed in this part of the world where shipping routes converged and the U-boats were looking for easier targets than those found on their North Atlantic patrols.

Carson's words proved to be prophetic. The *Rapier* was frequently summoned to the scene of a convoy which was being mauled by the enemy. The attacks mostly took place in the vicinity of Freetown and the convoy's position was usually indicated well in advance of *Rapier's* arrival by an ominous red glow in the night sky and the dull thud of distant explosions.

The vile work of the U-boats was evidenced afterwards by the debris which littered the ocean's surface. Water barrels, lifeboat fittings, gratings and personal possessions from torpedoed ships sunk days, weeks and even months ago, were grim reminders of the men who lost their lives in these shark-ridden waters.

23

Something moved on the greenish-grey surface of the sea and the sun lit up a dark triangular patch. Turner pointed towards it.

'Look at that bloody thing, Jack, still not satisfied after all it's had.'

Jack Corbett shaded his eyes against the glare of the sun and stared apprehensively at the massive shark some twenty yards away propelling itself round the raft.

'Blood lust, that's what's keeping it here. Just look at the size of the bastard! It could knock us off this bloody raft any time it wants and we'll be up shit creek!'

Turner nodded without speaking and shifted his gaze to the marks which he had made with his knife on the wood of the raft. Forty-eight marks each representing a day. Forty-eight days adrift in the South Atlantic since their cargo ship had been torpedoed at night, east of Ascension Island.

The U-boat had surfaced to identify its victim but the captain refused to take any survivors. Dave Turner, ship's carpenter, had been thrown out of his bunk when the torpedoes tore the guts out of the tramp steamer, sending it to the bottom one and a half minutes after the hits. The life raft they were on was the only one to be dropped before the ship broke up. In the light of what happened afterwards it would have been a mercy if that bastard of a German skipper had shot them before he submerged, thought Turner, as he stared again at the killer shark.

Over thirty men had gone to their deaths on the ship as the cargo of heavy machinery, loosened by the explosions, smashed bulkheads and sides. The dead ones were the lucky ones, he reckoned. As part of his job Turner was in the habit of keeping pencil and paper in his pockets and he'd kept himself sane by writing a day-to-day diary since the sinking. Originally, there had been fourteen men on the ten foot by eight foot raft — most of them under nineteen years of age.

The second officer, whom Turner had helped out of the water, was hoping they would reach the coast of Liberia. He'd reckoned on forty days but by that time only two men were alive. The emergency rations on the life raft provided two ounces of water, three times a day, three Horlicks tablets and one inch of pemmican per day. Turner reflected there had been no jokes, no reference to runs ashore. Just silence and a feeling of hatred for each other had developed. They had slept sitting opposite each other — chin on the opposite shoulder and arms round each other's shoulders.

The days were spent under a merciless, equatorial sun with up to eighteen sharks at a time surrounding the raft; some so hungry that they had to be kicked away as they tried to slither on the raft with jaws gaping, eager to amputate limbs. Now there was just that big, sinister-looking bastard over there, the rest had gorged their fill and disappeared. The nights had been dark and cold, with the dull roar of the sea, the oily lapping of water and the terrible feeling of isolation which threatened their sanity.

The first death had occurred after twenty days. With the death of the second officer, Turner as the oldest man was left in charge.

Some of the men began to sip sea water, gradually increasing until they were drinking half a cup at a time. The thin veneer of civilization soon wore off as a raging thirst caused some of them to fight for the meagre supply of water. One man had his hand lashed to the water container to prevent theft by others. After the water had been drunk and the rations eaten, some of the men including Turner and Jack Corbett, a fireman, had lived off the green vegetation which grew on the sides of the raft. Occasionally, the diet was varied when flying fish stranded themselves on the raft. They gargled with their own urine, suffered salt water boils and their hair turned white with the salt.

One man went berserk and jumped over the side, taking with him another man. The crazy man was torn to pieces by the sharks. The other man scrambled back on the raft but a shark bit off his leg up to the knee. Turner knew the blood would bring the sharks on to the raft and he pushed the injured man back into the sea. God forgive him, but there wasn't anything else he could do, was there?

One day there was general agreement to use some of the blood from one of the dead as saliva but it made them sick. They decided that they would not indulge in cannibalism and as each man died he was put over the side of the raft. The men who drank sea water died horribly, choked by their swollen tongues. Some lay quiet with a philosophical calm and eventually became silent for ever as the days passed without a sign of a ship. Daylight would sometimes reveal the corpse of a man who had shown determination to survive the day before, but with the darkness had found the futility of his plight unbearable; relinquishing hope he had sought refuge in death.

After forty days, only Turner and Corbett were alive. Turner guessed that Corbett was on the brink of a complete mental breakdown; especially after the previous day when an Allied aircraft flew over but in the vast, open sea the tiny raft and its occupants were missed and the plane continued on its course. The two men had exhausted their dwindling strength by waving their arms and shirts. As the plane disappeared they lay on their backs without the energy to voice the hatred which they felt towards the plane's crew. Desperation and fear had distorted their minds into believing that they had been deliberately left to die. They were unable to reason that from several thousand feet above the sea they were less visible in the varying colours of the ocean than the proverbial needle in a haystack.

'God help us, it's coming at us!' screamed Corbett.

Abruptly Turner's thoughts came back to the present.

The massive shape, propelled by a double-bladed tail which slashed the sea, was speeding forward towards the raft. They could see its eyes, a catlike golden colour with black pupils above the nostril slits in its pointed snout.

'God help us,' screamed Corbett as the monster came out of the water its huge mouth opened revealing row upon row of white fangs with serrated edges. It tried to fling itself on to the raft, pitching it violently from side to side, before sliding back into the sea.

There was a huge swirl near the raft and the tri-angular fin came up and knifed the surface. It rolled on to its side and they could see the white belly and the wide, grinning jaws. This time it drove straight under the raft. There was a crash as it hit the underside of the raft with its back and the two men clung on with clawed fingers. The shark turned and came back. Again the hurtling speed then the impact. The raft came out of the water; after tipping to one side it righted itself and fell back on an even keel. The shark's great head rose out of the water and its jaws opened and closed on the side of the raft. There was a crunching of timber as the shark hung on.

'Christ, he's going to get us — he'll not stop 'til he does,' shouted Turner, dragging himself away from the grinning head.

The great head began to shake and the two men slipped and slithered as they gripped the opposite side of the raft which was now being lifted out of the water and swung from side to side. Suddenly Corbett lost his grip and fell over the side. The shark released the raft from its jaws and whirled towards Corbett. Corbett screamed as the terrible jaws grabbed him round the middle of his body like a mastiff with a bone and Turner watched helplessly from the raft as it drifted away.

The shark and its victim sank gradually out of sight into the bloodstained green water.

Turner lay face downwards on the raft, his mind numbed by Corbett's horrific death. He hadn't see the shark for the last hour but he knew that this was only a temporary respite. This rectangle of death on which he floated had been the scene of thirteen deaths. Soon it would be his turn. The blood spattered over the raft would draw the shark like a needle to a magnet. Why wait for the inevitable?

This marathon fight for survival had been useless. This was the end. He wouldn't wait for that bastard to come back and tear him to pieces. One roll of his body and he'd be off the edge of the raft into the sea. His lips curled into a bitter smile as he thought of Corbett saying they'd be up shit creek if they were knocked off the raft. Maybe so, but if he could drown before that bloody shark returned it would be an easier death than Corbett's. Already a feeling of numbness was encircling his body — if he waited a few more minutes that numbness would spread and act as an anaesthetic to make it easier. He turned his head and saw the forty-eight scratch marks recording the battle for survival. Pity he couldn't have reached his half century.

What the hell was that noise? A deafening roar overhead blotted out the noise of the sea. Had the shark come back to finish him? Please God he hadn't left it too late to drown himself. He turned painfully on to his back and stared upwards with uncomprehending eyes at the aircraft which was flying so low that he could make out the pilot's face through the canopy and another member of the crew waving his arms. They'd seen him — praise be to God — they'd seen him. He heard the metallic sound of a voice through a loud hailer and dimly realised that some sort of a miracle had occurred to give him a reprieve from death.

The *Rapier's* decks throbbed with the vibration of engines driving on maximum revolutions and her screws flung a churning white sea from the stern.

After weeks of unspectacular but important convoy work the destroyer was moving towards the Equator like a greyhound off leash.

'Could be a U-boat on the surface,' said Lofty Jackson. 'Let's hope they stay up sunbathing 'til we get there,' he added.

Speculation about a forthcoming enemy encounter was eventually dispelled by Commander Thompson speaking over the ship's broadcast system.

The rescue of a survivor from a torpedoed ship was to be the *Rapier's* mission. The man had been seen recently on a liferaft by a Coastal Command aircraft. He had succeeded in abandoning the raft for an inflated dinghy, clearly marked in phosphorescent red and yellow sections, dropped by the aircraft. The dinghy contained fresh water, hard rations and a transmitter automatically tuned to make continuous transmissions while its battery lasted. The *Rapier's* high frequency direction finder was now being used to locate the dinghy's position from these transmissions. Estimated time of arrival would be during the next two hours. A sharp lookout by hands on deck whether on or off watch was ordered.

'There it is!' shouted Grainger as he pointed to the red and yellow object clearly defined by the sun against the blue backcloth of the sea.

As the *Rapier* closed the distance they could see a man standing in the dinghy. He was frantically waving his arms as if he feared that the destroyer would pass without stopping, leaving him to continue his lonely vigil in the unbroken expanse of the ocean.

'I know how you must feel, mate,' muttered Grainger, remembering his recent ordeal.

The destroyer was slowly circling the dinghy.

'Now comes the tricky bit when we stop. God help us if there's a U-boat there, using the survivor as bait,' said Jackson.

The man in the dinghy was stockily built and dressed in torn shirt and trousers. His beard and hair were caked white with salt and his face was haggard and lined with suffering but still showed the determination which had helped him to survive.

The outward sheer of the *Rapier's* bows, with its grey super-structure and square-cut stern, as it closed the distance was the most welcome sight that Dave Turner had ever seen in his life. This was his passage back to civilization. His appearance, not surprisingly in that moment of joy and relief, was of no concern to him. He'd won through against the odds — that's what counted now, but he knew that eventually the images of terror and death would return and never be far away for the rest of his life.

'Yon bloke looks in a bad way,' said Anderson.

Grainger picked up a heaving line and secured one end to a stanchion then stepped over the guard rails and prepared to dive over the side and secure the line to the dinghy, but the man in the dinghy shouted a warning for him to remain on deck and pointed to the surrounding sea. The dark, triangular fin of a shark could be seen uncomfortably close and Grainger quickly stepped inboard. He untied the line and threw the end with the Turk's head knot into the dinghy. The man below bent down to secure the line and the dinghy was pulled into the ship's side.

The *Rapier* was now stopped and a folding chain ladder was hung over the side. One of the ship's crew was halfway down the ladder, intending to help Turner inboard, but Turner was already feeling the benefit of the fresh water and hard rations he had found in the dinghy. With new found strength, born of hope, he waved the man back and indicated he was fit enough to climb inboard without assistance; and so it proved.

Climbing the ladder unaided he eased himself on to the destroyer's deck through the gap in the guard rails where stanchions had been lowered. He was led to the sick bay while the dinghy was hoisted inboard.

The shark, deprived of its anticipated prey, darted away as the *Rapier's* screws churned the sea into white froth and the bows of the ship cleaved a course north towards Freetown.

· · ·

'Wonder what that smart arse in the ship's office is up to?' asked Mick Shaw, looking over Grainger's shoulder. He pointed to a slip of paper pinned on the ship's notice board within the last few minutes.

Grainger saw that Sub Lieutenant Manders, in charge of the ship's office, was asking for someone who could type — temporary basis only.

'Probably needs someone to shift the typewriter,' said Grainger. 'You know the old come-on about anybody interested in music and the volunteers find themselves humping a dirty big piano on board for an ENSA show.'

'Maybe not,' said Mick scratching his chin thoughtfully. As a former newsman he was no stranger to using a typewriter and he could type at a reasonably fast speed. 'Anyway, a typewriter's easier to lift — think I'll take a chance to find out what he wants.'

Mick made his way to the ship's office and knocked on the door. The sub lieutenant's voice summoned him in. The typewriter was on a shelf at the side of the sub's desk. Shaw noted the pieces of screwed-up paper in the wire basket on the deck and guessed that Manders wasn't making the grade as a typist.

'You need a typist, sir?' he asked innocently.

Manders looked doubtfully at him. 'Are you volunteering, Shaw?'

'Yes, sir.'

'Experienced?'

'Newspaper reporter in civvy street, sir. Used one every day.'

'Sit down then.'

As Mick settled himself comfortable in the only other chair Manders began to explain. He pointed to several small diary-type loose leaves of paper which had been written on in pencil.

'These comprise a record of the day-to-day experiences of Mr Turner, the man we rescued yesterday. He is the sole survivor of his ship which was torpedoed. The captain wants it typing with carbon copies. Can you do it?'

'No problem, sir,' replied Mick confidently.

Manders was satisfied with the result of a brief typing test he gave Shaw and then requested him to attend at the ship's office the following morning.

'I'll clear it with the TGM for the time you need.'

157

The diary made fascinating reading. Shaw groaned to himself as he thought of how he could have used a scoop like this in the newspaper business. Still, there might be a chance later on so he decided to make an extra copy and began to type. Time would enhance a story like this.

'The rest we know,' said Manders after he had finished reading the typed sheets. 'Thanks, Shaw, you've done a good job – no mistakes either.'

He collected the sheets. 'Is this the lot?'

'Top and three copies you asked for, sir,' said Mick, – a fourth copy hidden in his cap as he left the ship's office.

The work had been well worthwhile and he had proved to his own satisfaction that none of his skill in typing a report had been lost.

24

Shortly after Dave Turner left the *Rapier* at Freetown, on his way to the UK – a place which at one time he thought he'd never see again – the destroyer made its final departure from the West African port and sailed south for the Cape.

While Turner had recuperated aboard the *Rapier,* the ship's company had taken part in a 'crossing the line ceremony.' Very few of them had escaped a ducking in the canvas tanks filled with sea water on the fo'c'sle. Only the captain amongst the officers had escaped and that was by locking himself in his sea cabin seconds before the mob reached his door.

Turner, looking comparatively fit and relaxed after his ordeal, had been an amused spectator on the fo'c'sle.

'Seems as if we've taken his mind off the last few weeks,' said Mick Shaw, still dishevelled after his ducking.

'Don't we get a certificate or something after this bloody lot?' asked Anderson.

Mick snorted. 'Bit late in the day, Jock, we should have been bloody-well certified when we volunteered for this bloody lot – as you so quaintly put it.'

Life aboard the destroyer had gradually returned to normal after the uproar and lunacy which had marked the ship's crossing of the equator, and now three days after leaving Freetown she had taken over escort duties again. This time with a convoy of six merchant ships from Takoradi.

The twelve days' trip through South Atlantic waters, with days of blazing sun, was untroubled by alarms. After shepherding the convoy to a safe anchorage in Table Bay, the *Rapier* moved south, rounding the Cape of Good Hope before berthing on an oiler in Simonstown with two other destroyers from the convoy escort.

'This is what I call living,' said Joe Myers as he and Ted Grainger looked out of the railway compartment on to the green and brown scrub of the South African veld, stretching as far as the eye could see.

They were travelling on two weeks' leave from Cape Town to Johannesburg. Their compartment exuded comfort, opulence and solidarity with the rich polished colour of mahogany wood and well-sprung leather upholstery. The quality of the meals and drinks service had been impeccable with no food rationing to contend with.

'Join the navy and see the world!' said Grainger, emptying the remaining contents of the beer bottle in to his glass.

'Drink now, pay later,' he added and drank the iced beer.

'You're a cheerful character,' laughed Myers. 'You haven't been listening to Jack Oliver by any chance?'

'Not recently – why? – What's he been on about?'

'Reckons we're on a one-way ticket once we go east and he doesn't want any part of it.'

'If he's right I don't blame him, but it's a bit late for opting out,' replied Grainger.

'He reckons not. When the ship leaves South Africa he says he won't be on it. He's up-homers near Wynberg – some bird he's shacked up with.'

'They'll pick him up – bound to.'

Myers laughed. 'He knows it, but he reckons that by that time the *Rapier* will have gone and he'll do his detention in barracks.'

'Afterwards, leave every night and enjoy the rest of the war in comfort,' said Grainger.

Grainger could imagine Leading Seaman Oliver trying something like that. Oliver was a smooth talker who could charm the birds off the trees. He fancied himself with the girls, and he was a man who was constantly looking for ways to make money. Card games, washing service – hammocks, clothes etc. – and hair cutting were just a few of his side lines.

'He's probably made enough money to set up in business,' said Myers.

During the afternoon of the following day the train arrived in Johannesburg and as it moved slowly into the station they had a glimpse of modern concrete, steel and glass buildings similar in design to American skyscraper blocks.

'There must be gold in them there hills,' commented Myers

160

as they took in the prosperous image which the streamlined buildings gave to the city centre.

There were four other men from the ship on the train and the sailors were met by their hosts as soon as they stepped on to the station platform.

Each man received an invitation to stay with a family and their hosts suggested that the sailors should use a city centre pub known as the Shakespeare for a meeting place during their leave. Apparently, the Shakespeare was so well-known that most passers-by would be able to direct them to it.

'Fancy a trip down a gold mine, Ted?'

John Sanderson straightened from the task of carving a massive joint of roast beef and his knife and fork were raised questioningly in mid-air.

Sanderson, a leading surgeon in Johannesburg and his wife Betty, both descended from English families, were Grainger's hosts during his leave.

The Sandersons' detached house stood in green lawns surrounded by a blaze of colour from flowers and shrubs.

Grainger was watching Sanderson's skilful carving of the joint and he could visualise the surgeon amputating a patient's limb with the same expertise.

The thought vaguely disturbed Grainger, but the invitation to see a gold mine appealed to him and John Sanderson made arrangements for the visit to take place the next day.

Grainger, with ten Dutch sailors, was listening carefully to the foreman in one of the mine's offices. They were all dressed in boiler suits, long rubber boots and short oilskin coats, with sou'westers, in their hands. A form was given to each man for signature containing a disclaimer of liability by the mining company for death or injury to the seamen during their visit.

The foreman was an Afrikaner and he obviously preferred to converse in Dutch, occasionally speaking in English for Grainger's benefit. The signed forms were collected and the foreman led the group across a yard to the shaft gate.

'You might think this gear is unnecessary, but wait while you get near the rock drilling and you'll be glad of it,' said the foreman.

He passed around a cardboard box containing cotton wool. 'Here, put some of this in your ears – you'll need it when the pressure increases.'

They each took a piece but did not block their ears with it as the foreman continued to speak. Grainger listened to the guttural voice now speaking in Dutch and decided to put the cotton wool in his ears.

The first descent of 2,000 feet was vertical, and Grainger had anticipated the smooth descent of a departmental store lift. The foreman grinned as he saw the momentary look of alarm on their faces as the lift plummetted like a stone to the first level. The Dutch sailors hurriedly stuffed the cotton wool in their ears as the increasing pressure hurt their ear drums.

At the first level they saw a huge chamber with an arched roof sub-divided into sections containing giant-sized fans. The fans provided air-conditioning throughout the mine, inputting fresh air and outputting foul. There were electric motors which operated the lifts and a man manipulated levers as he watched a huge dial on the wall. Indicators moved round the dial showing the position of the cages in different shafts. Lights flashed and buzzing noises sounded as calls were made from different depths to summon the lift cages.

'This is the nerve centre of the mine. If anything goes wrong here, we're all in trouble,' said the foreman. 'There's only one lift shaft up and down at each level and we have to get the relieving shift down before the others come up,' he explained. 'Could add another hour to a shift before you see daylight, but we're paid on the clocking-off time up top.'

Their next descent was made at an angle of almost thirty degrees in a truck similar to those used on a fairground roller coaster, the seats being built up in steps. Two men sat on each step leaving a gap in the middle for men to move to the back or come forward when they arrived at their stop. The truck was roofed with thick meshed wire and its sliding door at the front opened and closed like that of a tube train.

'We go so far down and then the seam disappears,' said the foreman. 'Then we have to dig in different directions and try to pick it up again. The rock formation where the seam runs is

162

shaped like a basin and if we're lucky we hit the seam again, if not, the mine closes.'

The truck came to an abrupt halt. Two coloured labourers and a white supervisor entered. The labourers climbed to the back of the truck and the supervisor, who spoke in Afrikaans, sat with the foreman at the front by the door. The truck slid alongside the platform at the next level and the supervisor jumped out shouting for the two labourers to follow. They struggled towards the front of the truck while their boss stamped his feet impatiently.

When the two men finally stepped from the truck the supervisor shouted abuse at them. One of the men protested and as the truck moved away Grainger looked back and saw the protesting native knocked to the ground with a vicious blow from the huge fist of the supervisor.

'Poor bastard,' muttered Grainger, disgusted by what he had seen.

He glanced round at his companions. A few of them had seen the incident but they passed no comment.

'We have every nationality and creed working in this mine except one,' said the foreman.

The group was watching the drilling of the rock by the native labourers as jets of water were sprayed to disperse the dust and cool the drills.

'Which one is that?' asked Grainger.

'A Jew – there's no Jews here. We get on well without them – there's always trouble when they're around, man.'

Grainger remembered John Sanderson's previous conversation when he had mentioned that the owner of this particular mine was a millionaire several times over. He was a Jew who lived near Muizenberg, a seaside resort for the wealthy on the Cape Peninsula.

Grainger smiled to himself. 'No need to work down the mine when you can get some silly bugger to do it for you,' he thought.

At the end of the tour they thanked the foreman and other officials for the visit and went their separate ways. As he walked through the yard away from the mine shaft Grainger saw the endless chain of iron buckets which travelled from the bottom of the mine. The buckets, tipped over by the weight of the contents at the top of their run, spilled out greyish gold-bearing rock for chemical processing before making the long descent for re-filling.

He looked at the piece of marble-like rock powdered with gold-coloured particles in his hand. Each member of the party had received a similar piece as a souvenir.

'Fool's gold, calcium carbonate with a dusting of iron pyrites – worthless,' the foreman had told them and invited them to take a piece each. Then he described how the original prospectors had found this rock on the ground and mistakenly thought they had struck gold.

Appearances could be deceptive but the owner of the mine living in Muizenberg knew the difference alright, thought Grainger.

Grainger was walking down a busy street in the centre of Johannesburg when he saw a black man with a heavy crate on his shoulder stumbling towards him. He stepped into the road to make way for the native as the pavement narrowed at that point. He regarded his action as common courtesy but as he stepped back on the pavement he heard a man's voice with a heavy Dutch accent.

'You British are too damned soft when it comes to dealing with blacks.'

Grainger turned abruptly towards the speaker and saw an elderly man in a white suit with a hard, sun-tanned face and penetrating eyes regarding him with a look of annoyance from under his wide-brimmed hat.

The man was powerfully built and looked as broad as he was tall. He gave Grainger the impression of being a tough Boer war veteran who had fought against the British at the turn of the century.

Grainger's face reflected his anger and the man recognised this and smiled.

'Come, my friend;' he stretched out a muscular arm and patted Grainger's shoulder.

'We're both men of the world, have a brandy with me and I'll explain.'

164

Grainger reluctantly accepted the invitation and the man led the way into a nearby bar. When the brandies were placed before them the man removed his hat revealing a shock of white hair. He raised his glass in salute to Grainger and promptly swallowed the contents in one gulp. Grainger drank more slowly having experienced the potency and fiery properties of South African brandy which was usually sold before it had been allowed to mature.

Grainger ordered two more brandies and his companion began to speak.

'With all due respect, you made a mistake out there when you stepped off the pavement for that black. No white does, or should do that in this country. It would be a sign of weakness and those black bastards would soon take advantage.'

Grainger began to protest but the man continued unabashed. 'People outside South Africa who criticise the way this country is run have no idea of the problems which exist here. I'll give you an example. A house boy who is a thief would be more likely to steal from a British master than an Afrikaner.'

'Why?' asked Grainger.

'If the boy stole from the Britisher, the worst that would happen to him is that he would be taken to court. The Afrikaner would give him a damned good hiding and then take him to court.'

'Wouldn't the Afrikaner be prosecuted for assault?'

'No, because the judge would realise that the Afrikaner was helping to uphold the law by providing a . . . how do you say it?'

'A deterrent?' suggested Grainger.

'Exactly, a deterrent which would make that black think carefully before he commits another offence. It works, believe me.'

Grainger downed his second brandy and politely refused the offer of another. He was about to develop the argument then he realised that the Dutchman was too prejudiced in the matter to take any notice of another opinion.

There'll be trouble here one of these days, he thought, as he excused himself and left for his appointment at the Shakespeare with Joe and the other lads from the *Rapier*.

'Have you lot read this?'

Joe Myers pointed to the front page of the evening paper he had been reading.

'It might be civilised in the town and residential areas round here but it can be rough in between – especially at night, according to this. If any of you get stranded in town without transport, don't even think about walking home – it could be your last walk.'

Grainger took the paper from Joe with a smile which gradually disappeared as he read the article.

'Come on, Ted, what's happened?' asked one of the sailors in the group.

Grainger did not reply; he was too absorbed with the article.

'One of the tribal compounds near the mines was raided by the police yesterday,' explained Myers. 'Three whites seen late at night in the city two weeks ago disappeared, and now they've been found.'

'Well, that's alright then,' said the sailor.

Grainger looked over the top of the paper.

'Seems the police are near enough certain that three bodies which were hacked to pieces and found in different parts of the compound are those of the missing persons.'

'We're supposed to be going to one of the compounds for the tribal dancing tomorrow,' said another man uneasily.

'Better not get too friendly with the natives then,' advised Joe.

'What a way to go – have you seen those topless beauties?' asked Grainger.

'Not much of a thrill if you've lost some of your parts in the family stewpot,' replied Joe. 'I've heard of some blokes whose ambition is to be shot by a jealous husband, but castration is something else!'

The visitors were visibly impressed as they sat on benches with their hosts, in open fields at one of the mines, watching the tribal dances. Native employees were performing rhythmic dances wearing full regalia and war paint.

'Most of them come from places outside the Republic, like South West Africa and Bechuanaland,' explained one of the mine officials. 'They earn good money, then go back home.

Some like it so much they sign on for another spell.'

Grainger wondered if the native who had been hit by the supervisor would be signing on again.

The two weeks in Johannesburg passed all too quickly. The sailors thanked their hosts and boarded the train for the return to their ship in a gloomy frame of mind.

'I can understand Jack Oliver wanting to stay in this country,' said Myers. 'It's been a good leave.'

The train for Simonstown was crowded and the men from the *Rapier* were making their way through the compartments looking for empty seats when they saw a massive Great Dane sprawled full length, occupying the whole of a seat designed to hold three people.

Grainger looked with amusement at the dog with its tail and one hind leg hanging off the seat, while the front legs on which its head rested overlapped the aisle end of the seat.

'Able Seaman Nuisance, I believe,' he said as he bent down and patted the dog's head. Nuisance opened one eye briefly and closed it again.

'Obviously not impressed,' said Myers. 'We'll stay here, anyway, I don't think there'll be any room farther up.'

The train jolted its way through Observatory, Rosebank, Newlands, Kenilworth and Wynberg. On reaching Plumstead, Nuisance raised his head and looked out of the window. He stretched himself then reluctantly slid off the seat and lay full length on the floor.

Nuisance was a symbol of the Royal Navy in the Cape Peninsula. He ruled supreme in Simonstown and in any train he selected to travel on along the suburban lines. Adopted by the navy as a mascot, he was allowed privileges which no other dog ever had, and he was even registered as an able seaman in the navy.

'What's up with him?' asked Myers. 'He's not due off until Simonstown.'

A sailor in the opposite seat laughed. 'He's had the seat for half the journey, now you can have it for the other half. Nuisance believes in fair shares with his chums, don't you, old chum?'

The sailor leaned forward to pat the dog's head but Nuisance put his jowl on his paws and closed his eyes. For him the incident was over.

'And they say the age of chivalry is dead!' said Myers as they carefully stepped over Nuisance and sat down.

The train pulled into Simonstown and the sailors followed Nuisance out of the station. The dog ambled towards a waiting bus which went to the nearby barracks at Froggy Pond.

'Thanks Nuisance,' said Joe as they turned towards the dock-yard entrance.

Nuisance appeared to shrug his shoulders. He looked back at them as if he was making sure they were going in the right direction then he jumped on the bus and settled himself comfortably on the special seat reserved for him.

25

The *Rapier* sailed from Simonstown without Leading Seaman Oliver. After rounding the Cape she made an unscheduled stop at Durban, which overlooked the Indian Ocean from magnificent beaches.

'You've got to hand it to Oliver,' said Myers as he and Grainger looked with interest from the ship's fo'c'sle at the buildings which marked the outer limits of the city centre. The multi-storied blocks reminded them of Johannesburg, contrasting sharply with the Victorian solidarity of Capetown.

'There's something puzzling me,' said Grainger. 'Why are we calling at Durban when everybody was certain that the first stop would be Mombasa?'

'You're making a mystery out of nothing, bach, we've probably got a convoy to meet off Durban. Anyway, we're here for a couple of days – and that's official.' The speaker was Taffy Jones, a member of Joe's team on X gun, who had overheard.

'I still get the feeling that the skipper's got something up his sleeve and we haven't heard the last of Oliver,' declared Grainger.

'One thing's certain,' remarked Myers, 'it's a bloody sight warmer than Capetown – feels like we're back on the equator.'

The other two nodded in agreement. Jones pointed below to the wharfside. 'How would you like to tangle with those two beauties?'

They looked down and saw two Zulu women walking past carrying baskets on their shoulders. They wore nothing except strings of beads and brief plaited skirts. Their bodies and limbs were magnificently proportioned and their brown skins gleamed in the sun as their powerful back muscles and well-formed breasts moved in rhythm to a majestic stride.

'Bit too heavy for me – I'd be giving too much weight away!'

grinned Joe.

'You should see the size of the men, bach,' said Jones. 'They're like mountains. They've got a weakness for boots, though. More than one drunken matelot has woken up with bare feet and no money. They flog the boots.'

'Getting their own back for Rorke's Drift, I expect,' said Grainger.

'What ship was Rorke on?' asked Taffy with mock seriousness.

'Hardship, you Welsh wonder!' replied Myers with a grin.

At midday excited voices sounded from the direction of the gangway. Grainger was checking the gun firing circuits in the transmitting station when the gunner's mate poked his head round the door.

'Clear lower deck in five minutes, Lofty, hands to muster on the quarter deck.'

'What's happening, chief?'

'Patrol's just brought Oliver on board – skipper's going to weigh him off.'

Grainger joined the rest of the ship's company to witness the naval ritual of a rating being sentenced to punishment.

Oliver, standing pale-faced but defiant between two escort guards, winked cheerfully at some of his friends as they assembled on the quarterdeck. Details of the charge were read out by the coxswain, and Oliver gave a smirk for the benefit of his friends. Instead of being flogged at the grating, as he would have been in Nelson's day, Oliver was sentenced by the captain to ninety days' detention, demoted to able seaman and deprived of two good conduct badges.

The smirk on Oliver's face disappeared when the captain said that Oliver would remain on board until the ship reached Mombasa. He would then be transferred ashore to commence his detention in the naval prison.

'You might be interested to know that I have made arrangements for you to re-join the *Rapier* at Trincomalee, so that you will not be deprived of the opportunity of seeing action with the East Indies Fleet,' added the captain.

Grainger looked at Oliver's face and saw that the confident look had gone and his shoulders slumped momentarily when the captain said that he would be re-joining his ship. Oliver had barely time to straighten himself before the coxswain's order to stand to attention sounded prior to his being escorted at the double off the quarter deck.

'Looks as if you were right, Ted, about calling here, skipper must have had word he'd been picked up in Capetown,' said Myers.

Grainger nodded. 'Did you see Oliver's face when he heard where he's going to do his time? It would have been easy for him at Durban, but near the equator with the strong arm sadists leaning on him will be a different proposition.'

'Aye,' replied Myers. 'Skipper's determined to make him pay through the nose for this one.'

Grainger was unsympathetic. 'He's asked for it – serves him right.'

Taffy Jones had also been right when he had mentioned the possibility of meeting a convoy off Durban. A crowd of people , who usually gathered on the wharves whenever a warship or troop transport departed, waved as the *Rapier* left Durban. She sailed due east and joined a convoy of three troop transports and four destroyers off the southern tip of Madagascar, avoiding the U-boat-infested Mozambique Channel. *Rapier* steamed in a solitary position several miles ahead of the convoy carrying out a continuous anti-submarine search as she steered in a wide zig-zag pattern. Contrary to expectations, the *Rapier* remained with the convoy until it arrived in the furnace-like heat of Aden two weeks after leaving Durban. The ship stayed in port for two days but the blistering heat discouraged most of the liberty men from going ashore.

'I've been reading a book about a chap who must have been in a different part of Mombasa to this,' said Mick Shaw. 'He reckons that Mombasa is a pulsating exotic island with beautiful beaches and protected by coral reefs from the pounding rollers of the Indian Ocean. He also mentions the crystal-clear blue of the sea.'

'So what?' remarked Jack Swann.

Brown water churned past the *Rapier*'s, stern as she entered the East African port of Kilindini. Foc's'le and quarterdeck

171

parties were lined up in the stand-easy position ready to be brought to attention when bosun's pipes shrilled in acknowledgement of the customary salutations from other navy ships.

'Looks as crystal-clear as bog water and don't tell me it was any different when this bloke waxed poetic in his book,' continued Mick.

Jack Swann laughed. 'Your author's description of Mombasa is quite accurate — I was there in peacetime. This is Kilindini which is Mombasa's port and handles the major part of East African trade as well as being a naval base. The city of Mombasa lies over there in the north east. That's where your beaches and blue seas are, old son.'

Lofty Jackson joined the group. 'Buffer wants a word, Ted, I believe he's got a nice quiet number lined up for you when we drop anchor.'

Grainger looked over Lofty's shoulder to see the chief bosun's mate, Petty Officer Railton, stalking towards them.

'Ah, Grainger, just the man I'm looking for. Better change into tropical rig for going ashore, you're part of the escort for Oliver when we get in.'

Grainger stared at the Buffer. 'Why me?'

Railton grinned. 'Because, lad, you're the right size, you're duty watch in the harbour and . . .' he added with heavy sarcasm, 'I knew you'd jump at the chance of a run ashore. Now get changed — you haven't got all bleeding day — we're pulling out of here this afternoon. Skipper's champing at the bit already.'

Grainger wiped the sweat from his forehead with the back of his hand then glanced at the other occupants of the *Rapier*'s motor boat which was now leaving the ship's side.

Stripey Clough, the boat's coxswain, moved the wheel with an expertise born of long practice. His expression was one of concentration as he brought the boat's bows on target for the landing stage. A stoker sat by the hatch cover of the motor in case of mechanical problems, taking furtive drags on a cigarette hidden between his fingers from the prying eyes of authority on the ship. The bow man gave every appearance of being disinterested in anything except the arrival of the motor boat at the landing stage. Leading Seaman Williams, in charge of the escort, sat with a moody expression on his face, apparently absorbed with the shine on his highly polished shoes while Donovan, the third member of the escort, periodically exchanged muffled conversation with Oliver.

After a few minutes the motor boat swept alongside and the bowman, using his boat hook, pulled the boat against the landing stage while escort and prisoner disembarked.

'Half an hour then, Bungy,' said Stripey and Williams nodded in agreement. The motor boat commenced its return journey to the *Rapier* and Williams looked round expectantly and then appeared satisfied when he saw a covered truck coming towards them.

'Give him a hand with his gear,' he ordered as Oliver struggled to lift his kitbag, hammock and case at the same time. Donovan shouldered the hammock while Grainger took the case.

The truck, with the letters R N marked in white on the sides, had stopped in a cloud of dust and they climbed into the back and sat down on the side benches. Ten minutes later after a bumpy ride over cracked road surfaces they were flung sideways as the truck stopped abruptly with a squeal of brakes.

'Has our guest from the *Rapier* arrived?'

The sarcasm in the voice was emphasised by the hard eyes and uncompromising features of the man who stared at them over the tail board of the truck.

Williams nodded in confirmation and the tailboard was lowered by a pair of muscular arms.

'Bring him to the office then.'

The party jumped down from the truck and the escort again helped Oliver by taking his hammock and case.

The office stood at the entrance to an enclosure which was fenced off with barbed wire like a stockade and closed at the rear by squat single-storey buildings with narrow barred windows.

The man who had come to the back of the truck was waiting for them at the office door with a disdainful look on his face. The white vest he wore covered bulging muscles and the badges on his vest confirmed his rank as petty officer physical training instructor. White shorts revealed thick, muscular legs and his feet were encased in plimsolls.

'Escort — drop that bloody hammock and case — prisoner, pick them up!'

The petty officer's voice sounded like the roar of a demented bull. Grainger and Donovan dropped the case and hammock respectively and watched Oliver attempt to balance the hammock with the kitbag already on the opposite shoulder.

When he had accomplished this the petty officer picked up the case and placed it on the hammock. He then forced Oliver's fingers round the handle of the case.

'Prisoner — double march — about turn — about turn — about turn!'

The escort watched sympathetically as Oliver ran up and down the enclosure until it seemed that he must collapse under the weight of his load and the equatorial heat. The colour of his face had changed from red to purple then finally to a sickly yellowish-white as saliva began to form round his mouth.

Williams was about to protest when the petty officer called a halt to the torture. The kitbag, hammock and case crashed to the ground from Oliver's shaking arms and he was ordered to pick them up or face another spell of double marching.

Williams was summoned into the office, papers were exchanged and the escort party returned to the truck. As the truck reversed round for its return journey to the landing stage they saw the stumbling figure of Oliver, still fully loaded with his possessions, being directed to one of the single-storey buildings.

Reckon he'll be glad to get back to the *Rapier* wherever we are, thought Grainger as he scanned the paper which Williams had given him to read for general interest. It was a form of receipt signed by the petty officer at the prison. The standard form of wording was typical of the iron-hard naval discipline of previous centuries.

Below the date and address of the prison were the words 'Received the body of Able Seaman Oliver'.

'Sounds like the poor bastard's already dead,' protested Donovan.

'Before he's finished there he might wish he was,' observed Williams grimly.

The *Rapier* left Kilindini that afternoon and returned to Aden where she awaited the arrival of capital ships from the Mediterranean.

26

Paddy Doyle, one of the *Rapier*'s special duty men in harbour, was a man who paid a great deal of attention to his appearance which could well be described as dapper. A peacetime rating, he had signed on for twelve years rather than face unemployment in civvy street. When he went on leave to his native Eire it was necessary for him to wear civilian clothes which he kept in the same impeccable condition as his naval dress.

Of medium height, fresh complexioned with fair hair and Irish blue eyes he looked as if butter wouldn't melt in his mouth. His soft Irish brogue, when he wasn't bawling out orders in the course of his duties as bosun's mate, gave the impression of an individual who had a generous philosophical approach to life.

When he was sober these characteristics were true enough. Even at tot time he was inclined to be generous in offering sippers to his friends. When he was on shore leave and unlimited supplies of strong drink were available he did his best to maintain the tradition of the fighting Irish. Paddy's runs ashore were legendary, frequently resulting in the naval patrol van bringing him back to his ship. He was one of those matelots who should have had zippers sewn on to their badges — they were off and on so often.

He had been an acting PO on Grainger's previous ship and after one monumental run ashore in Jarrow when he got fighting drunk, took on an entire shore patrol and had a swing at an officer, his PO rank had been blown and Paddy had gone right down to his present rate of AB with the loss of two good conduct badges.

'Trinco here we bloody well come,' muttered Paddy Doyle to himself as he paused to watch the ten Fleet destroyers trace intricate white patterns in the sea as they moved into a screening formation for the battleships and aircraft carriers which were passing through Aden's boom defences.

Paddy had heard about Trincomalee on the north east coast of Ceylon. One of his mates had described it as being like Scapa for bleakness and desolation except there was plenty of green jungle and it was a bloody sight warmer.

One thing's certain, thought Paddy, at the end of this war if he was still in circulation, his twelve would be completed and no way would he re-engage for another term. He'd had it up to his eyeballs. Peacetime had been alright but he'd look for something else after this lot. He'd got nothing lined up but surely he could make a go of it in civvy street and settle down with a wife and family. He'd stop in the UK, there was nothing back in Eire. His father and mother were as poor as church mice, they couldn't afford to keep him at home unemployed — that's what he'd be.

Serving in the navy wouldn't help him either. The British were unpopular back home and always would be and the local folk wouldn't think him a hero even if he had been sunk by the *Scharnhorst's* guns on one ship and sunk on another by the Luftwaffe's bombs.

Some might say he was a Jonah after that sort of record. Maybe, or would it be third time lucky? Lucky for him or the Japs? There was going to be a showdown alright with those slit-eyed bastards. That's what those ships were over there for. No doubt at all, at all.

He turned to pass the group of men working on the torpedo tubes amidships. His bosun's pipe shrilled and he shouted for the first lieutenant's requestmen and defaulters.

'D'ye mind making less noise, you Irish git?' requested Lofty Jackson. 'We're trying to work here and can't hear ourselves think for your bleeding racket!'

'Sure, it's yourselves need waking up,' replied Paddy. 'You'll all be seeing action shortly with this lot or hadn't you realised that?'

He pointed to the other ships. 'And we'll be the first into the shit or I'm an effing Englishman.'

'You are an effing Irishman,' said Lofty. 'We've all heard about you and your runs ashore. Wanted by mothers in every port for putting their daughters in the spud line!'

'There's no truth in it,' said Paddy. 'Sheer lies made up by jealous morons who can't even get their ration of black ham because they don't know how to get it up. But I'm not a man to take offence.'

'Except when you're three parts pissed ashore,' grinned Lofty.

'There have been people who needed to be taught good manners,' admitted Paddy. 'But enough of all this crap. Have you lot heard the latest buzz from the wardroom?'

'That will be a load of crap if it's from the wardroom,' said Grainger. 'Everybody knows the navigator specialises in leaking duff gen for the benefit of us poor sods on the lower deck. Once heard him say to Jimmy that it was to brighten our miserable little lives. Sadistic bastard!'

'This is the truth and not from the navigator, Ted. It'll cost you sippers though.'

'I thought there was a catch in it — alright Paddy me boy but it had better be good. No con, mind.'

'No con, right then. I have it on good authority from the captain that we're steaming on a south-easterly course for Trinco. Manoeuvres on the way for three days — then one of the battle wagons and a carrier are leaving the main fleet for Bombay and we're part of the escort that's going with them.'

'Is that all?' asked Lofty. 'The way you cadged the sippers I thought you'd be telling us that we'd been recalled to the UK for three weeks leave either watch.'

Paddy grinned and continued his way to the for'ard part of the ship. The shrill notes of his bosun's pipe were followed by his deafening shout for requestmen and defaulters. He turned back and added impishly. 'And three weeks' leave for both watches when the ship secures in Gladstone Dock. There now,' he grinned. 'Will that not satisfy you ungrateful English? I'll be round for sippers, Ted!'

The diversion to Bombay took place as Paddy had forecasted and there was some relaxation from the exercises of the last few days.

Three days later the ships entered Bombay harbour, the largest and most beautiful harbour in the whole of the Indian sub-continent. An impressive shoreline featured the massive golden-towered block of the Taj Mahal hotel, extensive university buildings and the marble edifice of the Gateway of India built

177

to commemorate the visit of King George V, Emperor of India, and Queen Mary.

Bombay's status as a major port was further confirmed by the bustling activity in the harbour and the sprawling industrial areas adjoining the docks where the squadron eventually berthed.

Rapier secured on the outside of two trawlers so that it was necessary to walk across the cluttered decks of the trawlers to reach the quay side.

Shore leave in Bombay passed without incident except for one involving Jock Anderson who found that negotiating the decks of the trawlers at night after a session on the local brew was far more difficult than when sober and in daylight.

His unconscious body, lying hidden in the shadow of the first trawler's funnel, was found or rather stumbled over by two stokers walking ahead of Grainger and Shaw on their way back to the ship at the end of shore leave.

'Christ, there's a body here!' shouted one of the stokers who knelt down and then laughed as he looked up.

'It's one of your lot — dead drunk by the looks of him.'

'Well, well,' said Mick. 'If it isn't good old Jock, drunk again. Put that fag out, Chalky, or you'll cremate the poor bastard.'

Chalky laughed but he accepted Mick's advice and threw his cigarette over the side. 'We'll leave you lads to look after him then. He looks nice and peaceful — just passed out I reckon — can't see any cuts or bruises on his head.'

'Hang on, lads, we'll need a hand,' said Grainger 'One on each corner. We'll have him back on board in no time,' he added encouragingly.

'Right,' said Chalky reluctantly, turning to the other stoker. 'Come on, Dusty, grab an arm — we can't leave the stupid bastard here and don't drop him over the side else he'll sink like a stone with what he's shifted tonight.'

'It'll cost him his bleeding tot tomorrow,' grumbled Dusty Miller.

Each man took his corner round the slumbering Anderson. On the count of three they hoisted the deadweight clear of the deck and staggered towards the trawler's rails where a short gangway was negotiated on to the second trawler. Grainger's suggestion that they have a breather before tackling the gangway on to the *Rapier* was readily accepted by the others and Jock was deposited on to the trawler's deck with a dull thud.

'This is where the men are separated from the boys,' said Grainger, pointing to the gangway which rose at a sharp angle from the trawler to the destroyer's deck.

'Before we go I'll have a look to see if the coast is clear,' said Chalky. 'If the Officer of the Day sees him like this he'll put him in Jimmy's report.'

'You as well if you aren't careful,' grinned Mick.

Chalky stumbled up the gangway and disappeared from view as he edged round the torpedo tubes to satisfy himself that neither the officer nor the quartermaster were nearby.

Several minutes passed and they were about to try to find out where he had gone when Chalky returned waving some cards in his hand.

'Here's your station cards and I've got Jock's card as well.'

They pocketed the cards and took up their positions round the still unconscious body. Grainger and Shaw took the legs and the two stokers lifted the shoulders as they backed up the steep gangway. Suddenly, Dusty lost his footing and released his grip as he lurched to one side. Jock's shoulder crashed over the side of the gangway support causing Chalky to lose his hold. The body swung head down towards the water lapping between the two ships.

Grainger and Shaw hung on desperately to the two legs which were coming into an upright position as Jock began to slide into a vertical dive. The two stokers scrambled to grab Jock by the waist and force him against the gangway.

'Bend his legs back,' grunted Chalky. 'We'll try to lift him over.'

The body seesawed either side of the gangway but gradually enough momentum was built up for the two stokers to recover their hold on Jock's shoulders.

With muffled grunts from the four men the body was swung on to the gangway and still unobserved they staggered on to the *Rapier's* deck.

'We'll need block and tackle to get him down there,' gasped Mick.

They were standing by the hatch cover of the forward mess deck with Jock lying nearby.

'We'll go down first,' said Chalky. 'You two hold him on the edge of the hatch with his feet on the ladder and we'll ease him down from below.'

The plan worked well until Jock slipped from the grasp of Grainger and Shaw. Jock slid down the ladder and knocked the two stokers over like skittles. Grainger went down the ladder, quickly followed by Shaw, and they both laughed at what they saw. Jock was still asleep with his back propped against the ladder while the two stokers were struggling to their feet, winded but unhurt. They managed to heave Jock on to the lockers where he continued to sleep.

'The next time the patrol can bloody well have him,' gasped Chalky. Dusty nodded in agreement.

The following day Jock seemed none the worse for his experience, although he couldn't remember anything about the previous night's episode. He was surprised to hear how he'd been brought back to the ship.

'Lost my cap last night — you haven't seen it, have you?' he asked after he had invited Grainger and Shaw to share his rum.

Grainger laughed as he remembered Jock swinging upside down over the side of the gangway and visualised the cap floating round the harbour.

'Why don't you look on the trawlers?' he suggested.

'Aye, and next time we'll bring your cap back and lose you — it'll be a bloody sight easier,' said Shaw. 'By the way, Jock, I'd save the rest of that tot if I was you. Chalky White and Dusty Miller gave us a hand with your carcase last night. They're coming round for sippers!'

The destroyers in the squadron turned to seaward as they screened the capital ships now formed in line ahead to pass through the boom defences of Trincomalee and secure at the Fleet anchorage.

Joe Myers, as captain of the quarter deck, had his men lined up in the stand easy position facing outboard ready to be brought to attention.

The *Rapier* entered harbour and approached the lines of battleships, cruisers, aircraft carriers and destroyers He was disappointed to see that the *Rapier* had been the last destroyer in. Junior skipper — all the gash jobs coming our way, he thought.

He looked round the great natural harbour fringed by hills. The surrounding landscape, the moored ships and floating dry dock reminded him of Scapa Flow, except it was a bloody sight warmer and greener.

So this is the East Indies Fleet, he thought, looks like Somerville has got a fleet together after two years without one. This lot aren't here for the ride either. Means we're going to start fighting back. Funny thing about Somerville was his transfer out here without a fleet for so long. Some kind of a rap for the Oran job, I wouldn't wonder.

The mauling of the French fleet there by Somerville's guns must have been done on orders to Somerville. Such a hue and cry afterwards — it was bloody typical of the Admiralty to find a scapegoat for somebody else's mistakes. Wonder when they'd get back to the UK. When the war ended and not before, I expect.

He'd been lucky to meet Ruth. They'd been writing to each other regularly. Maybe something would come of it when he got back. She was in the Wrens, now doing well by all accounts, in line for a commission according to her last letter. Funny how things worked out. Sheer luck that he and Ted had gone to Ashdown that night and seen the notice about the dance in the village hall. They'd been over the moon after meeting the two girls. A run ashore, with every indication of being as dull as ditch water, suddenly came alive and full of promise. The war had faded into insignificance for a time until Julie was killed. Bloody pity – she was a fine girl.

He'd been shocked when Ruth told him about it. Like losing a relative, even though the four of them had met only a few weeks before. Ted must have been devastated and now by another twist of fate they'd met up again on the same ship. Wonder if that's some sort of omen? Maybe their bad patch was over, they were both survivors, weren't they?

The shrilling of bosuns' pipes as salutes were exchanged with the senior ships interrupted Joe's thoughts and he called the quarter deck crew to attention.

27

The tasks of the East Indies Fleet were numerous and complex. Their main objectives being to deny the Japs the use of the Indian Ocean, to cut seaborne supply lines to the Jap armies in Burma, to give close support on the seaward flank of the 15th Corps in the new campaign in the Burmese Arakan and to attack Jap shipping, oil and harbour installations.

Since the summer of 1944, the Japs had virtually abandoned the Indian Ocean so far as the passage of large ships was concerned. The attacks by Allied aircraft and submarines had forced them to use convoys of very small ships which crept inshore, hugging the land as closely as possible.

During the last few months of 1944 the *Rapier* was kept fully occupied with the routine work of fleet and convoy escort duties in and out of Trincomalee, sometimes round the southern tip of Ceylon, then beyond to Cochin and Bombay. Jap surface ships may have been scarce but enemy submarines lurked with their torpedoes.

The weeks of almost continuous confinement on board in crowded conditions and intense heat gave rise to frustration and boredom on the mess decks. Arguments over trivial matters became commonplace and tempers flared at the least provocation.

Some relief from this monotonous existence was provided by an occasional run ashore in Colombo, or boiler cleaning leave in the mountains near Kandy for a few days in the crystal clear atmosphere of the Diyatawala rest camp, six thousand feet above sea level.

At sea, bread was often rationed to a daily slice per man, issued under the watchful eye of the killick in each mess on the evening of the previous day. It was made by a sweating, cursing PO chef and his assistant in a galley so cramped for space they could scarcely turn round between the ranges. The bread was intended for breakfast and tea. Half a slice for each meal and nothing else unless the mess caterer had been careful with his meagre funds so that a tin of Tickler's jam made a welcome surprise. Butter was another scarce commodity. Having received the slice of bread, each man was left with the problem of storing it from the greed of others. The popular choice was the locker or ditty box which could be secured with a lock. Invariably, bread stored for only a short period under these conditions became green, stale and riddled with weevils before it was eaten.

In addition to the issue of bread, two hot meals — midday and evening — were catered for in each mess. Midday was usually meat of some kind with veg and sweet. The type of sweet was very much dependent on the inventiveness and culinary capabilities of the cooks of the mess.

The cooks were responsible for preparing the hot meals, putting them up to the galley for cooking, subsequent serving in the mess and washing up. Each member of the mess took his turn in a rota of three cooks for each day which ended with the scrubbing out of the mess the following morning ready for inspection by the first lieutenant.

Supper was usually a fry up with potatoes; ' train smash' — sausages and tinned tomatoes — with chips being a frequent offering. It was not surprising that eating and drinking ranked high on the list of priorities when shore leave was given. A small canteen shop on board opened at specified periods to supply chocolate, cigarettes and occasionally eggs for those who wished to supplement the navy's daily food allowance from their own pockets.

The main attraction ashore at Trincomalee for the liberty men was a beer canteen with each man rationed to one bottle of strong export ale on a ticket system. In practice the tickets exchanged hands surreptitiously and it was not difficult to obtain more than the stipulated ration.

Scouse Webber, a member of Grainger's mess, had managed to obtain a handful of tickets that particular night. Both he and Paddy Doyle were well and truly fighting drunk by the time the *Rapier's* motor boat brought them back to the ship.

Scouse, normally an easy-going character, was one of only a few survivors from a destroyer sunk by bombs at Dunkirk. Shell shocked, as it was described in the last war, bomb-happy in this one, and the subsequent dis-integration of brain and nervous system was not understood by the majority of doctors. To cover their own ignorance in these cases some doctors entered a diagnosis of 'lacking in moral fibre' in the man's medical history. A man whose mind had been driven beyond the limits of sanity with little hope of a return to normality was thus labelled as a coward through the ignorance of that doctor.

Scouse, apparently recovered from his ordeal, was likely to become emotional and aggressive under the influence of alcohol. It was customary on these occasions for his mess mates to give him a wide berth and concentrate on their own business with a quiet aside of 'bloody nut case'. Liberal quantities of strong export beer had provided the fuel for Scouse's aggressiveness as he stumbled towards the hatchway leading into the for'ard lower mess deck.

Grainger, duty watch on board, was replying to a letter he had received from Jill Davidson. Her letter mentioned that she and Joan Mitchell had been selected for officer training. It seemed that Joan and Mick Shaw were writing to each other regularly, which did not surprise Grainger. It was obvious to Grainger that those two were attracted to each other from the moment they met. Mick had never mentioned Joan's name since leaving Greenock. Kept it quiet, the crafty blighter.

He heard the sound of voices, then feet clattering on the steel ladder which led down to the mess deck from the open hatchway. Mick's voice could be heard above cajoling Scouse Webber to get a move on down the ladder. Scouse stopped halfway with his face turned upwards. 'Shut yer trap, yer fat bastard — don't tell me what to do. I don't take orders from the likes of you!'

'Get moving, Scouse, you're blocking the ladder, for Chrissake,' said Mick whose feet had now appeared on the ladder above Scouse's head. Scouse wobbled down and Mick followed.

'Right,' said Scouse swaying against one of the tables 'I want an apology or you'll get your face smashed in.'

'Apology for what?' asked Mick stepping off the ladder.'

'You just called me a big mouth up top,' snarled Scouse.

'All I said was that you Scousers always have something to say. Talk a bleeding gramophone to scrap you lot would!'

'You'll apologise for that or get thumped.'

'Will you two keep quiet,' snapped Grainger.

'Scouse, why don't you sling your hammock, get your head

down and we'll talk about it tomorrow when you've sobered up.'

'And what the 'ell's it got to do with you, Grainger?'

Grainger, who had returned his attention to letter writing, looked up to see Scouse standing on the opposite side of the table, his face contorted with rage. 'Get your head down and forget it,' he replied and stood up feeling angry at Scouse's behaviour.

He felt a jarring pain and saw bright flashing lights as Scouse's fist hit him in the mouth, splitting his bottom lip. Before he could recover, a barrage of punches was swung into his face as he stood trapped between table and lockers. He ducked his head but took further blows as he edged round the end of the table. The white hot rage which had begun to seethe inside him numbed the pain of the blows, now his one objective was to get his hands on Scouse and beat him senseless.

Grainger moved clear of the table and swung a vicious jab at Scouse which landed under the heart. Scouse gasped for breath and stumbled forward into a left hook which caught him in the eye. A looping right delivered with Grainger's full weight connected on the chin and the fight was over. Scouse's eyes glazed and he collapsed on the floor.

Grainger, thwarted by this early end to the encounter, grabbed Scouse's head with both hands intending to bang it against the steel deck; then he felt himself being pulled away by several pairs of hands and he was pushed on to a bench by other members of the mess. He watched Scouse pull himself to his feet and stumble to the opposite side of the deck.

He looked down at his vest and the sight of the bloodstains from his nose and cut lip filled him with rage. 'You do that again and I'll kill you,' he snarled at Scouse's retreating back.

'Take it easy, Grainger, or you'll be up on the bridge with your cap,' Lofty Jackson was imposing his authority as killick of the mess. 'If you two can't behave I'll have to make sure you do.'

Grainger turned away, experiencing a feeling of disgust at his own part in the incident. Pent up emotions had been released like a volcanic eruption by a trivial matter, but the worse part for him was that but for the intervention of the other men he might have killed Scouse. He needed fresh air and made his way to the upper deck.

The night was peaceful and warm as he leaned over the guard rails listening to the water lapping against the ship's side.

'You look a mess — what does the other bloke look like?'

He turned and saw Joe Myers standing beside him.

'Bad news travels fast,' he replied harshly.

'It's not all bad. Thought you might like to know that Jack Swann will be asking you to put in for leading hand shortly. I was having a chat with him and your name cropped up. What do you think?'

'Tonight's episode won't do my chances of promotion any good — I'm not sure I'm interested, anyway,' replied Grainger.

'Now you sound like Mick Shaw. Look, Scouse Webber's a nutter after he's had a few pints. Everybody knows that and he probably got what he deserved. If I know Scouse he'll be round tomorrow with his tot asking you to have sippers as if nothing had happened.'

Joe's hand clapped down on Grainger's shoulder.

'Think about it— before Jack Swann mentions it, eh?'

Grainger nodded and Joe walked for'ard.

'Sorry you got involved Ted.'

Grainger turned to see Mick Shaw behind him. He suddenly grinned in spite of his split lip. 'I don't want Jill to hear about it.'

'Why should I mention anything to Jill?' asked Mick defensively.

'Come off it, Mick, you're likely to say something to Joan next time you write.'

Mick looked surprised. 'So that's it — Jill's been telling tales out of school. Wait 'til I see that young madam.'

'Why all the secrecy, you chump? It was obvious to me that Joan likes you. God knows why.'

'You think so — you really think so, Ted?'

Mick's face creased into a wide grin then almost immediately he became serious. 'I'd like to think so. It was only that one evening we met. Just a few hours. Not time enough really, if you look at it sensibly.'

'Since when does sense come into it?' asked Grainger. He grinned. 'If the chemistry works, that's all that matters. Could be love at first sight, mate.'

'Didn't work out last time — we thought we were made for each other, Jean and me. Didn't work out — not her fault really. Me responsible as much as anybody and the bloody job. Couldn't go down that road again — no bloody fear. She's a good kid is Joan — I like her a lot but it's a long way back to the UK and

186

people change.She could meet somebody else — probably has. Anyway, I was keeping things quiet until I had a chance of talking to her again. God knows when that'll be.'

'Sooner than you think, Mick, you might have to salute next time you see her.'

'Why?'

Grainger chuckled. 'She and Jill have been selected for a commission. Hasn't she told you?'

Before Mick could reply, the staccato bark of a machine gun came from the direction of the fo'c'sle.

'Sounds like the sentry's having a go at somebody — come on!' shouted Grainger as he flung himself up the steel ladder of the fo'c'sle.

Warships in Trincomalee had a sentry on the fo'c'sle at night with orders to keep a sharp lookout for midget submarines and frogmen who placed their limpet mines under a ship's keel with devastating effect.

The sentry was usually like a walking arsenal with his .303 rifle, a Lanchester which could empty its magazine of thirty-two rounds at the slight touch of a finger on its trigger, plus half a dozen hand grenades strung round his waist.

A boat coming anywhere near the ship had to be challenged for identification and if the challenge was not answered to the sentry's satisfaction he was under orders to open fire on the offender. Duty watch keepers took a spell of two hours in turn throughout the night on this duty.

As Grainger and Mick rounded the starboard side of B gundeck they were faced with the sight of Paddy Doyle aiming the Lanchester over the guard rails on the port side of the fo'c'sle. Paddy had a drunken leer on his face as he concentrated on his aim. Jock McLaren, the sentry, was vainly trying to recover the Lanchester from Paddy while the grenades round his waist clanked together in the struggle and his rifle lay unheeded on the deck.

'It's that bloody crazy Irishman,' muttered Mick. 'He and that silly bastard Webber have had a skinful ashore.'

Paddy's face was inflamed with drink as he struggled with McLaren.

'Leave off, you Scotch bastard, don't you know the enemy when you see 'em? What sort of a bloody sentry do you think you are?'

187

'It's not the enemy, ye Irish clod,' shouted McLaren. 'It's the ship's motor boat bringing some of the officers aboard!'

'Tis the Japanese, I tell you,' thundered Paddy, trying to line up the Lanchester on the motor boat, whose occupants were now feverishly trying to hook the boat on to the ship's falls.

The midshipman and the navigator had dived into the sea and were in the process of passing the hooks on the falls across the gap to the men in the sinking motor boat. The bosun's mate's pipe shrilled and there was a shout for 'Clear lower deck and man the motor boat falls.'

'Drop the gun, Paddy, unless you want to be topped for murder,' shouted Grainger.

Paddy stared at the officers in the water. 'Jaysus you're right — now why the hell would I think it was the Japs.'

He dropped the gun on the deck and McLaren bent down to grab it before Paddy changed his mind. Chief Petty Officer Baines, followed by Joe Myers, appeared on the fo'c'sle.

'You've got some explaining to do, Paddy, by the looks of things,' said Baines calmly.

Paddy stared at the coxswain with a look of bewilderment on his face. 'I thought it was the Japs, chief — honest to God.'

'Aye, lad, that's as maybe. Now put yer cap on and you can explain to the Officer of the Day. He's looking forward to having a chat with you.'

''I'm pleased to hear it Chief, if I just explain . . .'

'Come on, Doyle, less of the bullshit — get your bleeding cap on and *move*,' shouted Baines.

'Now where would my cap be — not over the side for Chris-sake?'

Paddy stared anxiously round the fo'c'sle. Grainger saw the cap resting against one of the bollards and handed it to the Irishman. Despite his drunken state Paddy was careful, as always, to place it on his head with the bow over his left eye.

'I'm ready, chief,' he announced in a dignified manner.

Baines looked at Grainger and Shaw. 'You two give a hand on the motor boat falls. We'll talk about this later. McLaren, keep those guns under control.'

McLaren had already made sure the guns were secure — the rifle was slung over his shoulder and he held the Lanchester tightly against his chest.

'Aye, aye, chief,' he muttered as he resumed his fo'c'sle patrol.

Meanwhile, the motor boat had been hoisted out of the water leaking like a sieve through a line of bullet holes neatly drilled from stem to stern — evidence of Paddy's marksmanship.

The six officers, including two from another ship, and two of the crew had swum to the boom and climbed inboard. Only the coxswain of the boat remained to secure as the ship's company were ordered to run away with the falls and bring the boat up to its davit heads.

There was much speculation on the messdecks the following day especially at tot time. The general opinion was that Paddy Doyle was for the high jump and it was a miracle that nobody in the motor boat had been hit.

Joe's prediction about Scouse Webber proved correct.

The rum rations were being served when Grainger saw Scouse walking towards him holding a cup. 'Sippers, Lofty?' Scouse looked sheepishly through a swollen right eye then grinned with an impish expression.

Grainger took the proffered cup. 'Cheers,' he said and promptly grimaced with pain as the rum stung his cut lip. 'Thanks for reminding me,' he added, handing the cup back and they shook hands. Lofty Jackson, pausing in the measuring of the rum, observed the incident with approval.

28

The swing of sea power from the Japanese to the East Indies Fleet in the Bay of Bengal had put pressure on the enemy's lines of communication. On land the Japanese had been halted on the borders of India and they were now in retreat down the Burma coast.

The seaward flank of the British Army was supported by warships from the East Indies Fleet, ranging from the battleship *Queen Elizabeth* to motor launches and landing craft. The navy was landing troops. stores, mules and vehicles and carrying out bombardments.

The fleet's guns, guided by target spotters of the Army and Sea Reconnaissance Units ashore, pounded the Japanese through Akyab, Ramree, Myebon and Cheduba, speeding the British advance down the coast to Rangoon.

The *Rapier* had played her part in these bombardments and landings with maximum use of her 4.7 inch guns, firing from barrels long since stripped of paint by the melting heat of explosion. Moving close to shore in mined waters and in advance of the landing forces, the *Rapier* with other destroyers systematically bombarded pre-selected targets and then maintained a watching brief ready to provide assistance to the men in the landing craft which surged towards the shore.

One evening, shortly before dusk, the ship was anchored near the malarial and scorpion-infested swamps which lie between Ramree Island and the mainland. A reconnaissance officer had been picked up from the coastal mangrove swamps and was now on board discussing new targets for bombardment with Commander Thompson. From the *Rapier's* upper deck the crew were able to watch a variety of animals and reptiles take their turns to drink at a muddy watering hole near one of the creeks which intersected the swamps.

'Fancy a run ashore, Mick?' Grainger pointed to the huge crocodiles which were moving quickly down a beach of soft sand to slake their thirst at the hole.

'Not bleeding likely,' replied Mick. He looked with awe at the crocodiles then laughed. 'The war hasn't upset their routine. Look how they respect each other's drinking time, which is more than you can say about some pubs back home.'

'I wonder who's waiting for who over there?' Grainger pointed to the thick jungle which extended inland beyond the swamps to a range of mountains in the distance.

'The target spotter who's just come on board must wonder about that as well. What with that lot as well as the Japs to contend with, I wouldn't have his job for a pension.' said Mick.

Shortly afterwards, during the invasion of Cheduba Island, Grainger moved quickly to secure a bowline of a motor launch which was coming alongside the *Rapier* for fresh water and to unload casualties. The naval guns were silent, having completed the initial bombardment and the sea was dotted with assault craft moving shorewards.

As he bent down to secure the line to the stanchion, Grainger looked down at the limited space on the launch crowded by survivors from assault craft which had been sunk by mines. A blinding explosion suddenly erupted beneath the launch and pieces of metal showered down on the destroyer's deck. The rope line which Grainger had secured to a stanchion broke and the launch's bows were pointing skywards before it disappeared from view.

Miraculously, only three men died in the explosion. As survivors and corpses were brought inboard Grainger assisted a soldier who told him that was the second time he had been blown up in the last fifteen minutes.

'I thought we were in luck when the launch picked us up and now look what's happened. Sod this for a caper, mate, it's enough to put bloody years on a bloke.'

The soldier's words were prophetic. Later that day when Grainger stopped to have a word with him he saw that the soldier's hair had turned white.

Jack Swann was of the opinion that the mines were automatically primed after surface craft had passed over them.

'Those Japs are crafty bastards,' said Swann. 'They've fixed the minefield so that one craft can pass but if another follows in the same track thinking it's a safe course the mine will have been primed to explode.'

'Do you reckon we're in the middle of a minefield, chief?' asked Shaw.

'No doubt of it,' replied Swann. The minesweepers are working now but we'll have to move first before they can sweep this area and that's going to be dicey.'

During the early afternoon the *Rapier's* anchor was raised carefully and the ship inched its way forward. No one spoke and the tension increased by the second as crew and survivors stood in silence half expecting to hear an ear-shattering explosion at any moment.

The ship's slow progress seemed never ending. Eventually safe waters were reached and the minesweepers were able to work in the area where she had been anchored.

A signal subsequently received from one of the minesweepers confirmed that the *Rapier* had been lying over six mines which would have broken her back had they exploded.

When Grainger heard the news he thought of the soldier who had been blown up twice that day and was thankful that the hat-trick had not been completed.

'Some blokes should be hung by their balls from the yard arm,' complained Lofty Jackson in disgust.

'Don't be hard on yourself, Lofty, we won't say nowt, your secret's safe with us,' grinned Bob Carson, an LTO who hailed from Bamber Bridge near Preston.

Bob was in charge of the *Rapier's* low power system. He'd broken off from explaining the technicalities of repairing a gun circuit to Grainger and Anderson.

'You some sort of a comedian, you Lancashire git? I'm talking about Nobby Clark, that's who,' retorted Lofty. 'He'd rob his own mother, would that one.'

'Aye, but he's usually careful not to do any thieving when the ship's at sea,' added Carson.

'That's only because he knows he'll be the first suspect if

anything's missing and he can't get rid of his ill-gotten gains ashore. Remember the other week we tied up alongside that S class destroyer? Well, that was bad enough but the thieving bastard has really hit the jackpot this time,' said Jackson.

Because of the heat and overcrowding on the mess decks when a ship was in harbour it was customary for some of the crew to sling their hammocks on the upper deck at night and hang their shoes on the securing rope of the hammock.

Grainger recalled that the *Rapier* had sailed before the hands had been piped on the destroyer which Jackson had been referring to. Later that day Nobby was trying to sell a range of used footwear around the various mess decks. There was no doubt amongst some of the ship's crew where Nobby had obtained the footwear despite his denials when accused of stealing from the other vessel.

'If they ever find out they'll come aboard and lynch him,' said Carson.

'Exactly, and if that's not enough, he'll have those Gurkhas looking for him now,' added Jackson.

The *Rapier* had recently been involved in landing troops in the Allied advance through Burma, including a contingent of Gurkhas. Grainger remembered the Gurkhas standing passively on the upper deck waiting to disembark. Several crates of poultry which they had brought with them would ensure that there would be no shortage of fresh meat.

'Go on,' prompted Carson.

Jackson continued. 'Well, you know those Gurkhas wouldn't show the blades of their knives unless they drew blood. Nobby's gone one better, he's managed to get one of the knives and he's trying to flog it as a souvenir. Reckons he did a deal with those shoes he's trying to flog. Not only that — he's got one of those bleeding hens walking about with a piece of string round its neck!'

'Could it be true — about the deal, I mean?' asked Grainger.

'Well,' said Jackson, 'if I was Nobby I'd be praying that those Gurkhas never book a return trip on the *Rapier*.'

The shrill whistle of the bosun's pipe on the port side of the upper deck was followed by the Irish accent of Paddy Doyle calling for 'Up spirits'.

'And stand fast the Holy Ghost,' added Carson cynically. 'There's another one who's lucky not to be shovelling shit in Alabama as the Yanks would say.'

'Lucky it wasn't a topping job,' replied Lofty. 'If anybody had been hit in that motor boat he'd have swung alright.'

'I'm not so sure, Skipper gave him the benefit of the doubt when Paddy said he thought they were Japs,' replied Carson. He turned to Grainger. 'You were up on the fo'c'sle, Ted. Do you think Paddy knew it was our own motor boat?'

'Hard to say. He told the skipper that the motor boat crew never answered his challenge and nobody was able to contradict him.'

'Expect he never gave 'em a chance to reply before he opened up,' said Lofty Jackson drily.

'Doyle had no business challenging anybody. He wasn't even duty watch,' protested Carson. 'I reckon he knew what he was doing alright. When one of his mess mates asked him how he'd mistaken his own officers for the enemy, Paddy wanted to know if there was any difference.'

'You planning to shoot anyone else, next run ashore, Paddy?' asked Lofty as Paddy was walking past the torpedo tubes about to repeat his call for 'Up spirits'.

'That's a nasty slur for a man who put duty before self in trying to save his ship,' retorted Paddy. 'Visibility was poor from the fo'c'sle and there was no answer to my challenge. You people could have been blown up and sunk!'

'Blown up and sunk — that's typical bloody Irish,' grinned Lofty. 'Everybody except you knew it was our motor boat.'

'Rubbish, man,' replied Paddy. 'Orders were to shoot if the challenge wasn't answered. As I said it was poor visibility from the fo'c'sle. Impossible to see who was coming along the ship's side.'

'That's because you'd had a skinful of export ale,' accused Carson. 'You'd got no business to be on the fo'c'sle — you were watch ashore — bosun's mate with a machine gun in his hands — I ask you?'

'I was perfectly sober. McLaren's a good mate of mine. I made some tea in the mess when I came off shore leave and brought him a cup. Took over his watch while he drank it. Where's the harm in that?'

'I dare say those poor sods in the motor boat could tell you if

194

you ask 'em,' said Lofty. 'I doubt if Jock McLaren will be a good mate of yours after that roasting the skipper gave him about dereliction of duty!'

'Lack of communication was the cause and nothing else,' said Paddy, 'Anybody who doesn't answer a sentry's challenge is asking to be shot — especially in wartime.'

Paddy swung on his heel and strode away in the direction of the quarter-deck. He blew a shrill call on his bosun's pipe and repeated his shout for 'Up spirits'.

'And stand fast the Holy Ghost,' said Carson.

'You know, there goes a man who can persuade himself to believe anything. The worst kind of liar, in fact,' he reflected.

There was a strong rumour that the *Rapier* would be returning to South Africa for a re-fit in the near future.

'There's somebody just arrived on board who'll be able to give us the date when we return to the land of the Springbok,' announced Mick Shaw. He looked across at Grainger. 'A pal of yours from Mombasa.'

'Not Oliver by any chance?'

'The very same — about four stones lighter and twenty years older.'

'Right,' said Grainger, 'let's go and see him.'

He and Shaw went on to the upper deck in time to see some of the crew surrounding Oliver who was being told by the quartermaster to pick up his possessions and report to the coxswain.

Oliver grinned when he saw Grainger 'Hi, fancy giving me a lift with my case again?'

Grainger smiled but made no move to help. 'You managed to survive the strong arm squad then?'

'Sure — nice blokes once you get to know them — even said they were looking forward to seeing me again when I left.'

A haunted look showed briefly in Oliver's eyes and Grainger got the impression that even the thought of returning to the prison at Mombasa was too bad for Oliver to contemplate — even from a distance.

The smile returned to Oliver's face. 'Caught the ship in time for going back to South Africa — decent of the skipper to arrange it for me.'

Oliver grinned mischievously at Shaw. 'Do you the world of good at Mombasa, Tubby. Get rid of your belly.'

Shaw sniffed contemptuously. 'What about that bird of yours at Wynberg? She'll think you're past it when she sees the new Jack Oliver.'

Oliver laughed as he lifted his kit bag.

'She'll find out different then, won't she?' and he followed the quartermaster who was making impatient noises as he motioned Oliver to get a move on.

Two days later the ship left Trincomalee but not for South Africa as confidently predicted by Oliver. The big ships were left in harbour as the *Rapier*, in company with three other fleet destroyers slipped their moorings and headed due east. 'Operation Suffice', the first of the destroyer sweeps which were to become known as 'club runs', had commenced.

Commander Thompson on the *Rapier* informed the ship's company that the purpose of the exercise was 'to look for the enemy and give him a bloody nose when we find him'.

This announcement was received with mixed feelings by the ship's company. Some of them looked forward to action as a relief from the boredom of the last few months. Others were less than enthusiastic especially after they realised that the ship's re-fit in South Africa had been postponed indefinitely.

'Looks as if the skipper's serious about keeping his promise to Oliver and seeing some action,' said Anderson as the group of torpedomen were closed up at action stations by the torpedo tubes.

'Skipper and Oliver can have all the action they want. I've had enough to last me a life time,' grumbled Shaw. He stared at the other destroyers in line abreast on the port side 'Reckon we're being used as bait.'

Grainger was about to reply when Jack Swann on his tour of inspection overhead Shaw's remark.

'Moaning again, Shaw, What might it be this time?'

Shaw regarded Swann with an angry expression. 'There's a buzz we're going to give the Jap shore batteries some target practice.' He pointed to the torpedo tubes. 'Not much use against shore batteries, Chief. We'll be even less use standing here.'

'There are other possibilities like surface ships and subs, or hadn't you thought of them? I'll make sure you're not standing around, believe me, lad.'

Shaw did not reply and as Swann walked away Grainger turned to Shaw. 'What's all this about us being used as bait, Mick?' he asked.

'Stands to reason, doesn't it? There's been no sign of the Japs in the Bay of Bengal for months. C-in-C's under pressure to send out a destroyer sweep to encourage the Nips to chance their arm. Their heavy stuff could see us off before the battle-wagons in Trinco raised anchor and cleared the gash. They should be out here with us, ready to use those bloody 15 inch pop guns!'

'I'd feel safer,' said Anderson with mock innocence. 'Why don't you mention it to the skipper. Might give him some ideas.'

'Sarcasm, Anderson, as someone once said, is the lowest form of wit and the highest form of ignorance and that just about sums you up.' Shaw paused then added. 'You'll see what I've said is right — that's if you live long enough!'

'You're a right bleeding Jonah,' laughed Anderson.

'Skipper's up-homers with a bird in Jo'burg. He's just as keen as we are to see South Africa again. He's not likely to take unnecessary risks, is he?'

'No, he'll do as he's told like the rest of us,' said Shaw. 'Captain 'D' over there is running this show. He's probably taking orders from some shore-based wallah, top heavy with gold braid, who doesn't know his arse from his elbow, and sleeps with a different Wren every night,' he added wistfully.

'Jealously'll get you nowhere, Mick', laughed Anderson.

During the next five days the four destroyers carried out an anti-submarine sweep across the Andaman Sea. The hope that they would meet targets suggested by intelligence reports or by chance did not materialise. In a final attempt to provoke the enemy into retaliation the destroyers bombarded Great Coco Island. Something like a thousand rounds of high explosive were expended without any apparent effect.

'The Nips have probably buggered off to the mainland weeks

197

ago,' was the general opinion voiced by Carson. The flotilla went to Akyab to re-fuel and another club run started after a break of two days.

Anticipation of meeting the enemy began to wane, particularly as the first two days of the second sweep proved abortive. Boredom began to blunt the previous enthusiasm of the destroyer crews until the situation changed abruptly during the third night.

The destroyers were nearing South Andaman when they came across an enemy convoy of three small coasters hugging the coastline towards Port Blair. Within minutes the coasters were set on fire and sunk by gunfire. Shortly afterwards, outside Port Blair, five sailing junks were destroyed in a hail of 20 mm cannon fire as the destroyers closed in to bombard the harbour.

This time there was some sporadic fire from shore batteries without any hits being sustained by the destroyers as they returned the fire. One tremendous explosion ashore which could have been an ammunition dump gave the attackers encouragement before the action ended and the destroyers set course for Trincomalee.

'Skipper didn't need your advice after all, Mick.' The speaker was Jock Anderson. He and Mick Shaw were greasing the firing mechanism on the starboard depth charge throwers. The *Rapier* and her three sister ships had arrived safely at Trincomalee in the early hours of that morning and the crews were now working part of ship.

'I reckon you're being sarcastic again, Jock. It's a nasty habit of yours — I should watch it,' said Mick placidly.

'You must admit that you were wrong about our ships being used as bait. The Japs didn't even show their faces.'

'You reckon it was a success then?' asked Mick

'Yes, we showed that we could do what we liked. Next time I reckon we'll really give them a belting.'

'A few junks won't upset them so much. They'd be empty for my money,' replied Mick.

'They could have been carrying troops or supplies.'

'Without escort? They'd have used one of their heavy cruisers if the convoy had been important. You take my tip, Jock, the Nips want us to come back with more ships. Ever heard of an ambush?

And I still say we're the bleeding bait!'

'What about the explosion at Port Blair then?'

'Anybody's guess. Who knows? Tell you one thing. I bet Captain 'D' can't wait to go back for a posthumous V.C. and we'll be helping him win it, worse luck!'

Mick was right about going back only this time the major part of the East Indies Fleet came with them, obviously encouraged by the reports of the previous operations. This time a series of successful hit and run raids were made on the Japanese air and fleet bases at Sabang.

'It's good to see this lot earning their keep,' said Grainger closed up at his after tubes action station. They were watching the *Queen Elizabeth* and *King George V* battleships thundering out 16 inch and 14 inch gun broadsides.

'Let's hope they keep the range and don't start dropping 'em short,' muttered Lofty Jackson as he saw orange flashes and clouds of smoke dotting the sides of the battleships and cruisers.

The massive shells screamed overhead towards the harbour of Penang where black smoke from oil installations was already belching high into the sky.

'What's happening now, for Chrissake?' asked Grainger as the *Rapier*'s funnel poured out dense black smoke and men clung to superstructure as the ship heeled round and moved quickly across the harbour entrance. Through the edge of the smoke screen a Dutch cruiser was launching itself at full speed towards the harbour.

The cruiser crossed the wake of the destroyer and they could see the torpedo tubes on the cruiser trained outboard on its starboard.

'She's going to fire the fish inside the harbour,' shouted Grainger and even as he shouted the cruiser was entering the harbour in a daring attack.

'Ours or theirs?' asked Grainger as a noise like an express train thundered overhead.

'Definitely theirs,' said Lofty, 'it's travelling in the opposite direction — sounds like the Dutchman's hit something.'

Muffled explosions through the smoke screen confirmed his remarks. The smoke thinned revealing the Dutch cruiser weaving its way towards the open sea closely followed by great spouts of water hurled upwards by bursting shells from the shore batteries. The air was filled with the roar of huge shells travelling inland as the fleet replied to the shore batteries.

Abruptly, there was silence.

'The shore batteries might have been wiped out,' said Grainger hopefully.

'Let's hope so — we could be in next with tin-fish now the Dutchman's stirred 'em up,' replied Lofty.

But suddenly the *Rapier* veered to starboard and made for the formation of ships lying out to sea, eventually resuming position in the encompassing destroyer flotilla.

Shortly afterwards normal sea watch duties were resumed and the crew were fallen out from their action stations.

29

The probing and testing of the Japanese strength in the Andaman Sea and round the coasts of Sumatra and Malaya continued but there was no sign of the Japanese Fleet and no air attacks
on the Allied ships. The belief held by the East Indies Fleet
Command that the main strength of the Japanese Fleet and Air
Force were being used in the Pacific was strengthened by the
success of the Allied hit and run tactics in the Andaman Sea
operations.

Two years out of the UK has seen a mainly novice ship's
company in the *Rapier* become a useful team, confident in their
ability to deal with any crisis. Even the usual condescending
attitude of regulars to 'hostilities only' men was now modified to
a grudging respect. There were exceptions, as might be expected when it was obvious that certain men did not, and never
would, have the ability to become proficient seamen.

Now the war in Europe was in its final stages and it looked as
if the Japanese had run out of steam. Many of the regulars
intended to waste no time in leaving the service as soon as
possible after the war ended.

But for the war some of them would have left on the previous
completion of engagements varying from seven, twelve or twenty
one years. They had entered as boys and they had little knowledge of civilian life. The new logic and different ideas of the
'H.O's had brought a change of perspectives to a life governed
by customs and procedures followed without question because
nobody had considered an alternative. Regulars and H.O.'s alike
looked forward to a future free of the restrictions of naval
discipline.

Another club run was planned, and this time the ship was in

company with two Fleet destroyers, S- and V- class respectively, recently arrived at Trincomalee from the UK. *Rapier* was the junior ship in terms of seniority of command but senior in experience of these probing sorties.

Captain 'D' in the S-class destroyer was known to some of the *Rapier's* ratings from previous ships.

'Bit of a mad bastard and his ship has a reputation for being a Jonah,' said Joe Myers as he stopped for a chat with Ted Grainger on the upper deck prior to the ship leaving harbour.

'What do you know about him, Joe?' asked Grainger.

'Only that he's been involved in several actions recently off Norwegian and Channel ports. Usually, he moves into trouble first and works out what to do afterwards.'

'A posthumous V.C. type?'

'You might say that. Only so far his ship has come through without a scratch but other ships who followed him bought the lot.'

'Do you think he's been picked by the top brass to stir the Japs up if they're still there?'

'They're there alright, boyo, and he'll stir the bastards up given half a chance — maybe at our expense!'

'Any more good news, Joe? You're beginning to sound like Mick Shaw.'

'Might sound daft, Ted, but I've a feeling in my water that our luck's going to change.'

'Like a re-fit at Simonstown then a trip to the UK when we get back?'

Joe's smile belied the serious look in his eyes. He made no reply as he walked towards the steel rungs leading up to X gun deck. He gave Grainger the impression of a man who had been given a look into the future and didn't like what he saw.

The club run began like the others almost without incident during the first three days. Closed up at action stations and sustained only by corned beef sandwiches, cups of tea and kye, with the odd hour of snatched sleep, the *Rapier's* crew suspected that the skipper's hopes of a clash with the Japanese would not be realised.

The three destroyers steered east towards Penang, then altered course for Sumatra where Japanese air activity was reported. A methodical bombardment of railway works at Sigli was carried out without opposition. Under cover of a rain squall the destroyers withdrew and next day searched the sea round the Nicobar Islands. The weather had cleared and the hot sun poured its heat on to a green sea.

A group of torpedomen were standing in the shade of *Rapier's* Oerlikon gun bridge which divided the two sets of tubes. As the three destroyers examined bays and inlets Mick Shaw gazed at the beaches of white sand and clusters of palm trees.

'Puts Brighton in the bleeding shade, that lot,' he declared.

Grainger nodded vaguely. He was beginning to think there was something in Mick's idea of an ambush. But from where? Those beaches were deserted. There was no cover for any defences. Nothing of a military nature to defend anywhere.

As if he had read Grainger's thoughts Mick turned from his examination of the shore line.

'Giving us a false sense of security like I said. You've heard of housewarming parties, I expect. Well, the one that's coming our way will be an arse-warming party if we carry on sticking our noses into every bay and creek we come across!'

'Captain 'D' won't turn back to Trinco unless there's a shortage of fuel,' replied Grainger.

'He'd sooner row back than miss a chance of mixing it with the Nips from what I've heard,' said Jock Anderson.

'From what you've heard,' mocked Shaw' and what else have you been hearing from that bunting tossing chum of yours on the bridge?'

'Only that the Haguro's likely to be at Port Blair with a destroyer escort,' replied Jock.

'And what the bleeding hell is the *Haguro* supposed to be?' sneered Mick.

'Heavy Jap cruiser with enough 8 inch guns to sink us and those two over there without breaking out in a sweat,' said Jock briskly.

'And how come you're so knowledgeable about its guns, my highland laddie?' asked Mick.

'Ship recognition chart in the SDO. Heard the yeoman talking to Jimmy about it when I was working up there,' replied Jock smugly.

'We might need the tin-fish after all if the cruiser comes out,'

203

said Grainger.

'We could still need them if it doesn't come out,' added Lofty Jackson. 'Remember the Dutch cruiser at Penang. This Captain 'D' won't stop outside harbour if he sees any advantage by going in.'

'And there'll be shore batteries, and what about that destroyer escort coming out to give us a welcome beforehand?' observed Mick. 'Christ, I wonder if there's time to put in a request for a draft chit.'

Jock Anderson laughed 'The only ship you'll get, Mick, is hardship.'

'It's citizenship I'm after,' laughed Mick. 'What do you say, Ted?'

Grainger made no comment. This was the fifth day at action stations and like the rest of the crew he was experiencing a lack of concentration. This might come to nothing, he thought hopefully, another day could see the destroyers still having nothing to report and being ordered to return to Trincomalee.

Within the next hour his feeling of optimism disappeared with the drone of aircraft overhead. The ships were almost in the same latitude as Little Andaman and the *Rapier's* gun crews were galvanised into action as the stream of orders from the transmitting station poured into the headphones. The gun barrels of the 4·7's swung round and upwards in unison with the two-pounder pom pom abaft the funnel and the 20 mm Oerlikons amidships.

Hardly had the orders been given before they were rescinded by the order 'check — check — check' when lookouts identified the aircraft as Flying Fortresses. The 4.7 inch guns were trained back to their fore and aft positions but to the dismay of the *Rapier's* upper deck crew they saw the destroyer on the port side of Captain 'D's ship open fire at the aircraft. Puffs of smoke marked the explosion of the first salvo of shells falling well short of the huge silver-winged aircraft.

'Reckon they must be flying over 20,000 feet,' said Jackson.

Shaw looked anxiously upwards, using his hands to shield the sun from his eyes.

'They reckon a Fortress can drop its bombs into a barrel from 20,000 feet. What's the matter with those stupid bastards over there? Are they blind?'

Even as they turned round to watch the offending destroyer the firing had ceased after the first salvo. Aldis lamps flashed between the ships as the aircraft rapidly dwindled to black dots in the sky and then disappeared.

'Somebody's getting a right bottling,' said Jackson.

Grainger could imagine the lookouts on the other destroyer receiving a tongue-lashing for wrong identification from their captain after his reprimand from Captain 'D'. It was a good job the Yanks identified us, he thought, or maybe they'd already got rid of their bombs and were on their way back to base.

'Ready for South Africa next time, Ted?' Grainger looked up at X gun deck and saw Joe Myers grinning down at him.

'When do you reckon that will be?' asked Grainger.

'This Welsh wonder reckons we're going back tonight,' replied Myers.

Taffy Jones poked his head over the deck rail. 'That's right, bach, heard it on the grapevine.'

The Welshman opened the pouch on his money belt and extracted a thick wad of rupee notes which he held up in his hand. 'I'm ready to celebrate the end of the war, man. By the time we're back in Simonstown it will be all over bar the shouting.'

'Bloody optimist,' said Myers drily and Grainger nodded his head in agreement as he walked back under the bridge of the Oerlikon gun deck.

Most of the crew, like Taffy, had saved money because apart from the occasional run ashore in Colombo and the canteen at Trincomalee, there had been little opportunity of spending it.

Pay over recent months had accumulated in anticipation of the long awaited return to South Africa.

Grainger wished he could share Taffy's optimism but for some reason which he could not readily define, he was beginning to feel apprehensive about the outcome of this operation. He scoffed at himself for being pessimistic with no good reason. After all, the *Rapier* had proved to be a lucky ship so far. Effective anti-submarine actions, successful bombardment of enemy coastlines and harbours without seeing enemy aircraft, and the recent escape at Cheduba after lying over those mines had been a near miracle.

She was lucky alright, thought Grainger, and yet... He looked

205

across at the other two destroyers in line abreast moving north-wards. On the starboard side the rays of the rising sun were like thick stripes painted across the sky spreading from a golden centre.

In any other circumstances it would have been a picturesque sight but at that particular moment of time it seemed to Grainger as if the Japanese were unfurling their flag as a challenge to the three destroyers.

30

The destroyers closed Port Blair during early morning but there was no sight of the Japanese cruiser or any other targets. By 1400 hours they were off the eastern end of Stewart Sound, a narrow stretch of water opening from the south-east of the Andaman Islands, dividing the land masses of North and Middle Islands in the rough form of a letter J.

'The Japs are here, look!" Grainger looked up at the pom pom gun deck and saw the gun layer pointing to the port side. A flag, showing a red-striped sun was secured to a buoy which bobbed from side to side in an eddying current less than fifty yards from the ship.

'There's a fault on the headphones — port side Oerlikon gun deck — see what you can do, Ted.' said Jack Swann from the starboard side of the tubes.

Grainger picked up the repair bag and climbed up the ladder to the gun deck. He was dismantling the headphones when one of the Oerlikon gunners spoke excitedly. 'If anybody's going to catch a packet it will be those two!'

'Being junior ship seems to have paid off this time,' said another man. 'We've got the guard job while those two get the glory.'

Grainger looked across the water at the green walls of jungle which rose steeply either side of a narrow channel. Captain 'D's ship was continuously nosing into the mouth of the channel while the V-class destroyer remained outside the entrance.

Both *Rapier* and the V-class were within 2,000 yards of the peninsula which formed a hook-shaped side to the channel entrance. The channel curved its way inland and there was a period of waiting after Captain 'D's ship had disappeared from view. Suddenly, they heard the sound of gun fire — the sharp crack of 4.7 inch guns was preceded by the rapid thudding of

Bofors from the depth of the jungle, then flame and smoke could be seen from the 4·7s on the V-class.

She appeared to be firing airbursts over the prominent point of the peninsula. Grainger tensed as he saw red winking lights dot the top ridge of the peninsula, then great mushrooms of black smoke with vivid orange centres appeared. Dull, thudding explosions were heard from the land followed by a sound like a freight train travelling overhead.

Great fountains of water shot into the air near the *Rapier*. 'God, why don't our 4·7s open up?' shouted one of the Oerlikon crews. His question was answered immediately as they were half-blinded by the red lash of the *Rapier's* 4·7s blasting out a port broadside in reply.

Grainger almost choked with the heat and acrid smell of cordite as the ship was enveloped in clouds of drifting orange-brown smoke. A sickening thought crossed his mind and he felt a numbing fear in his stomach. The Japanese must have held their fire until the destroyers were within a mile of the shore. Point blank range — for Christ's sake. Captain 'D' and his bloody Jonah of a ship were safe below where the guns of the shore batteries on the peninsula point could not bear and we're sitting targets on his bloody orders. Even the V-class was comparatively safe nearer the base of the peninsula.

Christ — the buoy — it was a marker for the shore batteries! It was the *Rapier*, almost stopped in the open bay, which was now the sole target. The Japs knew the exact range and bearing — thanks to the buoy — and now they had the destroyer at their mercy.

There was a piercing whistle and a crr . .ump. Columns of water shot up on both sides of the ship. The surrounding sea was churned into a white mass. Within a few minutes *Rapier* was hit four times suffering damage to both boiler rooms. The ship lost power and came to a stop.

Grainger, crouched low with the guns' crews, deriving a false sense of security from the shallow steel side surrounding the gun deck. The steel cover would have offered little more protection than cardboard against the huge shells which were now strad-dling the ship.

The blue sky and blazing sun had disappeared, to be replaced by a yellowish darkness of the kind that often preceded a storm. As the light continued to fade there was an eerie silence then a rustling sound like autumn leaves being swept away by a chill October wind and Grainger knew instinctively that he was in the presence of death.

Shells were exploding like thunder claps. The hull of the ship shook and reeled to the force of the detonations and shrapnel clashed against the steel then whined away over the water.

'Why don't we scarper out of range?' asked one of the gun crew. But the *Rapier* had been forced to stop and must now be presenting a perfect target for the enemy's guns with the full length of the port side drifting into view of the shore.

'Christ! the boilers must have been hit,' cried another man in dismay.

They crouched round the two Oerlikon guns, uselessly out of range, and waited like cattle to be slaughtered.

The current moved the ship round into the line of fire and as the bows moved slowly to starboard each section of the ship from fo'c'sle to quarter-deck presented itself to the shore batteries.

The firing from the *Rapier's* guns had become spasmodic as the shore batteries gained hits on or near gun decks. The fo'c'sle gun was the first to stop firing. There was an ear-splitting detonation nearby. B gun and the bridge had escaped as the ship rolled under the line of fire but the high direction control tower which fed the range, bearing and elevation details to the guns' crews, had received a direct hit.

As the ship continued to heel round, the pom pom deck was swept by a blizzard of jagged steel. Grainger heard the shrieks and groans of pain from below, then the ship rolled to port sacrificing the starboard Oerlikon gun crews and the searchlight above but saving the lives of the men crouched on the port Oerlikon gun deck. X gun, bravely answering the enemy's fire was hit and silenced.

The ship rolled to starboard, offering its quarterdeck to suffer more damage before the current mercifully pulled her round. Only the narrow stern of the ship now faced the shore as it drifted from the area where such grievous blows had been inflicted.

Terrible cries of pain came from the deck below and amongst them Grainger recognised the piteous voice of Jock Anderson. He was the first to scramble to his feet and found himself covered in broken glass. A glance at the space where the searchlight had been, told him where the glass had come from but looking beyond he saw the motionless figures of the starboard Oerlikon gun crew lying in dark pools of blood.

Over on the pom pom deck only one man was moving, the rest lay like waxen dolls, dismembered and discarded by their owner in a fit of rage. Grainger thought he must be going mad but for some strange reason he was no longer afraid.

Captain 'D's ship was steaming in towards *Rapier* with all guns blazing in the direction of the shore batteries. Now the S-class came alongside *Rapier's* disengaged starboard side — bow to stern.

The V-class crossed ahead, laying a smoke screen with funnels and floats in an attempt to draw the enemy's gun fire to herself. The guns of the S-class were masked by the *Rapier* and some of her guns' crews scrambled over the guard rails intending to man the *Rapier's* guns where the crews were dead or dying.

The main objectives were the pom pom and X gun. They were unsuccessful in both places and unprepared for what they saw. The pom pom's crew were hung round the gun mounting — eight bodies in all — and the wounded lay in pools of blood on the iron deck.

Part of a man's chest covered a gun sight and half a man was sitting in the trainer's seat. Whole corpses were easy to man-handle over the side but in one case a body lifted by the shoulders came away from its lower half. Hunks of raw flesh were removed with bare hands from the torn steel round the gun. Soon the salvage party's overalls were soaked with black blood. But the gun was useless with some of its barrels split by shrapnel.

X gun's mounting had been hit and most of the crew were dead or badly wounded. One half of the gun's shield was missing while the barrel swung grotesquely at an angle from its smashed mounting. Hair, skin and teeth were embedded in the breech block.

First aid parties were now taking care of the wounded and the salvage party from the S-class clambered back to their ship covered in blood, shaken by what they had seen.

The S-class destroyer, now secured to the *Rapier*, was working away towards the open sea. Both ships were moving at about six knots. Meanwhile, the V-class was still making smoke and engaging the battery. She was now the enemy's only clear target and received three direct hits. One of the shells, landing on the wheelhouse, killed three men and wounded several others. The steering was put out of action and before the emergency steering could be connected the V-class swung dangerously close to the *Rapier* and her wash parted two of the tow wires as she passed. The V-class regained steering control, the other two hits having caused only minor damage, and she followed Captain 'D' and the *Rapier*, still firing astern at the now silent enemy battery.

Grainger looked at the carnage on the surrounding gun decks and felt despair at the thought that such a superb piece of engineering as a man's body could be hacked to pieces in a fraction of a second by rusted lumps of jagged spinning metal. And for what? Had they achieved anything? There was nothing to achieve. No military targets — nothing to destroy that would do any damage to the Japs. Only the sacrifice of promising young lives to satisfy the ego of a Captain 'D' who aspired to be another Nelson no matter what it cost in men's lives.

And now thanks to that misplaced ambition all three destroyers stood a good chance of being lost. If they managed to escape from this confined waterway, Jap planes would be alerted to make short work of the *Rapier*, unable to move; the S-class unable to manoeuvre, being temporarily attached to *Rapier* and the V-class with damaged steering.

He looked up at the rear of the bridge and saw the captain, apparently unscathed, waving his arms upwards then pointing to the deck below the Oerlikon gun. He went to the ladder and looked down to see the first lieutenant's upturned face.

'Anyone hit up there, Grainger?'

'No, sir, starboard side caught it though.'

'Right, see if you can find Gunner 'T' — he's somewhere aft — tell him to come to the bridge.'

'But Anderson's been hit on the other side – he needs help!'

The first lieutenant's face was impassive.

'A first aid party's already there – he's being helped. Now get my message to the gunner.'

Grainger nodded and scrambled down the ladder. A man was kneeling as if in prayer against a depth charge thrower with part of his head blown away. Pieces of paper scurried round on the deck.

For no particular reason he bent to pick up some of the paper and then saw the gunner walking away from the quarterdeck. Grainger caught him up and passed on the first lieutenant's message and then his attention returned to the shreds of paper in his hand.

211

'Shredded rupee notes – oh, Christ! – not Taffy's!' he shouted then ran to the ladder leading up to X gun deck. As he climbed the ladder he yelled out 'Joe – Joe Myers – you alright?' But before he reached the top he knew with a numbing certainty that Joe would never answer his question.

A control party in charge of the Buffer, Petty Officer Railton, were using canvas bags to remove what had once been the crew of X gun.

Nearby, waiting to be collected, lay the corpse of Taffy Jones, his hand still clutching his chest with part of his shirt screwed into a bright crimson ball, the lower half of his body missing.

'What the hell are you doing here, Grainger, you've no business here.'

'Joe – Joe Myers – have you seen him?' asked Grainger.

Railton's hard face softened slightly. He pointed to the missing section of the gun's shield. 'I'm sorry – there's no trace – he'd be here on this side – got the full lift.' He saw the despair in Grainger's eyes and added sympathetically. 'He wouldn't know much about it.'

Grainger did not look back as he descended the ladder. He was still numbed with shock but he was aware that if he survived that day the real impact of Joe's death was still to come.

As he stepped off the ladder he looked at the shreds of rupee notes in his hand and remembered Taffy's optimism about the ship returning to South Africa as he waved the rupee notes. Well, Taffy could have been right about the ship, but the Welshman wouldn't be going nor would Joe with his hopes of seeing Ruth Mason again. He flung the shreds of paper over the guard rail and was distracted from his grief by the raucous voice of Lofty Jackson.

'Come on, Ted, there's a bloody war on – half the torpedo party's been wiped out!'

As he followed Jackson for'ard he saw the first aid parties working under the instructions of the doctor and sick bay attendant.

After a brief examination by the doctor the dead were rolled on to stretchers; heavy practice shells filled with sand and painted black with a yellow band, were tied to their bodies and they were tipped over the side into a shark-infested sea.

The upper deck and superstructure including the torpedo tubes were scarred with shrapnel. Where everything had been calm, ordered efficiency when he left for the Oerlikon gun deck, there were now the bodies of men hurled down and scattered like butcher's meat amongst twisted metal and debris. Cries and groans filled the air, fading as the doctor injected morphine to numb pain. Grainger gasped in anguished horror as he saw the mutilated bodies of Jack Swann, Mick Shaw and Jock Anderson being tipped over the side. He remembered the screams of agony underneath the Oerlikon gun decks and visualised the jagged lumps of shrapnel scything through their bodies. Only the summons to the Oerlikon gun had saved him from suffering the same fate.

Jackson's face was expressionless as he turned to face Grainger. 'It's the only way – it won't help morale keeping them on view. Come on, the lighting's gone on the for'ard mess deck. Primary and emergency circuits are kaput and doc needs some light to start operating.'

Torch lights probed the darkness of the mess decks as men stumbled through with stretchers and deposited the wounded on side lockers. Mess deck tables were already converted into operating tables and there was a strong antiseptic smell everywhere.

Grainger and Jackson were joined by the Gunner 'T', Bob Carson, and two other members of the torpedo party. The plan for restoring the lights by checking circuits from the switchboard was decided on and the group split into pairs to tackle the work. Within ten minutes emergency lighting had been rigged to assist the doctor and his assistants giving treatment to the wounded. The main circuits had been so badly damaged in parts that re-wiring was necessary.

As Grainger and Jackson made their way aft to the high power switch board they saw that the tasks of collecting identity discs from the dead and tending the wounded still continued. A party of men had started to wash down the blood-soaked sand from the decks and wipe away the stench of death with disinfectant and water.

'Nothing's changed since Nelson,' said Lofty bitterly. 'Just look at that stupid bastard over there.' Scouse Webber was swishing a hose pipe round the deck. He grinned as he noticed Jackson and Grainger.

'I'm as good as out of this effing outfit, I've been hit up the arse!'

'You always were a lucky bastard, Scouse,' replied Jackson with a grin.

'Have you seen the doc?' asked Grainger anxiously.

'Not worth wasting his time. He's tied up with worse cases than me. I'll see him later on when he's finished with 'em.'

The hatchway to number one boiler room was swung back and two corpses, stripped of their skin, were being lifted on to the deck. A third man, badly scalded but still alive, lay on a stretcher being carried to the for'ard mess deck. The three stokers were victims of the super-heated steam which had escaped when the boiler room was hit.

They paused by a group of stokers surrounding the first lieutenant, engineer officer and the chief stoker, all staring intently at the closed hatchway to number two boiler room.

'What's happening, Chalky?' asked Jackson.

Leading Stoker Chalky White, a tall, thin gloomy man was looking more disconsolate than usual.

'Looking for some silly bugger to open up number two. Fancy yer chance for a medal, Lofty?'

'Anybody down there?' asked Grainger.

'No – it was closed down before the action started and held in reserve.'

'What's the trouble then?' asked Grainger.

'Super-heated steam,' answered Chalky. 'That's the trouble, mate. Could be like number one down there. Both boilers are connected and number two has been hit as well. We don't know where. If the boiler's okay we'll be able to raise steam and make our way without a tow.'

Grainger felt a surge of hope. 'We might make it back if the Jap airforce is kept grounded.'

'Fat chance of that,' said Jackson.

'Anyway, somebody's got to go down and find out what's happened even if he finishes up skinned alive,' added Chalky.

'What about the spy hole in the boiler room door? – can the steam be seen without opening the door?' asked Grainger.

'No chance. Super-heated steam is invisible – the door has to be opened to find out.'

'Like looking for a gas leak with a lighted match,' observed Jackson. 'What about the engineer officer or the chief going down?'

'Skipper's refused them both permission, according to Jimmy.

Reckons they're needed for their experience – bullshit – it always comes down to the rank and file, doesn't it?'

Chalky's face took on a determined look.

'Might as well chance it. I'm fed up of buggering about here!'

He stepped through the group and spoke to the engineer officer. There was a brief conversation between Chalky and the officer before the top hatch cover was opened. Chalky looked round at the surrounding faces then took a deep breath and stepped over the coaming to quickly descend the vertical steel ladder rungs to the door which sealed off the entrance to the boiler room. The top hatch was closed after him to equalise the pressure, a normal procedure which was necessary before the boiler room door could be opened even without any damage inside.

The group of men on the deck waited anxiously for the news which would decide the fate of the ship. Suddenly the hatch cover swung back and Chalky's expressionless face appeared. 'It's okay to go in,' he said in a matter-of-fact voice as he hauled himself up on deck. The engineer officer and the chief stoker wasted no time in leading a team into the boiler room to investigate the damage and within the hour they had managed to raise steam and connect number two boiler so that *Rapier* was able to make eighteen knots unaided.

'Chalky deserves a bleeding VC for opening up number two – he could have been skinned like a rabbit when he opened that boiler room door!' said Lofty as he and Grainger surveyed the chaos which had once been the high power switchboard.

'He might deserve it but he won't get it, or anything else for that matter,' replied Grainger bitterly. 'The whole bloody thing has been a shambles. They don't give medals for such as that. Thanks to the supidity of one man good blokes like Joe Myers, Jack Swann and Mick Shaw and Jock Anderson with everything to live for have been cut down and fed to the sharks like butchers' meat. Not even a decent burial.'

'Not to mention the lads who've been maimed for the rest of their lives,' said Lofty quietly. 'Anyway,' he turned away to avoid the embarrassment of the tears which threatened to well into his eyes. 'We're lucky. It would have meant a tow if it hadn't been for

Chalky and that would have been suicide with the kamikazes buzzing around.'

'We're not out of it yet. It's going to be a long haul back to Burma on one boiler,' said Grainger.

Lofty clapped his hand on Grainger's shoulder. 'I have a feeling we're going to survive, mate, but not if the Gunner 'T' comes down here and finds we haven't started to clear up this bleeding mess!'

The sound of firing ceased as the other two destroyers closed in either side of the *Rapier* behind the thick smoke screen which hid them from the shore. Captain 'D's ship was unscathed from its duel with the shore batteries. Twisted, blackened metal in the vicinity of the for'ard guns on the other destroyer confirmed where hits had been sustained when the smoke screen was being laid.

The throbbing of the ship's engines as she began to make her own way was a heart warming sound to the crew. The galley, which had escaped damage, began to function again as hot soup and drinks were organised. Rum rations were issued and the survivors began to think about a future which only minutes ago did not seem possible. They were just thankful not to have shared the fate of their fallen comrades. Recriminations might come later, but they would never forget the green confines of Stewart Sound, the shell fire and the bloody shambles on *Rapier's* decks.

The three destroyers made their way north as anxious eyes scanned the empty sky for the expected ominous black dots which would mean the start of air attacks; but the sky remained empty.

Darkness fell, offering temporary protection. The smug voice of Tokyo Rose was heard over the broadcast system on the ship's mess decks informing her listeners that HMS *Rapier* had been sunk off Stewart Sound with heavy casualties and another destroyer badly damaged when they had the temerity to challenge the Japanese shore batteries on Kwantung Point. The other two destroyers were also identified.

'Stewart Sound – that's the name of the place is it, by God,' said

Grainger savagely. 'That's one place we'll never forget.'

'Aye, but you can bet your life that the top brass will want to forget, especially yon Captain 'D',' replied Carson.

'The shore batteries were wiped out according to a signal from the S-class,' argued Jackson.

'I'm not so sure,' replied Carson. 'The Japs could have been keeping under cover when they saw we were out of range like they did when we came in. They're not as thick as that bugger on the S-class seems to think. Anyway, what if they were wiped out? The price was too bloody high. When they come to write the history of this war know what they'll say, do you?'

'What for Chrissake?' snapped Jackson.

'They'll say it was murder. Bloody murder. All them blokes like Captain 'D' on the S-class what led matelots and brown jobs and even the bleeding Brylcreem boys to their deaths to further their own ambitions!'

'Depends who writes it,' argued Jackson.

'Truth will out whoever chooses to write it, mate. There's always some ambitious bastard who'll dig deep enough if there's something that seems too good to be true.' added Carson.

'Skipper seemed keen to make a good impression during the action,' said Lofty. 'I saw him on the bridge with all the flak flying round and cool as you like. Even came to the back of the bridge and waved for everybody to keep their heads up. Stupid bugger, didn't he see that poor bastard on the pom pom deck who'd lost his?'

'Cox'n'll tell you about that one,' said Carson. 'Mate of his was on Captain 'D's ship off Norway last year. Seems they were in a mix-up with German ships and Captain 'D' tore a strip of some of his officers for ducking their heads when the enemy shit streamed over the bridge. Stands to reason our skipper wanted to show off with Captain 'D' alongside when they were giving us a tow.'

'How did Tokyo Rose have the names of the ships so soon after the action?' asked Grainger. 'The Japs must have been watching us from day one of the operation.'

'Captain 'D' did everything but hand out leaflets when he disappeared round that bend into the channel after instructing us and the other destroyer to lay beam on to the shore batteries,' said Lofty sarcastically.

'Right among their ranging buoys,' added Carson drily, 'He

was certainly round the bend alright.'

During the morning of the following day after leaving Stewart Sound aircraft were sighted and action station bells jarred, but tension was relaxed when Allied planes were identified.

'Don't ever let me hear anything against the Brylcreem boys after this,' said the Buffer when a signal was received by the *Rapier* indicating that a series of Allied air strikes had kept Japanese planes on the ground during the last twenty-four hours. Shortly afterwards the three destroyers arrived safely at Akyab.

The wounded were transferred to hospital and work began on temporary repairs to the ships. The day before *Rapier* left for Simonstown Lofty Jackson returned from a visit ashore to the hospital with bad news.

'Two more dead – the stoker from number one boiler room – a blessing in his case – and Scouse Webber,' he said gloomily.

Grainger looked across in shocked surprise. 'Scouse, are you sure? He was joking about it.'

Jackson nodded. 'I know, I was there, remember? The sawbones at the hospital said that shrapnel had penetrated his bowels and there was internal bleeding – turned gangrenous.'

'And he said he wasn't an urgent case,' said Grainger quietly – almost to himself. 'When's the funeral then – I'll go as one of the party from this ship.'

'Funeral's already taken place – they don't waste time in this climate after a bloke's snuffed it,' replied Lofty sadly.

'But they usually ask for an escort from the man's ship to attend,' protested Grainger.

'That's what I said – some stupid bastard ashore fouled that one up. It seems that the hospital was told that *Rapier* would be sailing that day so they got a funeral party made up of crew from the other ships.'

'All strangers – none of his mates – that's a bloody poor show,' commented Carson bitterly.

'Scouse would have had a good laugh up there with his warped sense of humour,' said Jackson quietly. 'He expected no favours and he was seldom disappointed.'

31

The *Rapier* sailed for Trincomalee, but before leaving Akyab lower deck was cleared for Captain 'D' when he came aboard to address the ship's company. Damage to the after part of the ship meant that his speech would have to be given on the destroyer's fo'c'sle and not on the normal venue of the quarterdeck. Six and a half feet in height, he was a massive figure in white tropical rig and his physical presence and impressive manner inspired respect even in the men with glowering expressions who surrounded him. His speech began with condolences for the casualties and then he explained that incorrect military intelligence had led him to believe that the guns on Kwantung Point had been removed and the gun site was, to all intents and purposes, derelict. The consequence of this error was the near loss of all three destroyers.

Grainger listened to this giant of a man calmly recounting how yesterday's action had failed so miserably. Grainger's feelings were a mixture of seething anger and remorse. This Captain 'D' belonged to a special breed of naval officer he had encountered before. Their lives were dedicated to the service and in typical naval style they showed no fear in action, revelling in battle and soon showing boredom in peaceful surroundings. This man would have set himself the highest standards to live up to and he would not tolerate anyone who failed to live up to those standards.

To Grainger's mind there seemed to be a lack of sincerity in the condolences. Perhaps this originated from impatience and an eagerness to get on with the war free of the distractions of protocol which were now being imposed on him. It was just as well there were such men if the Allies were to recover from the humiliating defeats suffered at the hands of the Nips over the last three years. After all, the men who were dead or maimed were only a fraction of expected casualties which the war would claim. Grainger remembered his father talking about Field Marshal Haig in the last war who had chosen to sacrifice men to the lethal crossfire of enemy machine guns in the hope of making temporary gains of a few yards of ground at a time.

It became clear to most of the silent ship's company that Captain 'D's eagerness to achieve something from the operation coupled with over-confidence bred from complacency, had compounded the error in military intelligence.

As Lofty Jackson said afterwards, 'Even if he had been given duff information it was no reason to risk laying us and the V-class alongside a bloody shore battery at point blank range without knowing for certain that the guns had been shifted beforehand.'

The *Rapier's* men would never forget their dead shipmates nor the day they had been sacrificed without apparent reason, even taking into account the insanity of war.

Grainger thought about Joe Myers, Mick Shaw, Jock Anderson, Taffy, Jack Swann, the stokers, the guncrews; all of them, with dreams of a future back home, only to be slaughtered and thrown over the side for the sharks, with a shell fastened to each body to ensure sinking, and supplied as a concession from naval stores.

It was ironic that this Captain 'D' would probably make admiral, survive the war and live to a ripe old age in comfortable retirement. Wonder what Mick and Joe would have had to say about that thought Grainger sadly and for no particular reason.

The *Rapier* returned to Trincomalee and there were expressions of dismay and sympathy from men who watched from other ships as they saw the shell damage which had scarred the destroyer's hull and superstructure from bow to stern.

Mail which had accumulated during their absence was now being eagerly read by the survivors; a pile of letters addressed to men who would never read them was retained in the ship's office.

There were two letters from Jill; she was a second officer now based at Portsmouth. In the thick of the invasion operations. She'll cope with anything they throw at her mused Grainger to himself. She seemed to think a lot about Mick. Joan Mitchell did as well. Mick had been looking forward to seeing her again. Something might have blossomed out of that relationship. The way Mick had been so reluctant to talk about her. Didn't make sense, especially when you knew what an extrovert he was. And Ruth Mason whom Joe Myers was so keen on. Wouldn't have been surprised to see those two married if Joe had survived. Like Joan, Ruth's letters would be returned and they would both be stunned by the blunt notification of death.

Maybe they had other interests now. Two and a half years had passed without them seeing each other; long enough for memories to be dimmed. Perhaps he was being too sentimental. Life was cheap in this war. Countless thousands of people had suffered bereavement. The 'killed in action' letters would be commonplace back home. But he knew he was being cynical; those three girls would be shattered. How could anybody with a spark of humanity in them feel otherwise, when they heard of the death of a loved one?

Jill had said she was looking forward to seeing Mick and himself in the near future. She sent her love and looked forward to his next letter. Maybe she'd been told now that Mick wouldn't be coming home.

Grainger knew that it was going to be difficult writing that next letter to her. Bob Carson's voice interrupted his thoughts. 'Jack Swann and the other lads on the starboard side of the tubes were unlucky alright. How did you make out, Ted?'

'Jack sent me up to repair the headphones on the portside Oerlikons – I'd have been with them otherwise.'

'Christ! What a way to go,' said Carson. 'It wouldn't have been so bad if they could have had a decent burial, but to be slaughtered then chucked overboard for shark fodder doesn't bear thinking about.'

'That Captain 'D' has a lot to answer for. Trailed us like sheep and nothing we could do about it,' said Grainger angrily.

'Nothing short of mutiny, that is,' replied Carson.

Lofty Jackson sitting on the opposite side of the mess deck table sucked in his cheeks. 'Don't use that word, Bob,' he said sharply. 'Get us hung that will!'

'End result's the same,' said Carson sarcastically.

'Can I change the subject? Here, Ted, have a read of that.' Pearson, a telegraphist in the navy and an insurance man in peacetime, had a disgusted expression on his face as he pushed the letter across the table.

Grainger read the letter from Pearson's employers which stated that a payment of thirty shillings, each month, which had been credited to Pearson's bank account to make up the difference between his former salary and navy pay, would be discontinued from the date of the letter. It seemed that Pearson's navy earnings now exceeded his civilian salary and the insurance company did not consider that they were under any obligation to continue the payments.

Grainger handed the letter back. 'How did they find out?'

'Snooping at the tax office, I expect,' said Pearson angrily. 'I get three lousy pounds for a seven-day week, twenty-four hours a day, and a good chance of being blown to pieces thrown in.' He flung the letter on to the table. 'With friends like that, who needs enemies?'

'Cheer up mate,' replied Grainger. 'At least you got seven and a tanner a week out of them. Better than being poked in the eye with a pointed stick!'

'And you've helped them to keep their hands on all those bleeding millions, Sparks!' added Lofty Jackson with a malicious grin.

The *Rapier's* major re-fit was to be at Simonstown but the announcement of this news did not inspire much enthusiasm amongst a ship's company which only a few days ago had been eagerly looking forward to the event.

Sharing living quarters and action stations for over two years, then seeing so many colleagues killed or maimed in a matter of minutes was a harrowing experience for even the most insensitive characters in the ship's company. Hard men like Nobby Clark and Oliver had changed their ways. Nobby appeared to have lost interest in stealing other people's property when the ship was in harbour. Oliver, who normally looked upon South Africa as his second home, showed no emotion when he heard the news about the re-fit.

Oliver's action station was captain of Y gun, the last of the *Rapier's* 4·7 inch guns to keep firing. The quarterdeck had been hit but Y gun was missed, though two of the gun's crew had been badly wounded.

When Grainger had gone aft to look for the Gunner 'T', he

had noticed Oliver driving himself like a madman, oblivious to everything except the need to return the enemy fire. Since the action, Oliver seemed morose and only interested in recovering the authority he had once held as leading hand.

'Oliver's a changed man with all this dedication and devotion to duty these days,' remarked Bob Carson to Grainger as they were checking the depth charge racks on the quarter deck. They had seen Oliver applying a coat of paint to the shield of his beloved Y gun.

Carson laughed. 'Reckon he's jealous of that hook you've just put up, Ted, and wants his back again.'

Carson was referring to Grainger's recent promotion to Leading Torpedo Operator.

'Looks as if the action the skipper promised has done what detention couldn't do,' said Grainger.

Carson was not impressed. 'Flash in the pan, I reckon, after the first run ashore in Simonstown he'll be the same old Oliver, mark my words!'

'I'm not so sure,' replied Grainger. 'If he deserts this time he won't go back to the UK when the commission's finished.'

'It won't be long before we're back anyway, now that Gerry's packed in.'

'Let's have the UK leave first; the war here could have finished by that time,' suggested Grainger.

'Pigs might fly – it'll be the invasion of Singapore next and we'll be back to take part,' was Carson's gloomy forecast.

Two months elapsed before the *Rapier* was ready to re-join the East Indies Fleet. There were no desertions this time in South Africa. Oliver had learned his lesson evidently. There had been the usual generous invitations for the men to stay with white South African families and this time Grainger went with Bob Carson to stay with an Afrikaner family who lived in Worcester, the fruit-growing centre of the Cape Province.

The husband worked as a superintendent on the railways. He was quite a good natured man but his wife, in her early forties, and the teenage daughter could scarcely be described as friendly. During the absence of the husband at some of the meals mother and daughter would converse with each other in Afrikaans in front of their guests.

This practice ended when Grainger using his smattering of German, similar to the Dutch language from which Afrikaans is derived, held a pre-arranged conversation with Carson when all four were sitting at the breakfast table. The two sailors were elated by the look of embarrassment on the faces of mother and daughter as they realised their guests may have understood their previous conversations.

This lack of friendliness was reflected in the local pub when Grainger and Carson met four colleagues from the *Rapier* to hear Churchill's VE day speech being relayed on the public address system. The main bar was packed with locals listening expressionless to the resonant tones of the British premier, exultant in his announcement of victory and praise for the Allied Forces, then vitriolic in expressing contempt for the defeated evils of Nazism which had brought so much death, destruction and misery. The speech ended with hope for the future and a declaration to work for permanent freedom and prosperity throughout the world.

'A brave new world, in fact,' said Carson. 'We've heard all that crap before. Hope he hasn't forgotten there's a war on out here! Where's that lot going to?'

Carson turned round to watch the locals walking out of the pub, carrying their drinks into the yard outside and leaving the bar empty, apart from the sailors and the barman. They walked to the window and saw the crowd standing in groups.

'Must be over fifty of 'em out there, d'ye think they're trying to tell us something?' asked Atkinson, a burly leading hand. 'Is it the uniform, mister?' he asked, turning to the barman.

The man shrugged his shoulders without replying.

'In that case we'll have another pint and that lot can sup outside,' said Atkinson. 'Best place for 'em if you ask me!' He thumped the bar loudly with his empty glass. 'Set 'em up, squire!' he commanded the bar tender.

When the *Rapier's* men eventually left and saw the crowd still there they expected trouble. They walked in closed formation towards the roadway, ready to give as good as they got if there was any violence and watching intently for the first movement from the staring onlookers but none came. They reached the roadway and watched the crowd drifting back to the pub.

'Looked like a bleeding lynch mob back there,' said Atkinson.

'Reckon they're friends of Adolf, Bob?'

Bob laughed. 'Likely they haven't got over the Boer War yet. If you want some more of the local atmosphere come back with Ted and me to our place and we'll introduce you to the missus and her daughter.'

As a rule it must be admitted that South African hospitality had been extremely generous but there are usually exceptions to every rule. Some of the people of Worcester with their closed community mentality had proved to be one of those exceptions. The impression gained by the *Rapier's* men, who had been invited to stay there, was that a Kriegsmarine uniform would have been a more welcome sight to a large section of the white population.

Despite the attractions of shore leave elsewhere, the *Rapier's* original ship's company were impatient for the ship's return to Colombo and the end of the commission. They had been too long in a ship which now held sad memories for them. In tropical temperatures, overcrowded and difficult conditions, they had served over three times the length of an average peace-time commission. It was time for them to leave the scene.

The only cloud on the horizon was the prospect of returning for another commission in the Far East after leave.

Nobody believed Paddy Doyle when he blew his bosun's pipe round the *Rapier's* decks and announced the end of the war shortly after the ship's return to Colombo.

'Sure, it's the truth I'm telling yer,' he protested when Lofty Jackson challenged him on the source of his information. 'The Yanks have hit them with a new type of bomb – if you don't believe me, listen to the skipper when he gives it out over the relay.'

Paddy's sensational news was confirmed by Commander Thompson shortly afterwards.

The cloud on the horizon for the ship's crew had been dispersed by mushroom-shaped clouds over the towns of Hiroshima and Nagasaki which had signalled the explosion of atomic bombs and the surrender of Japan.

When the *Rapier's* crew left the ship at the end of the commission, unmarked by ceremony, they knew their return home would be permanent.

· · ·

Grainger leaned against the guard rail of the County class cruiser bound for the UK. He looked down at the military base camps on the banks of the Suez Canal and the flat desolate landscape beyond, stretching as far as he could see.

He grinned and gave the thumbs-up sign as he heard a shout 'You lucky bastards!' from a soldier on the quayside who was waving his arms above his head. The cruiser was stopped in one of the canal locks to allow a merchant ship through on its way to the Red Sea. The merchant ship slid by and the cruiser moved back into the canal, then nosed its way towards Port Said and the second leg of its voyage through the Mediterranean.

The ten days' passage from Colombo had given Grainger time to speculate on the changes he was likely to find at home after an absence of three years. The prospect of seeing family and friends again was exciting but his pre-war working experience gave him no illusions about the opportunities of finding a decent job, especially as he didn't have one to go back to like many of the other 'Hostilities Only' men.

Not much in the way of qualifications either apart from health, strength and intelligence. No pull with friends and relatives in good jobs who could put in a word on his behalf where it counted. He'd been lucky so far – he was still alive and well, thank God, not maimed or dead like Joe and Mick and the others. As long as it was legal he was determined to make the most of any chance that came his way.

Grainger descended a ladder to the deck below and entered the canteen. Still in a thoughtful mood about future prospects, he selected a newspaper at random from a nearby table then sat down. The paper was an old copy of the London Gazette and after scanning the various lists of medal awards he was about to replace the paper and pick up a magazine when his eyes focussed briefly on a column heading.

Despite the heat he felt his blood chill and his hands lose their steadiness as he read that HMS *Velperton* had been torpedoed and sunk in the West Atlantic – there were no survivors.

It was a warm September afternoon as the cruiser moved down

the coast near enough for the men on the upper deck to see the green fields and reddish-brown earth of the countryside surrounding Plymouth.

As Grainger took in the welcome sight he realised that the village of Ashdown must be somewhere near in the folds of those hills and the feeling of sadness was re-awakened as he remembered Julie.

The cruiser slipped past the breakwater and made its way slowly through the mass of ships in the Sound. Drake's Island drifted past before the ship entered the River Tamar to finally secure in Devonport Dockyard.

Carson pointed to the wharf, deserted except for a group of dockers who had finished securing ropes and wires and were now pushing a gangway towards the cruiser's upper deck.

'What did I tell you?' he said bitterly. 'There's no 'welcome home'. They've forgotten about the bloody war already.'

'Hang on,' grinned Lofty Jackson, 'I'll ask the skipper if he'll arrange for the bootnecks to play us into barracks. What would you like? Entry of the bleeding Gladiators or Home is the Sailor?'

Carson muttered a caustic comment and then remonstrated, 'There'll be no bleeding virgins either after the Yanks have been here!'

'Not to worry, Bob,' replied the irrepressible Lofty Jackson. 'Virginity's only like a balloon when you come to think about it – one bang and it's gone forever!'

Grainger smiled as he looked at the grey mass of HMS *Drake* visible behind the parade ground and playing fields which stretched down to the dockyard perimeter. It seemed like a lifetime since he had arrived there for the first time.

Orders were given over the tannoy system for men on draft to barracks to muster at the gangway with their kit.

'Come on, Ted, – unless you're stopping on board for the return trip,' said Lofty Jackson.

Grainger shouldered his kit bag and hammock.

'Not this bloody time, mate!'